Twisted Texan

AND OTHER STORIES

Rich Mussler

PublishAmerica
Baltimore

First printing

ISBN: 1-4137-4213-0
PUBLISHED BY PUBLISHAMERICA, LLLP
www.publishamerica.com
Baltimore

Printed in the United States of America

For Benjamin and Emily

Table of Contents

Twisted Texan:
The News Lady and the Chicken

At breakfast we all rested elbows on the simulated wood-grain formica countertop of the only Denny's left on the south side of town. You know, that one on Lamar at Grand. It wasn't light yet, and we were coming off a nightmare shift.

Though exhausted I recognized that it was probably not a good idea to talk about what had just happened. Best leave certain things unsaid.

"More coffee?" the waitress asked. Only it sounded like "Mo-ah *caw*fee." This was the same top-heavy girl that always calls everyone "honey."

"Sure."

"Why not."

"Personally, I could use something stronger," the news lady said. But she pushed her mug forward and the honey-waitress filled it.

"There ya go-*ah*, honey," she said and moved on.

I could see the short-order cook behind the counter, slinging hash, and recognized him. He was a doper I'd put away a few years back, out now on parole I guessed. Good for him. At least he's working at honest labor, and maybe he's clean and sober. Maybe. I sort of hoped he wouldn't recognize me as just then he was making my *Grand Slam* with eggs scrambled. God knows what he might put in those eggs if he recognized me. He looked up from the grill briefly and half-smiled, then turned his back so all I could see was a line of sweat down the spine of his t-shirt.

"I always *wondered*," Kathy Borman said and stopped. I was listening, but apparently she wasn't going to finish. She lit a cigarette instead. She sat between me and Howard Thorp at the counter, and I saw her glance at him.

He saw it, too, that sidelong glance. "Always wondered *what?*" he asked, pointedly.

9

Kathy picked a bit of tobacco off her tongue and wiped it on a napkin. She took the diplomatic route and lied, finishing the sentence with another thought. "I always wondered if you're to tip the waitress when you sit at the counter. Do they expect it?"

Howard Thorp had, not three hours earlier, peed in his pants. That's right, he *wet* himself. It was a good thing he kept an extra pair of slacks in his locker. Several of the production crew slapped him on the back and gave him encouragement despite the embarrassing mishap, saying things like, "I woulda done the same thing, Howard," and, "it coulda happened to anybody, Howard." But the two cameramen who were closest to him when it happened and caught it on video didn't say anything. They gave him looks of disgust.

We'd been sitting there with them in the back of the production van waiting until Kathy came in, expecting to be interviewed like always.

Kathy did come in, but she didn't interview anyone. In fact, she didn't speak at all. After awhile the two cameramen shrugged their shoulders and left. Howard and I waited silently. She was perched in front of a small vanity with one leg curled up under her. She removed the "on air" makeup.

Then we all drove to the Denny's.

"So," I said to Howard, "you made your first bust," and I sipped bad coffee. I leaned back in my seat and peered over Kathy at Howard Thorp. "And it's a good one, too."

The news lady between us shook her hair, turned her head and looked at me. She turned the corners of her lips down and rolled her eyes. *My, oh damn!* She is one fine looking woman. I recalled, at that moment, reading something about a five million dollar, three-year contract with the local CBS affiliate and felt in my gut that she was probably worth every penny. Chocolate brown hair and icy blue eyes. Beautiful. Seasoned news investigator. Intelligent.

"It was a good bust, wasn't it?" Howard Thorp said. There was a sort of hope in his voice. "Someone said street value of a couple hundred thou?"

"Yes, it was," I said. And added for emphasis, "At *least*."

The news lady turned her head to shift her gaze from me to him. I couldn't see her expression now but could guess it. Then she turned back to me, rolled her eyes again and blew smoke.

She didn't know me very well. I hoped she wanted to know me better, though I admit I'm not much of a catch. Maybe there's a chance, I thought, but not likely. I shook the thought from my head.

God knows what Kathy ever saw in Howard Thorp, other than news anchor good looks, fame, money, etc. The rumors about them, I knew for a fact, were true. They went at it like bunnies. I heard them myself in that little production van a few times.

That was then and this is now, so I smiled at her. She smiled back. I saw her eyes drop and follow my arms down to the counter then back up to the coffee mug I cradled in both hands. There was something sensual in the way she did that. Of course, with those crystal blue eyes of hers just about anything she did would strike me as sensual. She's at least fifteen years younger than I am, I noted to myself. What was I thinking?

She pulled her shoulders back and looked at me, in my dark-blue DEA jacket with the bright yellow letters, as if she were seeing me for the first time. She chewed the inside of her lower lip thoughtfully. Then she turned her head and snubbed out her half-smoked cigarette.

"Well, thank *God* it was a good bust," Howard Thorp said, repeating the phrase. "My first one, after all." He smiled at the news lady, but she did not return the smile.

Instead she looked at him thinking (I'm guessing this part): *Six months planning, two months of daily on-air time and a budget of three-quarters of a million to get... this.* But again she said nothing. Just looked at him.

And then, after a long moment, she turned back to me and rolled her eyes one more time. I peered around Kathy to look at the subject of her disdain. Mr. Howard Thorp, Channel 6 sports anchor, was a short but athletic-looking fellow built like the Olympic swimmer he had once been. His hair was closely cropped, his jaw square and dimpled, and his face highly photogenic. He was everything I am not and never will be.

He had volunteered for this assignment, I was told. Good PR for our department. I was told that, too. The camera favored him from any angle, they said. His numbers are high with women, they said. So they followed him with their cameras through abbreviated training for the DEA. I supervised his training myself. And every evening a news crew showed up with Kathy Borman who asked Howard searching questions (edited and fed to millions of TVs throughout Dallas-Ft. Worth via the six o'clock evening newscasts).

"How are you holding up to the rigorous physical training, Howard?"

"Do you enjoy the firearms instruction?"

"Was the sensitivity training useful, or is it a guise for racial profiling?"

Howard answered every question with thoughtful, intelligent sound bites. He looked into the camera and connected with the viewing audience. It was pure gold. Ratings for channel 6 soared.

And Kathy closed each session with a curt nod, saying "I'm Kathy Borman on location with Howard Thorp, *live and undercover*, on special assignment with the DEA." Howard wore the same jacket I wore, except his was new and fit better.

Howard Thorp was probably a nice guy. Hell, what do I know? He was maybe thirty (I'm no good at ages), was recently profiled as one of North Texas' *most eligible bachelors* in one of those cheesy magazines, and was fit and trim from swimming God knows how many miles every day. A natural athlete, the man holds three gold medals and two silvers from the nineteen-eighty-something Olympics. What can I say?

But what made things interesting to me, twisted Texan that I am, sitting there at the counter that night, was that just a few hours earlier Olympic gold medalist Howard Thorp, Channel 6 Sports Anchor, a guy who routinely partied with the Cowboys, the Mavs *and* the Rangers, and was a known womanizer, this very same Howard Thorp had proven himself (video-recorded for posterity, I might add) to be *cowardly*. Like the lion from Oz. Or as we say here in the great state of Texas, *chicken*. Preparation and media hype aside, the man was yellow.

So when I looked at him all I could think was: *cluck-cluck-cluck.*

But now, seeing him there on the other side of Kathy, I felt sorry for him.

"Thank God it *was* a good bust," he said to me, again, responding to my longer-than-polite gaze. "And I want to say to *you*, Fritz," he swallowed hard but managed to spit it out, "thank you for what you did out there tonight to help."

Kathy checked my reaction.

I shrugged and gazed into my cup. "Just doing my job, Howard."

"Quite right," she remarked. "Fritz was just doing *his* job."

Howard Thorp dropped his eyes to his own coffee.

Kathy, smiling at me again, leaned against me. "Aren't you carrying a gun?" she asked, kind of purring. "I mean, I thought you said you always carried a gun."

She must have noticed I'd removed my .45. No bulge, at least none under the armpit.

"Oh," I said, absently slapping the empty space. "It's in the car. But I always carry a back up." She looked at me curiously. "A second gun," I said, explaining. "Most cops carry one."

Howard Thorp tilted his head at this, making a mental note to buy a second gun.

Kathy raised her eyebrows and looked intently about my person. This scrutiny made me a little uncomfortable. "Where?" she asked.

"Trust me," I said. "It's there."

The waitress delivered our *Grand Slams*, then punished us by refilling our cups with that rancid, brown water they call coffee. "There ya go-*ah*, honey," she said to no one in particular.

Kathy ignored the food but lit another cigarette. She rested her chin on her palm and studied me a moment, stirring creamer into her cup absently. Something was gelling in her mind, and I had a feeling I was about to hear about it. "You know, Fritz," she said, her voice trailing off.

(She sounds even better, up close right there in your ear like that, than she does on the air.)

"What?" I prompted her to complete her thought and shoveled hash browns into my mouth.

"I was thinking. You have a very photogenic face."

Like hell, I thought. "Sure," I said to her.

Howard Thorp peered at me over the top of Kathy's head. It was as if he read ahead and didn't like where this script was going.

Kathy continued. "You ever think about…"

I put a stop to it. "It's Mr. Thorp's job to look good on camera. My job is to keep him from getting into too much trouble."

He seemed relieved to hear me say that.

"Well," Kathy said, countering, raising her mug to sip from it. "Unfortunately, Howard seems more than capable of keeping himself out of trouble. The only usable footage we got tonight was of his backside cowering behind a dumpster."

That icy comment came without warning, and I choked on my wheat toast. So much for leaving things unsaid.

Howard Thorp gritted his teeth and turned a bright red. Not an angry sort of red but the embarrassed kind. "Shit," was all he said under his breath.

"No problem, really," I said, not knowing what to say. "We got a good bust out of it. And it isn't uncommon for someone to freeze up their first time out." It was a lie meant to save face for poor Howard.

Kathy Borman gave me a look that would chill margaritas. She wasn't buying it. And I'm sure Howard saw what was coming and was dreading it.

"It *is* a problem," she said, putting her coffee down hard, spilling it. "Because *my reputation* is involved. And my career. Right now I have no story for this evening's broadcast – unless I choose to show our-man-undercover wetting himself."

She pivoted on her stool to face the Olympian directly. "Congratulations,

Howard. You've given new meaning to the term *yellow* journalism." She slid off her stool and marched out of the restaurant.

Now, *that* was cold.

Howard sat there a moment, stunned. He didn't look at me. He drew a deep breath then let it out slowly, composing himself. "I suppose," he said quietly, "I deserved that. I expect I will hear it for the rest of my life."

He stood up. "It's crazy," he said with a puzzled look on his face. "I was so excited to be working this assignment with you DEA guys. It never occurred to me that something like this would happen, but it did." He shrugged, and then walked off.

I watched him over my shoulder until I saw him pass through the Denny's front door. *Poor sonovabitch,* I thought, and went back to work on my eggs.

ờ   ờ   ờ

I awoke late that afternoon to the sound of my cell phone gurgling. I was disoriented, hot and sweaty. It felt like it was a hundred in my apartment. I rubbed my eyes and scratched. The cell phone gurgled again, a sort of muffled electronic pulse. For a moment I couldn't think where I left it.

I'd dropped Kathy off at the television station after breakfast, then drove home to sit with my laptop. I wrote my report and fired it off via email to my boss in Austin because I wanted him to hear exactly what happened from me before the rumor mill kicked in. That took me about forty minutes.

I must have crashed after sending it off because there I was on the couch in the living room of my apartment. The sun beat through the southwest window. Again the cell gurgled and this time I pinpointed the phone's location. It was under my DEA jacket on the floor.

I rose from the couch, staggered across the room, and picked it up.

"This is Fritz," I said, checking the thermostat on the wall. Christ, it *was* a hundred. *The damn air must be out again.* I made a mental note to kill the landlord.

"Fritz, I need to talk to you."

I recognized that polished baritone. It was Howard Thorp.

I wasn't really in any mood to talk to anyone just then. "Did you get some sleep?"

"A little. Look, can we talk somewhere?"

"About what?"

"You know about what," he said, his voice terse. "You've got to help me. It's all over town already. They're calling me *Howard the Coward*."

I couldn't help but smile at that. I agreed to meet him.

"I'm at the Mark downtown," he said. The Mark was across the street from the news station.

"Give me an hour," I said, and dropped the cell into its charger.

I walked into the kitchen and found my mother at the table, a sweater over her shoulders (hot as it was) and her hands folded in her lap. I moved her into the apartment next to mine when her second husband (whose lavish lifestyle and costly final days had burned up all the money Dad had squirreled away for her) had died.

"How long you been sitting here, Mom?" I asked her. She's seventy-three.

"I made you breakfast."

I looked at my watch. "It's three-thirty. I'm hungry, but I don't want breakfast."

"That's good," she said. "Because I made it this morning and it's cold by now." There was a batch of Betty Crocker biscuits in the oven and some scrambled eggs and bacon congealing in a frying pan on the stove. I took two of the biscuits and popped them into the microwave.

"I worked all night."

She shrugged. "I figured. Already read the paper."

I made some coffee and sat down at the table with the warmed-up biscuits. She pushed the *Dallas Morning News* across to me, but I prefer getting my news from the little black-and-white TV on the kitchen counter. It's the only television I own.

"Want coffee, Mom?"

She held her cup out and I filled it for her. She added three spoons of sugar.

I tried channel 6 first, hoping to catch something about Howard Thorp *"on special assignment with the DEA."* That will be interesting, was my thinking. But it was too early for local news. I flipped to CNN. Leslie Stahl was delivering a soliloquy on JFK Junior, who had flown his plane into the sea killing himself, his wife and her sister just two days before.

"I met her once, you know," I heard my mother say. She blew on her coffee with a soft whistle, cooling it, something I remember her doing all my life.

I looked at her and tried to guess what she was talking about. She was studying the box of biscuit mix rather intently. "Who?" I asked, taking a stab at it. "One of the Kennedy women? Or Leslie Stahl?"

She turned the box around for me to see. "Betty Crocker," she said, pointing to the small image of a brunette in the corner. "And it was quite an honor."

I slapped some butter on the biscuit, watched the news from the corner of my eye, and thought about that a long moment. Should I or should I *not* attempt to tackle this? Yes, I should, I decided. "Mom," I said, turning down the volume on the set, "you didn't meet Betty Crocker."

"I most certainly did." My mother held her body bone straight in the chair and looked at me across the top of her cup. "The woman ran into the back of my car."

I washed the biscuit down with some coffee. "What are you talking about?"

"On my way to work."

Mother had been a stewardess in the 'sixties for Northwest Airlines, before we moved to Texas. "You mean in Minneapolis?"

She nodded. "*Wham!* She smacked into me so hard my head snapped, right there on the parkway. Crumpled the bumper and gave me such a fright." Mom sipped her coffee, but it was still too hot for her so she whistled at it some more. "I was very angry with her until she told me who she was. I didn't recognize her, but she wrote her name and phone number on a slip of paper and gave it to me."

I closed my eyes and rubbed my temples. I thought I'd heard all of Mom's stories, but this was a new one. My father was married to this woman for forty-odd years. I remember him saying that often, adding "and the emphasis is on the word *odd*."

"What did Dad do when you told him about it?"

"Oh, he blew up, of course. You know your father." She tested her coffee again, tentatively. "He never even called her! A rich woman like Betty Crocker, and famous, too. He *never* called her." Mother shook her head and shrugged. "Acted as though it didn't happen."

I ate the other biscuit. "He didn't call her, Mom, because it wasn't Betty Crocker. She doesn't exist."

She frowned at me. "You're so much like your father," she said disparagingly. "That's what he said, too, but I was there when that woman smacked into me. Of course, she exists! How do you think that bumper got crumpled?"

ও   ও   ও

Howard Thorp sat there, alone in the darkness, looking rather glum in a corner booth at the back of the bar. The Mark is an upscale place atop a hotel downtown where corporate attorneys used to meet their rich, oilmen clients in Stetsons for three-martini lunches. Now they meet their rich dot.com clients in baseball caps, but the conversation hasn't changed much. Neither has the Mark.

The bar is long, curved, and solid oak. A half dozen frozen margarita machines purr along a back wall, spinning constantly, producing with unerring uniformity the infamous "frozen concoction" that sustains sanity. In case you haven't heard, the margarita is the official state beverage of Texas, and a watering hole that can't produce them in bulk will not survive here. The Mark's oak bar forms the inside curve of a half-moon shaped room, and the outer perimeter is floor-to-ceiling glass. Twenty-four stories up, the view of the city is terrific from any seat in the joint, and Dallas does have one lovely skyline. A stainless steel dance floor, with a smooth jazz band to go with it every night after nine, rounds out the place. It was nearly five o'clock when I got there and already a small crowd was forming at the bar to jumpstart happy hour.

Howard did not look happy. Perhaps the hour would be wasted on him. I pushed through the twenty-somethings at the bar and ordered a margarita, then crossed the room to him.

"What were they saying?" he asked me.

I sat down, puzzled. "Who?"

"Them." He indicated the group of twenty-somethings. "They work at the station. Everyone's talking about it."

I shook my head at him. "I doubt it."

He was despondent. "I took a risk, you know. Taking this assignment. I certainly didn't have to."

"Why did you?"

"I've been sports anchor for six years. Nobody takes you seriously."

A waitress brought my margarita over and I thanked her. I could see I would need it to fortify this conversation. Howard ordered another, but he was already several ahead. The waitress winked at him, smiled, turned on her heal and marched jauntily away. Wasted effort. Howard didn't notice.

I took a drink. I still wasn't sure I liked this fellow. Certainly I didn't care for the yellow streak, but no one can fully account for what he is inside. And I've seen others go to pieces. It's what you do after that counts. I took another gulp from the margarita, a big one, then put my glass down in front of me. "What did you want to talk to me about, Howard?"

Now it was Howard's turn to gulp his drink. He drained the glass and wiped his mouth with the back of his hand. "Well," he said, "I was wondering if you filed your report yet."

This was interesting. I shook my head no, lying. "What about it?"

"What about it? Christ, you can destroy me with that report."

I tried real hard to remember what I put in it before I'd emailed the damn thing. With paperwork I tend to be straight forward. *Just the facts,* like Dragnet. I don't write novels. But I am thorough and tend to make note of minor details such as DEA agents who break ranks, wet themselves and run, even pretend ones like Howard. I probably did say some unflattering things in that report, but it was the truth.

"Are you suggesting I leave out the part where you ran away?" I asked him.

The man went ashen. He glanced around the room, then lowered his voice considerably. "Look, Fritz. Under the Freedom of Information Act your report once filed is public property. It's one thing to have people whispering about it. But I'm dead if it's printed."

I thought about that a moment. "Don't be ridiculous," I said, but could see his point.

"Honestly. My career is dead if this incident gets into a public record."

He was beginning to win me over. But he pushed a little too hard.

"Dammit. I'm willing to pay you to go easy on me."

I felt my blood run cold and I sat back in my chair. I hadn't expected this. I said to myself: *So, he's not just a coward. He's scum, too.*

He could see in my face that he had made a mistake, saying that. He crossed his arms, swallowed hard twice, then sat back in his chair and rested his chin on his chest. His lower lip protruded unattractively.

After a moment I said, "It probably isn't a good idea to bribe an official of the Drug Enforcement Agency. Because that sort of thing winds up in reports also."

"Oh, Jesus," he said. I thought he was going to cry.

The waitress brought Howard's drink but could sense by the dark cloud over our table that he was in no mood to chitchat. She left it without flirting.

I decided then to put an end to this "special assignment" business. I could do it easily, now. I could rid myself of this television crap and get on with the business of busting dope-heads. God knows there is plenty to do. I didn't need this distraction.

Howard, too, could get on with his life, I figured. He was just in this deal to move his career forward. I doubted that bad publicity would really impact his career as dramatically as he supposed, though it might make things dicey for him here in Texas. So what if he had to pack his bags? I wasn't interested in risking my neck with him tagging along playing cops and robbers, never knowing when he might break and run or sit and quiver or maybe next time crap his britches. This was serious business, fighting drugs. There are some very bad people involved.

Howard could be a risk to himself or me or others if his nerves cracked at the wrong moment. It just wasn't worth it.

All of this ran through my mind as I sat there across from him, fuming. Then his eyes focused again and he looked squarely at me. He took a deep breath and his chin stopped quivering. With all sincerity and humility, he said, "I'm sorry, Fritz. That was a stupid thing for me to say, and I apologize."

Perhaps it was his boyish good looks or those dirt brown eyes that got to me, but in that instant my resolve to ditch the project melted away. Of course, I will be forever criticized for that decision, now, knowing the outcome. But at the time, I thought: *What would you do, Fritz, with any other kid who screwed up one time? You'd give him shot at it, another opportunity to prove himself, that's what.*

So that's what I decided to do. I decided to talk to him straight, and slipped instinctively into my east-Texas drawl.

"Don't worry 'bout what I put into any official report, Ol' Son," I said, and lifted my margarita to him. "Y'all just git over it. Forget what people are sayin', or what you think they're sayin', 'cause people always talk but nobody pays no attention to it. Even what they write in the papers. Forget it! None of it matters. All that matters in the end is this: *When you get tossed off a bull you get right back on and ride him again.* My daddy taught me that."

He looked bolstered a bit by my words. Motivated. He even smiled. Hell, I should have been a football coach! God knows the Cowboys could use a real one about now.

Howard lifted his glass to mine and smiled. "Here's to Howard the Coward," he said. *"R.I.P."*

"I'll drink to that," I said, and did. Then I lifted my glass and added, "And here's to the *new* Howard. Special Agent Howard Thorp, on assignment *live and undercover* with the DEA."

And we drank to that, too.

"I'll show 'em on the next bust," he said enthusiastically. "Back on the bull, like you said. We're close to cracking this wide open, aren't we?"

ࢤ   ࢤ   ࢤ

I fell asleep that night reviewing my personal notes regarding the target of our investigation, a major player named *Alberto Antonio Garza.* Our case against Mr. Garza was on hold, awaiting an indictment from a grand jury convened secretly by the federal prosecutor assigned to the case. She felt we had enough evidence to press for an indictment (I wasn't so sure), but the process of convincing the grand jury meant a careful, exacting review of the evidence that involved my frequent testimony. I was being called back to testify, once again, that very week. I wanted to be prepared.

This Garza character was someone I'd been pursuing for six long years. He was important to us because of his ties to the Miramontes cartel in Columbia. Emanuel Miramontes is, for our purposes here in Texas, untouchable. But we've been making some progress busting up his distribution channel, harassing his mules, roughing up the kingpins and street dealers whenever and wherever we can find them. Garza was at the top of this heap of Texas-based thugs and miscreants. He owned a six million dollar home in upscale Highland Park and ran a half-dozen legitimate businesses to launder the dirty money – auto dealerships mostly.

As I said, I'd fallen asleep – with the Gonzalez file tucked under my arm – on the couch. I seem to be doing as much sleeping on my couch as I do in bed these days. But I was awakened by a knock at my door, not a serious kind of knock but a gentle *rap-rap-rap.* Couldn't be my mom, I knew, because she has a key and just walks in. I pulled myself off the couch and peered through the peephole.

Kathy Borman was standing there.

I checked my watch – it was almost midnight – then opened the door.

"What are you doing here?"

She folded her arms. "Can we talk?"

That was the second time in twenty-four hours I'd heard that request. I shrugged and she stepped inside.

"I am going to fix myself a drink," I said. "Want anything?"

"What do you have?"

"Beer, dark beer, lite beer, imported beer or scotch."

"Scotch, on the rocks if you've got ice."

"I got ice. Have a seat."

I poured what was left of my *Cutty Sark* into two tumblers, with ice.

She took a sip and sat on the couch. "Jesus Christ, it's hot in here," she said and removed her jacket.

"Air's out. Landlord's working on it," I said sitting next to her. "What'd you want to see me about, Kathy?"

She thought about this a moment, then jumped into it. "I'm in trouble, Fritz, with this nightmare television production."

"*You're* in trouble? Why?"

"The whole story was my idea. I sold it to my boss. He sold it to his boss. His boss sold it to your boss. Christ, I even suggested Howard."

"So if it doesn't work out?"

"I'm history as a producer. I'll never get a shot at big story again. Not in this town."

I thought about it a moment, swirling the ice in my cup. "What can I do about it?"

She leaned forward. "I want to start putting more emphasis on your role in the DEA. I want to put a camera on you, follow you wherever you go. Especially during the busts."

I shook my head. "Can't do that, Kathy."

"Why not?"

"That much focus and notoriety will get me dead someday. Unlike you, I need to be invisible to do my job."

She slid closer to me on the couch. "But I've thought about that. We'll just fuzz you up. You've seen that on TV. Distort your image so you're unrecognizable. We can even electronically disguise your voice."

I was skeptical.

She finished the scotch in her glass. "Look. Fritz. This is a huge market. Lots of money is involved. And if Howard pulls one more stunt like he did last night, it's over for me. I got nothing. But if I've got back up coverage, a story on you, then… well, at least I can make the deadline for the evening news."

She put her hand on my arm. I felt the warmth of her touch.

છ   છ   છ

At three o'clock in the morning Howard Thorp, who had been asleep, awoke with a start, fell back asleep briefly, then awoke again. He was frightened by a dream about Alberto Garza becoming an alligator, of all things. A baby alligator two feet long had once taken a chomp out of

Howard's forearm in his grandfather's backyard in South Florida. He was six at the time. It wouldn't let go of little Howard, even after his grandfather had cut the miniature green monster in half with garden shears. And in his dream Alberto Garza was an alligator clamped on Howard's arm refusing to let go.

He reached for Kathy and realized she was not there beside him. Howard had gone to bed without her for the first time in six months. He lay awake thinking alternately about that, and about the alligator with the face of Alberto Garza, for two hours.

Just before sunrise Kathy Borman opened the door of the apartment they'd been sharing and, after brushing her teeth, slipped into bed beside him.

"Where in hell have you been?"

"Sorry, baby," Kathy said into the darkness. "Did I awaken you?"

"Where were you?"

"Editing. I'm putting the entire thing into a two-hour format. Once the investigation is completed we can run it as a special."

"Like hell."

"Look, what do you want from me, Howard?"

"The truth. Where in hell were you?"

"I told you."

"Liar. *Slut.*"

"Fine. I'm Kathy the Slut and you're Howard the Coward."

Howard lay quietly a moment, infuriated. "So I'm a coward. Now what?"

"Now nothing, as far as I give a damn. I'm tired." She rolled to her side, putting her back to him.

"Don't think I'll put up with this," Howard said to her in a growl.

"Let me sleep."

"If you're with me, you're with me. If you're not, you're not."

"Well, I'm with you now, Howard. And an hour ago I was editing video. Let me sleep."

~ ~ ~

I met Howard for some additional training two days later when I'd finished with the grand jury. I hadn't seen him since our conversation at the Mark, but I felt with the pending action against Garza I'd better build up his confidence and sharpen his skills. So I had him meet me downtown at the city police interactive weapons training unit for some target practice. I had no idea, at that time, how much the man had grown to hate me.

"Ready to shoot?" I asked him, and slapped him on the back.

"Sure," he said. His face was passive. "Are you?"

I hadn't planned to do any shooting that day, and told him so. "But I'm always willing to fire off a round, when I get a chance."

He didn't comment but looked at me oddly when I said that. His face said, *you bastard.*

I thought: *So, he knows about Kathy and me.* I'm only a man, after all. Not many men would take a pass on a woman like Kathy Borman. *Well, if he doesn't want her snaked by the likes of me, he'd better become more of a man himself.*

Howard changed the subject. "Kathy says they're putting a camera crew on you."

"That's what I heard."

Kathy entered the unit just then with a crew in tow. Of course, they intended to videotape Howard's simulated raid training. They clamored to get set up and complained about the lighting. The interactive weapons training unit is a walk-through practice regimen for cops. It simulates an actual raid in a small house. It is close and cramped. Targets appear at random, triggered by a controller using a computer keyboard, and score is kept on both speed and accuracy. Some of the targets are bad guys, holding weapons and looking nasty, and some are innocent bystanders, usually a woman or a child. And, often, one or two simulated targets are policemen. It is *not* considered a good thing to shoot the innocent bystanders or the policemen.

"Are you shooting today, Fritz?" Kathy asked me.

I shook my head. "No, I want to put Howard through his paces. He needs the experience. Your crew about ready?"

"In a moment."

I went up into the control booth to stand with the controller. From there I had a clear view of the entire set. After a few minutes, the camera crew was ready and Kathy gave us a thumbs up. Howard put a set of sound mufflers over his ears and checked the magazine on his Colt .45.

I spoke into the microphone at the control booth. "All set, Howard?"

Howard turned to face me. He nodded, then raised his pistol in the air to signal his readiness. But he held the pistol oddly. His middle finger was extended straight up, toward me. He waved the gun like that a moment, then lowered it.

So, that's how it's gonna be, I thought. *Well, to hell with Howard the Coward and to hell with this whole reality TV bullshit.* I gritted my teeth and nodded to the controller. He signaled the start of the exercise with the ring of a very loud bell, and Howard walked onto the simulated raid set.

The camera crew photographed his every movement as Kathy watched quietly.

A plywood bad guy popped up almost immediately, about twenty paces in front of Howard. He fired, and the bullet passed between the bad guy's plywood eyeballs.

"Jesus," the controller said, surprised.

The set was lit realistically, like a darkened house. Howard stepped into shadow, moving forward silently with his back to a wall. Two bad guys were triggered simultaneously, popping up directly before him. Howard fired twice, in rapid succession, scoring kill shots on both with bullets passing through their wooden hearts. Seconds later a bystander popped into view, but Howard held his fire expertly. He glanced about, his eyes exploring the dark recesses of the set.

"This guy is pretty good," the controller said to me in a whisper.

Howard stepped tentatively into a hallway. Instantly, two bad guy targets jumped out before him – one near and the other at the end of the hall. Howard fired three times, once into the nearest target at eye level, and twice into the far target's chest area. Then, in a sweeping motion demonstrating his natural athleticism, Howard dove and rolled forward across the room while ejecting the empty cartridge from his pistol. As he rose to his feet he slid a second cartridge into his weapon with an audible *click*.

At once, behind him, three figures appeared. Two bad guys and one innocent bystander. Howard spun, falling back against the wall behind him, firing. The two bad guys splintered with kill shots but the bystander was not fired upon at all.

Howard carefully peered around the corner of the room into a simulated kitchen. It was *very* dark in there. He moved forward cautiously, his body tense and alert. Three figures jumped up, one behind the utility island in the center of the room and two, one after the other, behind the refrigerator. They were all bad guys, and Howard dispatched them with perfect shots.

He had one bullet left in his weapon. Moving swiftly from room to room Howard sought bad guys but no targets appeared. The house was empty. He then moved to the back door of the set. Cautiously, slowly turning the door handle, he pushed open the door with his foot. A target sprang up not two feet away. Howard raised his pistol to the target's forehead with an outstretched arm.

But he did not fire.

The controller let out a long breath of air in a low whistle, then said, *"Holly cow."*

Howard stood frozen with pistol extended to the target's forehead, but he had not fired. And it was a good thing. The target was a simulated police officer.

The controller rang the bell again, signaling the end of the exercise, and checked his stop watch. The television crew shouted excitedly and rushed onto the set to Howard. He holstered his weapon, removed the sound muffler and grinned at them sheepishly.

I looked at the controller, stunned, eyebrows raised and mouth agape.

"A perfect score, Fritz," the controller said to me. "Just under three minutes. Not bad for a sports anchor."

I laughed out loud. I thought, *damned this guy is weird – one day peeing his pants and the next coming across like James Bond.* I ran down to the set to congratulate Howard.

"How many times did you shoot?" I asked, testing him.

"Eleven. Got one in the chamber."

"How many dead bad guys?"

He grinned at me. *"Ten."*

I let out a rebel whoop and lifted my hand overhead. Howard raised his and we high-fived with a solid clap.

I turned to the cameraman, who was still videotaping, and pulled the lens to my face. *"Perfect* score," I said proudly. "Howard Thorp just nailed a perfect score, in under three minutes, on the City of Dallas Police Department's interactive weapons training unit. And not meaning to minimize his performance in any way, I must humbly point out that he was trained by the best. *Me."*

Howard threw his arm around my shoulders. "The *best*," he echoed, and we laughed, and I let out another rebel whoop.

"Big deal."

Howard and I turned to the source of this disgruntled comment, Kathy. She had a scowl on her face. "And *so what*," she added for emphasis.

I was surprised by her reaction. "It is a big deal, Kathy," I said. "This exercise isn't easy. Not many get a perfect score."

She looked from me to Howard and shook her head. "Well, at least we got some good video. Good thing those targets can't fire back. Right, Howard?"

જી   જી   જી

When I got home that evening my mother was sitting in my apartment nude. I can tell you that of all the things one should avoid in life, seeing one's seventy-three year old parent naked has got to be at the top of the list.

"Mother! What are you thinking?" I said to her. She was seated in a chair near an open window making little gasping sounds.

"It's very warm in here, Fritz," she told me.

"I know that, Mom." I checked the thermostat and it read close to a hundred, again. "That goddamn landlord was supposed to send somebody over here to fix it."

I picked mom's clothes up off the floor and helped her into them. "Why don't you just wait for me in your apartment? The air conditioning works fine in your apartment."

"Yes, I know it does," she said, stepping into her slacks. I pulled them up for her. "But I prefer it over here. My place is just so lonely all day."

I couldn't imagine how my apartment, down the hall two doors from hers, was any less lonely.

After she was dressed I got her a glass of ice water from the refrigerator and made her drink it down. "Ah," she said. "That's better."

I called the landlord and raised hell. But he assured me that he'd sent a repairman by my house two days in a row. Each time he was turned away. I hung up the phone and looked at Mom.

"Mom. Did someone come to my door today and yesterday?" I asked her.

"Yes. A man in coveralls. I could see him through the little peephole."

"Did you open the door? It was a repairman."

"I know that," she said. "And yes I opened the door. I opened the door and sent him away."

Well, that explains a lot, I thought, and took a deep breath.

"Why'd you do that, Mom?"

My mother looked at me disdainfully. "Because, Fritz, both times the man said he was here to fix my air conditioning. I told him that my air conditioning was working just fine. So he left."

I put my hand to my eyes and massaged my temples a long moment. "Mom," I said, "the man was here to fix *my* air conditioning. Not yours."

"Oh. Well. Then he should have said so."

I nodded. How can you argue with that?

"Let's eat out tonight," I said, and added, "I'm buying."

Mom was delighted.

26

২৯ ২৯ ২৯

Kathy Borman showed up at my apartment again that night, about eleven or so. I slept with her, and after, we held each other, smoked and talked. She told me all about Howard's alligator dreams, and about the conversation they'd had when she'd gotten home the other night.

"What did you tell him?" I asked her.

"Tell him? About what?"

"About us."

"Nothing." She gave me the details of their conversation. "Why should I tell him about us, Fritz?"

I couldn't think of any good reason.

"I think he knows," I said.

She nodded. "Sure he does."

২৯ ২৯ ২৯

The grand jury came through for us. They concurred with the federal prosecutor that we had enough evidence, finally, after six long years of investigation, to indict Alberto Antonio Garza on federal drug importation and distribution charges. We were ready to make an arrest.

I had long ago developed a plan for just such an opportunity. It involved six Texas Rangers, who routinely help us when making these high-profile arrests, and my own team of agents. Naturally, channel 6's Howard Thorp and his entourage would be along for the ride.

Garza's home on Turtle Creek was a two-and-a-half acre compound with a 12-foot perimeter wall. Garza's own security force of a half dozen armed thugs provided protection for him, his wife and two children. Neighbors shared the perimeter wall on three sides of Garza's property, so normally the only access was through the front gate. One of Garza's neighbors, however, happened to be a retired judge, a good man, a man of conscience. The judge granted us access to the security fence through his backyard, which helped a great deal.

That very evening, I sent the Texas Rangers over the wall to take up positions behind Garza's house. They would eliminate the possibility of Garza slipping through our fingers and making an escape. Next, I drove my car, with Howard beside me, down the narrow lane leading to the compound's front gate. A guard stopped us there. I displayed my

27

identification, the warrant for Mr. Garza's arrest and a second warrant to search the premises. The guard announced, as I knew he would, that Mr. Garza was not at home. We knew for a fact that he was indeed at home. It didn't much matter what the guard said because I possessed a search warrant. He complied and opened the front gate.

As the heavy gate swung open the rest of my crew – eight of the best agents in the DEA – pulled up behind me in our armored truck. They'd been waiting at the end of the driveway for my signal. Behind the truck was the channel 6 news van, with Kathy Borman in the driver's seat. We passed through the gate and approached a huge, rambling house, *Casa de Garza.*

I assumed our approach was being monitored inside the house.

We parked askew in the driveway and exited our vehicles. Two of my agents took positions, as planned, at opposite corners of the house. From there they could keep an eye on the front and sides for anyone sneaking out. Howard and the rest of us wore our blue DEA jackets, and we packed some heavy artillery because I was unsure exactly how much resistance we should expect. Garza was smart – smart enough to *not* start a shooting match, I hoped. But I just didn't know. The channel 6 news team (Kathy and two cameramen) wore bright yellow jackets.

As I rang the bell, both cameramen rolled tape.

One of Garza's thugs opened the door and I waved my paperwork under his nose.

"I have a warrant for the arrest of Alberto Antonio Garza," I said. "And to search these premises." The guard looked us over, very thoroughly, and eyeballed the television crew. Their cameras were trained on him.

He laughed. After a moment he said, *"Perdone, Señor."* He laughed some more, something striking him *very* funny, and then spoke English but with a heavy south-of-the-border accent. "So sorry. But you see Señor Garza is no here *esta noche.* You come at a bad time to arrest him, I am afraid. He fly away. He go just this morning on business trip to Columbia." Again, the man laughed.

I pushed past him and my crew followed me. Three more swarthy gentlemen stood inside the door. They glowered at us. "All right," I said to my team, "spread out. Search every room, every closet. Let's go." They went.

We found Mrs. Garza, and her two young children, watching *The Littlest Mermaid* on a huge television in a dark room. Mrs. Garza seemed none too surprised or concerned to see us. She turned her head and spoke to me, without rising. "Buenas noches, Señor. ¿Buscan usted a mi esposa? También.

Permita que mí sepa si usted lo encuentra." She laughed, thinking I wouldn't understand, but I've been speaking Spanish since high school. She had said, *"Are you looking for my husband? So am I. Let me know if you find him."*

ॐ ॐ ॐ

After an hour of looking, and no Garza, I reconvened the team in the living room. Garza's four thugs sat smirking at us and smoking. I checked in with the Rangers on the radio to make certain no one slipped by. The Texas Rangers were still at their posts. Nobody could get past them.

Kathy Borman was growing impatient. "I thought you said Garza was here, Fritz?"

"He's here."

Through the back window of the house I noticed a huge swimming pool. It was lit from below and glowed bluish-green in the night. I also saw that a small cabana overlooked the pool. I turned to the gentleman with the hearty laugh who'd met me at the front door and asked, "Any other buildings on the property?"

He shook his head coolly. "No, Señor. *Nada.*" The other three thugs glanced at each other, their eyes locking briefly.

He's in the cabana, I knew at once.

"OK, Mike," I said to the most experienced agent on my team. "You and Carlos stay here with these gentlemen. Keep an eye on 'em. The rest of you, come with me."

I opened the sliding glass door facing the pool and stepped outside. The four remaining agents on my team, and Howard, Kathy and the two cameramen, followed me out there. It was like making a raid with the Marx Brothers.

"What's going on, Fritz?" Howard wanted to know.

I put my finger to my lips and motioned toward the cabana. It was large enough to hold a shower, a couple of toilets, and an outdoor bar that looked fully stocked from where I stood. At the very least, I figured, if my hunch was wrong, we could all enjoy a drink on Señor Garza.

"What makes you think he's in there?" Howard whispered.

"He's in there," I said. "And my guess is he's got a couple thugs with him and enough hardware to rob a bank. He's gonna fight."

I drew my weapon and the rest of my team did, too. Howard turned ashen.

"Wait a minute," he said. "Why don't we set the cabana on fire? If they're in there, that'll bring them out."

I shook my head. "We don't roast suspects, Howard. We arrest them."

"Well, how do you propose to get them out?"

I looked at Howard a long moment. "Why don't you go knock on the door and ask them to give up?"

He shook his head. "I don't want to do that."

"Well, I don't either," I said, and smiled at him. "But that's my job." I could see Howard was actually trembling and looked a little sick to his stomach. I glanced at Kathy. She could see it too.

"Look, Howard," I said. "You stay here in case Mike and Carlos have any trouble with those guys inside. Don't let anyone out, you understand?"

Howard nodded, and swallowed dryly.

I split the rest of the group in two, sending two of my guys around the right side of the pool. The other two came with me around the left side. One cameramen and Kathy stayed with Howard, but the other guy gamely trailed along behind me, camera rolling.

We got in position, hiding behind whatever was handy. I hunkered down behind a cement gargoyle spewing water in a graceful arc into the pool, then shouted at the cabana: "*Alberto Antonio Garza!* This is Federal Agent Fritz Hauser, DEA. I have a warrant for your arrest. Throw down your weapons. Step out of the cabana!"

To be honest, I knew that the camera was on me and thought a little dramatic oratory would sound great on the 6 o'clock news.

But I didn't expect the hail of gunfire that erupted before I finished it. Garza and three others inside let loose with everything they had. Bullets flashed around us like roman candles. A series of tiny eruptions spit across the pool as somebody inside the cabana emptied a clip into it.

At the first *crack!* of gunfire, Howard the Coward spun on his heel and ran right over the top of his cameraman, sending the poor guy sprawling backward over a potted plant. Professional that he was, the cameraman managed to keep his lens focused on the departing backside of channel 6's sports anchor. Howard pumped his feet like he was leading the pack in a hundred-yard dash and disappeared behind the house into darkened shrubbery.

Simultaneously Kathy hit the ground, taking cover behind a huge palm. It was good timing, because everything around her shattered as gunfire reduced the glass door to shards. Chunks of it rained down upon her.

I saw flashes inside the house as well and knew that Mike and Carlos had their hands full with the thugs inside.

The mad spray of machine-gun fire continued unabated from inside the cabana. Fortunately, they were very bad marksmen shooting through the tiniest of little portholes in the cabana's bathrooms. The bullets tore up everything but people.

I swung my arms over the top of my spitting gargoyle and unloaded a clip from my pistol into the cabana. The rest of my team did likewise. The pool-side building splintered to bits. The bottles at the bar were decimated and liquor flowed into the pool.

Then it was quiet. I heard a series of clicks as we all slid fresh clips into our weapons.

I shouted again, this time not for any news camera. "Give it up, Garza! You're surrounded and we have forty agents out here! FORTY! *CUARENTA!*"

It was quiet again, and I readied myself for another round of gunfire.

Instead, the cabana door opened. Then, out flew rifles, shot-guns, pistols, machine guns and a variety of other lethal weaponry. They were tossed through the open cabana door and into the pool.

I heard a gruff, angry voice calling out from inside the cabana. "OK! No more shooting! We thought you guys was thieves! Criminals! *Not federales!*"

I signaled to my men to hold their fire and after a moment Alberto Antonio Garza stepped out of the cabana with his hands in the air. Seconds later, two of his thugs stepped out behind him, one bleeding from a bullet hole in his thigh. A fourth man in the cabana was dead.

I called to my agents in the house. "Mike! Carlos! You OK?"

"We're OK, Fritz." It was Mike. "But call an ambulance for these idiots who drew down on us."

I glanced across the pool at Kathy. She stood, shaking off glass, looking for Howard.

But Howard was long gone.

ھے   ھے   ھے

Poor guy. He really *was* a coward. When he heard the gunfire that night, I suppose all Howard could see was the face of Alberto Garza on the head of an alligator, teeth clamped tightly around his forearm. And when his fear induced him to flight, his only thought must have been to escape. He ran into the thicket to escape the danger at the pool side. He forgot about the Texas Rangers hiding out there in the dark.

And when Texas' most elite squad of police officers heard the gunfire, they drew their weapons. Seconds later they were charged by a madman in the darkness.

In less than a heartbeat Howard Thorp was full of lead and no longer *live and undercover.*

Texas Hondas

A whine and a roar pierced the silence in the hill country. Two roadrunners scurried through the mesquite underbrush, escaping, their spindly legs pumping. The wind that is always present pushed against a bent oak and dislodged a few of the remaining dead leaves. They fluttered across the narrow path. Brad, double clutching and dropping two gears, emerged under the oak's branches. That was the whine. He hit the path's little crest and both wheels lifted off the ground, then leaning back, he brought it down again on just the rear tire and kept it upright like that for thirty feet.

Running along the gully below was the roar. Brian, younger by nearly six years, dipped and rose and twisted out of sight momentarily. A wake of dust trailed him as he zigged the older Super Hawk half way up one bank and then zagged across the dry streambed up the opposite bank. He swooped over the top just behind the new 350, dropped a gear and wound it out to pull up along beside him. But it didn't last. Brad's new bike was geared much lower and so was better suited for the dirt. He grinned, twisted the handle, and sped away.

Both motorcycles crested the edge of the gravel pit and nosed downward at sixty degrees or so, no hesitation. It was a deep pit, 40 or maybe 50 feet to the bottom. The rush and weightlessness as they dropped lifted Brad's spirits considerably, left him with the feeling of flying, with his breakfast up in his throat. At the bottom he led along a narrow trail of packed gravel, nearly redlining in second gear. The old, heavy Hawk chugged and fell behind, not keeping up.

Brad approached the shear wall at the opposite end of the pit. Crouching over the 350's handlebars, standing on the pegs, shifting into third, he rocketed up the bank. He knew it was reckless but held to it. To let up meant, likely, that he would dump it half way up. The bike made it to the top, no sweat.

Brian followed, gamely, but the old Hawk sunk its front tire deep into dusty gravel. The bike slowed on the incline and three-quarters of the way up the engine stalled. Not enough revs. He spilled it and went sliding back down in a cloud. Hanging on to the rubber grips he instinctively let his body drag behind, flopping like a lure on a sinker. Boy and machine came to rest on the pit's floor, dirt and gravel jammed into ears, nostrils and tailpipes.

Brad straddled his bike near the edge and looked down at his kid brother. He killed the engine and drew a pack of Winstons from his shirt pocket.

"That dirt taste good, runt?" he called, blowing smoke, laughing, slipping the silver lighter back into his jeans.

"Aw, shit," Brian said, spitting bits of gravel and rubbing his eyes.

"Y'all got off the path where the gravel's too soft. Same thing nailed me once."

Brian picked himself up and righted the heavy motorcycle, putting his back into it. "What's it like further on?" he asked.

Brad drew long on his cigarette and instinctively looked over his shoulder toward the millstream. He ran his hand across his closely cropped head – it felt like brush bristles – then looked back down on his brother. "It's okay. Pretty bitchin'. There's a path and it runs close along the bank. You never been down there?"

Brian shook his head. "Comes out on the highway," he said by way of explanation. He was fourteen.

Brad considered that a moment. "Well, then, c'mon and we'll ride it together."

Brian looked up, thinking. Grinning. Brad was a silhouette with the afternoon sun behind him.

"C'mon, dammit," he said again, finishing the cigarette and flicking its glowing remains down on his brother. "No one's gonna know you ain't legal. But you got to get your butt up here first."

Brian threw his leg over and cranked the starter. It rumbled, then barked as he rolled the throttle. He sped back to the center of the pit, slowed, circled one-eighty, then opened it up. He screamed a rebel war-whoop. This time he hit the bank square-center in the hardened path and did not lose his courage. He kept the throttle pulled back and when the machine slowed two-thirds of the way up he dropped a gear, like he knew what he was doing, and crested the top with plenty of speed. The momentum sent him airborne. He hit the ground rear wheel first and didn't slow, leaving Brad to eat his dust. His older brother hooted, jumped the kick-starter, and went roaring after him. They hollered at each other for no reason but shear elation.

The millstream was a tributary of the Guadalupe. At one time its gentle waters were channeled to power a saw in the mill for cutting cedar into planks, but that was a long time ago. Brad edged past his brother to lead as they approached the stream, following a well-worn path through the mesquite. It was November but the cypress trees were as pretty as ever, he thought. It had been over a year since he'd been down this way. Where the path diverged in a Y he turned upstream and Brian followed.

It was cooler by the stream; the cypress trees shielded the sun. The path was hard dirt. The motorcycles cruised unhurriedly, avoiding the occasional massive roots and sharp-edged stones that pushed through in places. There was also lots of ducking low to keep from getting swept off by drooping branches. Eventually the trail turned sharply to cross over – the water at this point was no more than six or eight inches deep. They drove through it slowly and emerged on the other side at the edge of a large field. Brad put his foot down to stop a moment and Brian pulled up beside him.

"Did you see the deer back there?" Brian asked.

Brad shook his head. "You saw a deer?"

"Two of 'em, on the bank back there." He pointed.

Brad was disappointed because he would like to have seen the deer. "We used to have a lot of deer around here," he said.

They continued across the field to a fencerow, then followed that towards the highway. They could see it in the distance. There was no path now and the drought had made the soil hard. It was rutted, too, and the bikes bounced, making the ride uncomfortable. But they didn't mind. They took their own sweet time. At the highway the fence met another fence, but there was a gate with a wire loop over a cedar post. Brad opened the gate and after they'd passed through was careful to drop the wire loop back into place.

They drove north on the two-lane blacktop and met no other traffic. It was really hot for November. Little bubbles in the tar popped when the motorcycles' tires squished them.

When they came to the little diner called the *Kerrville Kozy Kafe*, a half mile from home, Brad slowed and pulled into its graveled parking lot. Brian followed him in. They braked to a stop, dropped kickstands while still coasting, and killed the engines.

"I'll buy you a coke or somethin'," Brad said to him. He was hungry.

Inside it was quite dark. A big jukebox shone in the corner of the room, playing *Stop in the Name of Love*. Two overhead fans spun lazily on the low ceiling. Chrome stools with red, vinyl tops and no backs stood in a curve around the horseshoe-shaped counter. Two cattlemen in a booth sat smoking and eating at the same time, their dusty hats on the table. The brothers sat at the counter.

A girl in a pink uniform with a white apron came out from the kitchen to see what they wanted. She was dark.

"Cheeseburger and coke for me," Brad said. "What d'you want, Bri?"

"Can I have a coke float?" he asked.

"You got coke floats here, don't ya?" Brad asked the waitress. She nodded and made a notation on her little pad with a stubby yellow pencil. "And bring us some fries, too. Please."

The girl went back through the little door into the kitchen and shouted something in Spanish.

Brad pivoted in the stool, leaned on his elbow and lit a cigarette. He looked at the bikes through the window. "Nothing like riding a motorcycle, is there?" he said. "The way it feels when you lean into a turn with the wind in your hair."

"What hair, red neck?" Brian sniggered.

Brad ran his hand across his bristle-top again.

"No shit. Feels weird. But they said I can grow it out a little, now I'm through basic."

Brian followed Brad's gaze and looked at the motorcycles, too. "Can't wait till I get my license."

The Supremes stopped, the jukebox clunked and whirred, and *Bridge Over Troubled Water* came up.

The girl brought two cokes to the counter and a soda glass heaped with vanilla ice cream. She removed the caps with a church key she kept on a string around her neck and slid one of the bottles across the counter to Brad. She poured half the coke from the second bottle over the ice cream. It fizzed as the ice cream rose from the bottom. She stuck a long spoon and a straw into the glass and slid it and the rest of the coke across to Brian.

"What were you saying in there," Brad was asking her as she did this, flirting. *"No hablo español."*

She flirted back. "That's for me to know and for you to find out," she said in clipped English.

"Now, I reckon I might just be tempted to try," he grinned.

She flashed white teeth and disappeared back into the kitchen.

Brian watched this while sucking from the straw. "She wants you bad, Brad."

Brad tilted his coke back, then wiped his mouth.

"Well, tell her to take a number and git in line," he said. And they both laughed.

The door opened behind them and three Texas state troopers came in. They had arrived in separate cars, parked outside. Identical blue Fords with white doors. They wore broad brimmed hats, which they removed, but they did not remove their sunglasses. One of them had glasses with mirrored lenses. They sat together in a booth and the waitress brought in a steaming pot of coffee and three mugs. They chatted with her amiably, but Brad could not hear them over Simon and Garfunkle.

"Pigs," he said, with no particular animosity.

Brad and Brian were happy. It had been a wonderful Thanksgiving, with Brad home and their aunt driving over from New Orleans. When they were younger, they fought like brothers do, but they were always fond of each other. They hadn't argued the whole holiday. And they had the motorcycle thing in common.

The waitress appeared again, this time with Brad's burger and the side of fries. Brian shook some ketchup onto the fries and poured the rest of his coke over what was left of the ice cream.

"When you got to go back?" he asked.

"Sunday," Brad answered. "Catch a Greyhound to Austin, then take the redeye to Fort Benning. Then infantry school, another eight weeks. And then, well, it's look out gooks."

They ate in silence. The music changed. Elvis. Orbison. Johnny Cash. The jukebox clunked and whirred between each 45.

"Know what I wish?" Brian asked.

His brother shook his head.

"I wish you could stick over Christmas. We could ride your cycle down to Corpus, or out to Padre Island maybe."

"Like where Dad used to take us?"

Brian nodded. "We could sleep on the beach and catch shrimp in the gulf. Maybe find a guy with a boat who'd take us out fishing."

Brad liked the idea. "It'd be a blast to ride on the beach through the tide pools."

"Yeah, a blast."

Brad finished his burger then worked on Brian's fries. Brian finished off the last of his float. He pivoted on his stool and leaned back on his elbows. He closed his eyes.

"Sleepy?" his older brother asked him.

"Naw. I feel full. But good."

Brad leaned back against the counter, also. "Me too."

The policeman with the mirrored glasses stood up. He placed his hat back on his head, then turned and looked over at Brad and Brian. He walked towards them, crossing the diner. Brad felt his stomach muscles tighten as he watched the trooper approach, but he did not shift his weight from his elbows. Brian's eyes widened.

The policeman took a toothpick from the dispenser on the counter and stuck it in his mouth. "Those your Hondas outside, gentlemen?" he asked.

Brad nodded. "Yes, sir."

"The plates on the black one's expired."

"Oh. Well, we mostly ride on my granddad's property."

The trooper stood silent for a long moment, working the toothpick. Brad could not tell if his words had registered with him. Brian began to squirm on the stool.

The policeman spoke. *"Mostly?"* he repeated.

Brad held his gaze steady. He could see his and Brian's reflection in the man's lenses.

The trooper shifted his gaze to the younger brother. "Is that your motorcycle, son?" he asked.

Brian glanced at Brad, then swallowed. "Yes, sir, it is," he said, his voice barely audible.

"I'm sorry. I couldn't hear you," the policeman said.

Brian cleared his throat and spoke up. "I said, yes sir, it is."

The broad brim of the trooper's hat rose and fell. "I see," he said, finally. He ran a knuckle across his chin. "Well, keep it off the highway."

"Yes, sir."

The trooper turned and strode out of the diner. They watched him cross the graveled lot to his cruiser, enter it, and drive away.

Brian let all the air from his lungs.

Brad shook his head and raised his eyebrows. "Pigs," he repeated, again with no particular animosity. He drew a Winston from the pack and lit it. "Want another coke?" he asked.

"Naw."

They sat awhile and listened to music, Brad smoking, not talking at all. The other policemen left, taking their two cruisers in opposite directions. All the other customers left, also. The place cleared out.

The girl came by and Brad paid her and tipped her a dollar. He didn't speak to her. Instead, he said, "You can ride the 350 while I'm gone if you want."

Brian's eyes lit up. "No shit?"

"Sure. I need someone to change the oil in it and just so long as you keep it clean."

Brian was agreeable. "I'll wash and wax it every time I ride it," he said. Brad smiled at this.

They walked outside and a breeze from the south felt cool for a change. There were clouds on the horizon. Dark clouds.

"Tell you what," Brad said as he straddled his bike. "When I get back you'll be old enough to drive and I reckon you'll have your license. We'll ride on down to Padre then, the two of us."

"Awesome!" Brian said. "You mean it?"

"Sure I mean it."

"We've got to," Brian agreed. "That'd be awesome."

Brad dropped his cigarette butt and stepped on it. "We'll do it, all right."

"Let's make a pact on it," Brian said. He held his hand straight out to Brad. "The minute you get back."

Brad smirked at him and shook his head once, slowly. He kicked the Honda's engine to life. "No sense making pacts," he said. "That's kid stuff."

Brian considered this. The remark smarted a bit. He didn't want to do anything that was kid stuff. He kick-started the Hawk. His big brother hit the highway but instead of heading home he turned and drove back in the direction they came from, towards the millstream.

He wanted to see those deer one last time if he could.

Christmas in Room 201

Everyone knew that Gerald was dying. Everyone, that is, except the little guy himself. The disease which had cast him down and confined him to his bed could not restrict his spirit, and his own intelligence would never conclude such a terrible fact on its own. Someone, we jointly agreed, would simply have to tell him.

Christmas was just a month off. Our prayers for weeks had been that we could share one last Thanksgiving, but now, our bellies full and knees pressed to the cold hardwood floorboards, we asked the impossible. Eyes closed, heads bowed, and huddled around Gerald's bed, we prayed for Christmas.

Mrs. Green, the matron, entered our room and spoke sternly. "Lights out now, children."

"Yes, in a minute," Randolf, my brother, replied. It was bold of him to answer back at all, and the matron paused at the door, her presence demanding an apology. None came. Instead, Randolf rose to his feet and folded his arms. "There is something we must tell Gerald," he said simply.

The matron looked at the four of us still on our knees at little Gerald in the bed, then nodded to Randolf.

"Five minutes," she said, and closed the door.

At thirteen, Randolf was the oldest of the six who slept in our room, and generally his word was law. He was thin and lanky, but very strong. "Stand up," he ordered, and I and the others obeyed at once.

"Now hold hands, and form a circle around Gerald's bed." We did that, too. I thought it was significant that my brother and I each held Gerald's hands, flanking him, with the three girls linking us together. We were the strong ones, I felt, though Gerald lay near death. Sandy, Sharon, and baby Susan seemed the weak ones who needed our protection. Still, it was Sandy who spoke first.

"We love you, Gerald," she said. And we all nodded in agreement.

Gerald's eyes were glazed; he seemed to peer at us through a thick haze. "I know it," he said. He was four, but his illness had aged him. His hair had come out in patches until none was left.

"You're very sick," my brother said to him.

Gerald nodded and sighed deeply. "But won't I get better?"

We all watched Randolf and held our breath. He looked to us for support, but we could offer none. Returning his gaze to Gerald, he shook his head solemnly.

"No." He spoke with authority and finality.

Tears leaped from Gerald's eyes and streamed silently down his cheeks. Sandy squeezed my hand.

"We asked God to give us Christmas together, Gerald," she said.

Gerald looked to Randolf for confirmation.

"You'll have Christmas," Randolf said to him. "I promise you that."

The next morning Dr. Sanderson, the orphanage physician, arrived and entered our room. We were shooed out to breakfast early, and since there was no school that day (it being holiday), we played in the gymnasium with the rest of the kids. We divided into teams and played tag-ball, but those of us who lived together in Room 201 kept a watchful eye on the door through which we knew Dr. Sanderson would emerge. He soon did.

Mrs. Green was with him. "Should he be in the hospital?" I heard her ask.

Dr. Sanderson shook his head. "There's nothing to be done in the hospital, I'm afraid."

Randolf dropped his ball and ran to the doctor. At first the physician had been annoyed by Randolf's directness, but by now he had become used to his questions. "Will Gerald live past Christmas, Doctor? We've promised him Christmas."

"You did that?" Dr. Sanderson replied gruffly, then softened. "Son, if he makes it to the end of the week it will be a miracle. He'll never see Christmas; he's too far gone."

For the rest of the day my brother was not to be found. Mrs. Green was in a quandary when he missed lunch.

Although I knew where he was, I would never tell, for Randolf needed some think-time. "Think-time" was something Father had taught us before he and Mother had perished, and we valued it beyond all else. But as dinner approached, I knew I'd have to fetch him, for Mrs. Green would not tolerate two missed meals.

41

At the apex of the rooftop, his back to the brick chimney, Randolf sat with arms looped about his knees, absorbed in his think-time. I crawled up beside him, and pretended not to notice the sooty streaks on his cheeks. He ran a sleeve under his nose.

"It's a rotten deal," he said to me. I looked over the rooftops at the glass-and-steel skyscrapers on the horizon and nodded in agreement. He spat into the wind. "I promised him Christmas. We asked God to give us Christmas. But he won't see it."

"We asked God for Thanksgiving, Randolf. He gave us that. Maybe He'll give us Christmas, too."

"It's four weeks off," Randolf said bitterly.

We sat silently together a long moment.

"Randolf, will Gerald go to heaven and be with his mother and father?" I asked.

"Yes, of course," Randolf replied.

I rested my head on my arms. "I sometimes wish I could do that."

Before lights-out that night the five of us from Room 201 approached the matron. She was rolling her hair into tiny curls, holding each with bobby pins, and listening to the radio. "What is it, children?" she asked when we interrupted her.

"We'd like to move Christmas up a bit," Randolf said.

Mrs. Green put her pins down. "Do what?"

"We promised Gerald Christmas," Sandy said. "So we'd like to have it this Sunday."

"Now, that's plain foolish," Mrs. Green dismissed us. "Christmas doesn't come in November. And you can't push holidays about like wagons."

But we wouldn't be put off. "We've talked it over," I said, to do my part. "We've *decided*."

Mrs. Green sensed a mutiny. "You've decided?" she said.

"Tomorrow will be Christmas Eve in Room 201," Randolf said.

"We'll decorate a tree there if you don't mind," Sharon said, but she wasn't asking.

"And we'll sing carols and open gifts at midnight," the baby Susan chimed in.

There was no dissuading us. As we marched to our room, Susan stopped in the stairwell. "Won't you join us?" she called to Mrs. Green.

She eyed each of us with squared shoulders, then seemed to collapse in upon herself. "Of course, I will," she promised.

Gerald was thrilled with the idea. "Will Santa come?" he asked.

Randolf shook his head. "It isn't *really* Christmas, Gerald. But we'll make believe that is it. We'll have a Christmas together, the six of us, just as promised. But there will be no Santa Claus."

We spent the whole of Saturday preparing for our Christmas. Randolf vanished over the perimeter wall immediately after breakfast, armed with his pocketknife. He returned hours later with a four-foot pine he had cut himself in Central Park and drug back as best he could. Its branches filled our room and its scent attracted the other children. They came begging to help.

"Make ornaments for the tree," Sandy told them.

Gerald, propped with the pillows in his bed, watched the preparations. He was too weak to help us, but he laughed and shouted encouragement to everyone.

After supper we trimmed the tree in Room 201. Dozens of kids from other rooms tramped through and proudly hung their ornaments, constructed of paper and hand colored. Paper streamers and strings of popcorn were added. A star of tin was placed on top.

The children each spoke to Gerald, wishing him Merry Christmas. Some kissed his forehead or held his hand, while others patted his tiny feet bundled under the blankets. He chatted with them excitedly.

"I hope Santa brings you what you wish," he'd say.

"Happy New Year to you!" I heard him proclaim.

"God bless you!" he told all as they left to make room for the others who clamored in.

With ten o'clock came lights-out and the others were ushered to bed. Those of us in Room 201 sang carols and held hands around our lovely tree, overburdened with so many ornaments.

At eleven Mrs. Green came to our room with a plate of cookies and hot cider. She giggled and laughed with us like a school girl. We sang more carols and then Mrs. Green read to us the Christmas story from Luke, chapter two.

And at midnight we each took our special gifts and laid them upon Gerald's bed. They were wrapped in whatever we could find.

The day had taken its toll on Gerald, but the gifts delighted him. I gave him the flashlight I'd gotten the previous Christmas. Susan gave him her kerchief, and Sharon a whistle made of wood which sounded exactly like the trains that steamed though the city. Sandy had traded her hairbrush for a red wool cap which when placed on Gerald's head made us all laugh. And Randolf's gift was his pocketknife, so highly prized that his sacrifice awed us all.

43

No sooner had Gerald opened his gifts then did we hear a *"thump, thump, thump!"* at the door.

"My goodness!" cried Mrs. Green. "Who on earth could that be at this late hour?" She crossed the room and opened the door in a broad, sweeping motion. There, beaming in the hallway, stood Santa Claus, red suit, white beard, and black boots.

"Ho, Ho, Ho!" he bellowed.

"Santa," we shouted, and jumped into his arms.

Laughing and singing, he drew from his bag candy for us all. He lifted Gerald from his bed and exclaimed, "So, you're the cause of this early Christmas! I'll have you know my reindeer are dog-tired from such an unexpected trip, but I never heard a word of complaint from any of them!"

He told us of a harrowing near miss with an airplane as he circled the Statue of Liberty searching for us and of the antiaircraft guns near Fort Sumter taking pot-shots at him in his sleigh. We laughed and laughed as he told us his stories, drinking our cider and eating our cookies, and when it came time for him to go we children giggled and shouted, "Goodbye, *Doctor* Santa!" Our awareness of his charade seemed to befuddle him, but it only added to our delight. Our sides ached and we lay on the floor in hysterics.

At last we again gathered in a circle around Gerald's bed, holding hands, Mrs. Green joining us. We sang "Silent Night" reverently and had a moment of silent prayer together.

Then Gerald spoke to us, thanking each of us individually for our gifts, and together for our Christmas in Room 201. "I'm afraid I have no gifts for you to open," he said to us. "But I promise you this, when I do get to heaven I intend to look up all of your moms and dads. I'll let them know you're all getting along well. I'll tell them what good friends you were to me. And I'll tell everyone about our Christmas here in this room."

Mrs. Green began to weep and left in a rush.

Finally, Randolf spoke and voiced what we all felt. "I suppose, Gerald," he said, "that your gift is about the finest one I'll ever receive." We all nodded in solemn agreement.

In the morning, Gerald was gone. Mrs. Green quietly returned to each of us the gifts we had given him.

I still have that flashlight, carried so many years and several times around the world. It sits now above my books on a shelf all its own, gathering dust. On the first Sunday after each Thanksgiving, I pull it down, clean it off, and replace the batteries.

If the phone rings on that Sunday, it is usually my brother Randolf calling from his home in New York. I can hear him opening and closing the blade of his pocketknife, its hinges so well-oiled that it snaps shut with a pop. He calls, he says, to check up on me, and to share news of the girls, but we both know his real reason is to keep alive the memory of that Christmas.

It was a Christmas by which all since have been judged, I suppose, that Christmas in Room 201.

The Hobo
(a film play)

FADE IN

EXTERIOR, RURAL COUNTRYSIDE - DAY
It is a hot, dusty-dry summer. The heat rising from the platinum-colored wheat fields distorts the image of a slow moving freight train, rumbling in the distance. It passes through a small rural community unnoticed.

INSERT: "1956"

INSIDE A FREIGHT CAR
It is hot and dirty. We hear the clickety-clack of the car's wheels against steel tracks passing underneath. A figure stirs in a dark corner. He's been sleeping in straw there. The man rises to his feet and moves unsteadily to the open doorway and spits. He is a HOBO, maybe 30 years old, tattered, torn, and in need of a shave. He squats at the edge of the doorway and watches the scenery rumble by. After waiting a moment for the right spot, he leaps...

BESIDE THE TRACKS
The Hobo tumbles into soft dirt, rolling to a stop. He takes a moment, seated there, to slap the dust from his trousers and pick thistles from his red wool socks.

TRUCKING WITH THE HOBO
The Hobo makes his way through the tall grass of a wheat field towards a small group of homes on the outskirts of town.

EXTERIOR, A RURAL COMMUNITY - DAY
A group of kids are playing marbles in the backyard of one of the houses. They are a ragtag bunch of youngsters, wearing jeans with holes worn in the knees, rolled at the cuffs. The yard they play in is yellowed from a lack of water. One of them, the only girl, is a tomboy named CYNTHY. She is seven years old. She spots the approaching Hobo and points to him.

      CYNTHY: *Look, a hobo!*

The others look and rise to their feet.

BILLY, a lanky youngster taller than the rest, watches the Hobo with keen interest.

      BILLY: *What's he want, I wonder.*

      CYNTHY: *Somethin' to eat, prob'ly. Or money.*

      BILLY: *Money?*

JIMMY, a stout little fellow spits.

      JIMMY: *To buy booze. My dad says hobos would kill ya for a quarter to buy booz.... They carry switchblades, ya know.*

This comment registers with the little tomboy.

      CYNTHY: *Switchblades!*

The information sharpens Billy's and the others' focus, and they watch the Hobo with mouths open.

ANGLE ON THE HOBO
He sees the kids but does not acknowledge them, averting his eyes. Kids are trouble, he figures. He walks past them in the yard to the backdoor of the older, rather rundown, rural house.

The Hobo raps his knuckles on the door. It is a polite, obviously practiced knock – firm, but gentle. It is meant to convey that the one doing the knocking has every right to be here at this door.

After a moment a woman in a thin, cotton dress opens the door. She is the TOMBOY'S MOTHER and she has a towheaded TODDLER, three years old, on her hip.

The Hobo removes his hat and crumples it in his hands.

> HOBO: *Ma'am. I'm a man down on his luck. Could you spare me somethin'?*

The woman eyes him briefly through the screen door, then disappears momentarily. She returns and thrusts a handful of sliced white bread and an apple through the doorway.

> HOBO (genuinely pleased): *Thank you, ma'am!*

He peers at her for a long moment – the woman and her baby peer back.

> TOMBOY'S MOTHER (sarcastically): *Somethin' else?*

The Hobo turns the corner of his mouth downward and shakes his head no.

> TOMBOY'S MOTHER: *Alrighty then. My husband is due home in a minute. He don't take kindly to strangers.*

She dry swallows. Her eyes tell us she is lying, being protective.

The Hobo replaces the hat on his head and with a polite nod turns away. He walks past the kids toward the next house, a half city-block away in this rural neighborhood.

The Hobo moves along with a lanky stride. He chomps on the apple but slips the bread inside his shirt for later.

ANGLE ON THE CHILDREN
They kneel and turn back to their marbles. But the tomboy Cynthy continues to watch the Hobo with keen eyes and a furrowed brow.

      CYNTHY: *He's goin' ta your house next, Billy.*

Billy looks, but quickly returns to the game.

      BILLY: *He won't git nothin'. Ma's drunk.*

DISSOLVE

EXTERIOR, BILLY'S HOUSE – DUSK
Billy runs through the twilight and takes the back-porch steps two at a time. He crashes through the screen door and disappears inside.

INTERIOR, BILLY'S HOUSE – IN THE KITCHEN
He slides into the kitchen, opens the refrigerator and retrieves a glass bottle quart of milk. From the cupboard he grabs a colored tin cup and pours milk to its brim.

But Billy freezes at the sight of the kitchen table. It is set with two soup bowls, one dirty and the other untouched. A large metal pot half full of cold stew is there also.

      BILLY: *Uh-oh.*

There is a sound behind him that paralyzes him with fear. He turns.

Billy's MOTHER, a woman in her early-thirties, stands before him with arms loosely folded across her chest. She wears a shapeless, cotton smock. Her face is hard-lined and unsmiling – and she grips a thick bamboo stick in one hand, like a club. She holds a tumbler of whiskey-over-ice in the other.

Billy shrieks and steps back.

      BILLY: *Ma, I didn't know! I didn't **know**, Ma!*

49

He backs into the counter near the sink. His mother shoots the whiskey and sets the glass aside.

> BILLY'S MOTHER: *I fixt yer supper, you little bastard. I warned you about missin' supper.*

> BILLY (near hysterical): *I didn't know! You didn't fix none yesterday!*

She raises the bamboo stick high above her head in a drunken frenzy.

> BILLY'S MOTHER: *I'll learn ya to miss supper!*

She swings the heavy stick and connects across the side of Billy's head. He yelps, throwing up his hands, trying to rush past her, but she swings again. The stick slaps across his shoulders with a sickening thud.

Billy cries out pitifully, pleading *No Ma! No Ma!*, but his mother cuffs him across the ear with her open hand. She is unsteady on her feet and absolutely and irrationally furious.

She backhands the bamboo across Billy's nose, splitting it, blackening his eyes almost instantly.

> BILLY'S MOTHER: *Never you never miss **supper!***

Billy stumbles back into the kitchen table. The stick, flailed wildly, cracks across his head. It almost knocks him out cold, but he staggers, reaching blindly. His hand falls across the handle of a large, serrated bread knife lying next to a loaf of bread. His fingers instinctively close around it.

Billy's mother charges upon him drunkenly with the bamboo stick cocked back like a baseball bat...

Defensively, Billy lunges forward into his onrushing mother, his own hands thrust forward. The knife he holds pierces the cotton smock, sinking to its hilt into his mother's ribcage just below her breast.

His mother stops, drawing a sharp breath of air. She studies the knife's handle protruding from her chest, at first not comprehending, then knowing. A crimson stain oozes from the wound. She looks up and focuses, her eyes connecting with those of her son.

Billy shrieks as his mother collapses. He falls upon her, wailing, screaming... *No Ma! No Ma!*

DISSOLVE

EXTEROR, BILLY'S HOME – NIGHT
A COUNTY SHERIFF'S POLICE CAR, its single red lamp flashing but chrome fender-mounted siren silent, is parked askew in Billy's front yard.

A huge CADILLAC AMBULANCE is also there, its rear door open.

The COUNTY SHERIFF is questioning Billy's neighbors. He's a big man, mid-fifties, and is well-known by these people...

ANGLE ON THE CROWD
Billy's neighbors are coming out in their nightclothes to see what all the commotion is about. They've been awakened by the sirens and flashing lights.

We hear a murmur in the crowd as someone raises her voice...

FEMALE VOICE IN THE CROWD: *Murder?!*

The others react to this, frightened. We hear various other voices, too, male and female, asking:

VOICES IN THE CROWD (spilling over each other):
*How was she killed? **Murder**, you say? Knifed! Who? Ella? **Ella Barton**? Oh, my Lord Jesus! Who done it? **Oh, butcher!***

The clamor for information rises. The Sheriff raises his hands to quiet the crowd.

SHERIFF: *Now, hold it down folks. Please.*

Billy's tomboy friend Cynthy is at the front of the group with her parents, the woman who gave the Hobo a meal and her barrel-chested husband, TOMBOY'S FATHER.

TOMBOY'S FATHER (to the Sheriff): *What's goin' on here, Ed?*

Two AMBULANCE ATTENDENTS bring Billy through the door. He is strapped to a stretcher, unconscious.

SHERIFF: *Stand back, folks.*

As Billy passes the crowd gasps at the sight of him. His eyes are puffy slits, his nose is spit and bleeding and lips swollen.

CYNTHY: *Billy!*

The ambulance crew loads him inside and prepares to depart. The Sheriff faces the crowd of neighbors, raising his arms…

SHERIFF: *Folks, please.* **Please!** *Your neighbor, ah, Ella Barton, is dead I'm afraid. She's been stabbed.*

Confusion and dismay rifles through the crowd as the rumors they've been hearing are confirmed.

SHERIFF: *Her boy, Billy. Well, he's been beaten. Does anybody know where the father is?*

Cynthy's father steps forward.

TOMBOY'S FATHER: *Sure, Ed. Don't you remember? That was Davey Barton, killed at the mill last year....*

The Sheriff recalls, and looks back at the house.

SHERIFF: *Sure, I remember. So that was Davey Barton's wife?*

The group confirms this.

SHERIFF: *Alright. Did any of you see if Mrs. Barton had any visitors today?*

Billy's tomboy friend pipes up.

CYNTHY: *I did, Sheriff! I did!*

TOMBOY'S FATHER: *What!?*

The Sheriff kneels before the young girl. She is clearly in awe of him.

TOMBOY'S FATHER (encouragingly): *Now honey, don't you be afraid. Tell the Sheriff everythin' ya seen.*

CYNTHY: *It was a **hobo**. All us kids seen him. Mama gave him a apple!*

The girl's mother recalls him excitedly.

TOMBOY'S MOTHER: *That's right! He came to the back door this afternoon. Lookin' for a handout so I gave him some bread and an apple. Why, he gave me the filthiest look, too. Scared me ta death!*

The crowd excites audibly at this report…

TOMBOY'S MOTHER (continuing, to her husband): I *told him you was due home any minute and he went away.*

CYNTHY: *Hobo's carry switchblades! They kill folks for a quarter!*

The neighbors are alarmed by this. Their rancor builds. They are becoming angry.

SHERIFF: *Now, wait a minute.*
(to Cynthy)
What's your name, honey?

CYNTHY: *Cynthy.*

SHERIFF: *OK, Cynthy. Now tell me. Did you see this hobo come over here after he left your place?*

Cynthy nods enthusiastically.

CYNTHY: *Yes sir, I did. All us kids seen him.*

One of the neighbors shouts…

ANGRY MAN: *That's does it! I know where them hobos sleep down by the river…*

TOMBOY'S FATHER: *That's right. So do I…*

SHERIFF: *Hey, hey! Hold up! You let me handle this.*

TOMBOY'S FATHER: *No bum's gonna mess with our women an' children!*

ANGRY MAN: *He beat hell outta little Billy, the coward!*

A second angry man jumps into the fray.

2ND ANGRY MAN: *Prob'ly raped poor ol' Mrs. Barton, too. Before he cut her throat.*

The crowd gasps.

SHERIFF (exasperated): *Now who said anythin' about her throat bein' cut?!*

TOMBOY'S FATHER (calling to the men in the crowd):
Git your lanterns and rifles, any of you with the guts for
it. And meet me at the Dixie in twenty minutes!

The men and women in the crowd shout and holler at one another as they begin to disperse...

SHERIFF: *Now hold on a minute!* **Hold on!**

He barks orders and protests loudly but goes unheeded by the crowd. They go their separate ways and leave him alone in the darkness.

DISSOLVE

EXTERIOR, THE DIXIE TAVERN - NIGHT
The Dixie Tavern is a local meeting place in this rural community. It is a one story building with dark windows. Moths flutter about the neon sign that alternately flashes *THE DIXIE* and *BEER & WINE.*

The graveled parking lot is filling quickly with arriving pickups, Dodges, Fords and Studebakers. They are driven by Billy's neighbors and others who have been called to the occasion. Each of the pickups has a rifle in a gun rack in the rear window.

The TOMBOY'S FATHER arrives and greets both the ANGRY MAN and 2ND ANGRY MAN as they enter the tavern.

INTERIOR, THE DIXIE TAVERN – NIGHT
The dimly lit Dixie is suddenly busy with arriving men. They all immediately head for the bar and order beer. A juke box glows in the corner as Marty Robbins croons "I Just Can't Help Singing the Blues."

The Tomboy's Father calls attention to all who are present...

TOMBOY'S FATHER: *Hey you men, listen up. In case*
you ain't heard, somethin' terrible's happened tonight.

Those patrons of the tavern playing pool put their cue sticks down. Others turn in their stools to listen.

TOMBOY'S FATHER (continuing): *This afternoon a hobo came ta my place and threatened my wife and kids.*

Someone hands him a mug of beer and he quaffs it.

TOMBOY'S FATHER (continuing): *Then the sonovabitch went over to the widder Barton's. He thrashed the daylights outta her boy Billy and then had his way with her.*

The group in the tavern shouts angrily in disbelief and dismay.

TOMBOY'S FATHER (continuing): *That ain't all. Then the bastard slit her throat, **ear ta ear!***

This moves those in the tavern to a strident fury. All in the tavern are livid. Their voices rise in pitch as they shout at one another.

TOMBOY'S FATHER (continuing, shouting): *We're goin' down ta the river where them bums camp and clean 'em out! Let's go, boys!*

They all shout enthusiastically and crowd through the tavern's narrow exit. Most carry six packs under their arms.

EXTERIOR, THE DIXIE - NIGHT
As the men pour out of the Dixie they are confronted by the lone Sheriff. He rests coolly against the hood of his patrol car, arms crossed and hat tipped back on his head.

The angry men hesitate at the sight of him.

SHERIFF: *Now just where d'you boys think you're goin'?*

The men study him. They glance nervously at one another. No one wants to be spokesman now.

SHERIFF (continuing): *And what is it you're plannin' ta do when you git there?*

Finally, the Tomboy's Father speaks up.

TOMBOY'S FATHER: *Well, Sheriff, we're goin' down ta the river and clean out them drunks down there.*

SHERIFF: *Gonna run 'em off, are ya?*

TOMBOY'S FATHER: *That's right.*

SHERIFF: *Lemme ask ya this. You want me ta catch whoever murdered Mrs. Barton? Bring 'em ta justice?*

The men nod and agree that that is *precisely* what they want him to do.

SHERIFF (angered): *And how do ya 'spect me to do that if you go down there and scatter my prime suspects ta hell and gone?*

The men look at each other. They hadn't thought of this.

2ND ANGRY MAN: *See here, Sheriff. You can't 'spect us ta sit 'round here and do nothin'! With our women and children attacked!*

SHERIFF: *That is ex-actly what I expect of ya.*

TOMBOY'S FATHER (mediating): *Alright, then. We won't run 'em off. We'll circle their hobo camp and capture the lot of 'em!*

A roar of approval goes up from the angry group of men.

SHERIFF: *You do that and you'll be breakin' the law! Interferin' with a criminal investigation!*

TOMBOY'S FATHER: *Just try ta stop us, Sheriff!*

More shouts and angry talk erupt from the crowd. They flood past the protesting sheriff and into their pickups. Starters grind, engines turn over and rumble, blue smoke erupts from tailpipes.

The sheriff pleads for sensibility, but the men are in no mood for reason.

DISSOLVE

EXTERIOR, A COUNTRY ROAD – NIGHT
The neighbors of Billy Barton roll along the two-lane blacktop in a long caravan, each pickup nose-to-bumper to another pickup. There is a bright, full moon and it is a clear, cloudless night.

The line of vehicles pulls off the highway and coasts to a stop next to a sheep pasture. A flock of sheep munches quietly in the otherwise empty field.

The men exit their pickups, most of them discarding empty beer bottles into the ditch alongside the road.

They huddle together around the Tomboy's Father and the two Angry Men.

ANGRY MAN: *This is it.*

2ND ANGRY MAN (pointing across the field): *They camp over there, down by the river. See them campfires?*

The men all look.

Across the pasture, beyond the grazing sheep, is a line of trees. Through the branches the flicker of campfires is visible, and blue smoke curls into the moonlit sky.

TOMBOY'S FATHER: *Yeah. I see 'em.*

Tomboy's Father hoists a Coleman lantern and pumps it. A Winchester 30-30 carbine rifle is slung over his shoulder.

ANGRY MAN: *What's the plan? We gotta have a plan.*

TOMBOY'S FATHER (pumping the lantern): *Right. You take half the men and come down from the north.*

He strikes a match and ignites the lantern.

TOMBOY'S FATHER (continuing): *And I'll take the rest and come up from the south.*

ANGRY MAN: *They may try to swim the river.*

2ND ANGRY MAN: *They do and they drown. River's deep and swift in there.*

ANGRY MAN: *What if they run? Or... charge us?*

TOMBOY'S FATHER (addressing the group of men): *You men better watch out, 'cause most of these bums carry switchblades, razors and such.*

2ND ANGRY MAN: *They might even have guns.*

This thought gives the men pause. It isn't something they had thought of before.

TOMBOY'S FATHER: *We're ready for them. They fire at us and we fire right back.*

This is something they all agree on.

WIDE VIEW OF THE PASTURE
The armed men split into two groups, cross under the barbed-wire fence that borders the highway and cut through the field. The sheep scatter in the moonlight.

They chatter nervously with one another, making no attempt at stealth. Their lanterns and flashlights cast eerie shadows across their faces and flash stray beams of light across the pasture to the trees lining the river...

EXTERIOR, THE RIVERSIDE HOBO CAMP – NIGHT

The hobo camp does indeed exist. There are three or four campfires burning with men gathered near each one. The river flows dark and swift nearby, but the opposite shore is not too far distant. Some of the men sleep, others recline against rocks while visiting with one another in hushed tones. A makeshift tent and bedrolls are visible.

We see by the light of the moon and the campfires that these are dirty, unkempt and ragged looking men with shaggy faces and patched clothes. Most of them smoke cigars, pipes or cigarettes.

Four men warm their backs near a large campfire, playing cards with a filthy deck. A bottle of Mad Dog 20/20 and other assorted bottles of cheap wine are passed amongst them.

The CAMERA PANS UP from the cards in the dealer's hand revealing that he is none other than the HOBO who begged for food earlier in the day. His crumpled hat sits back upon his head, and he draws on a stubby cigar. He distributes the cards amongst those playing then considers his own hand thoughtfully.

TRUCKING, IN THE WOODS

The armed residents from the nearby community have crossed the field and now enter the woods. They stomp through the thick underbrush with very little cunning or stealth. Tree limbs crack and twigs snap underfoot.

Their faces reveal the truth. They're angry, yes, but frightened too. Their eyes glance nervously from shadow to shadow. They jerk their flashlights, the beams jumping crazily. The moon slips eerily in and out of view behind the treetops. Thorny branches scratch at their faces...

THE HOBO CARD GAME

A poker hand plays out. The hobos mutter to one another: *I'm in for a nickel. I'll raise ya a nickel. I'll see yer damn dime and raise ya another! OK boys, read 'em and weep.*

Behind the hobo card players we see the beams of flashlights and lanterns approaching, flashing amongst the treetops.

CLOSE ANGLE ON TOMBOY'S FATHER
Leading a dozen others in his group, approaching from the south, he reaches
the edge of the hobo camp and surveys it from behind a fallen log. The others
creep up behind him.

The hobos are clearly visible from this vantage point.

ACROSS THE CAMP, ANGLE ON ANGRY MAN
The Angry Man leads his group also, coming downstream from the north. He
forces his way through thick undergrowth, rifle clutched in both hands.

But the Angry Man's feet tangle in the roots of the undergrowth, and he
stumbles forward to his belly. As he strikes the ground, his rifle fires: *BOOM!*

ANGLE ON TOMBOY'S FATHER
The bullet strikes the fallen tree behind which Tomboy's Father is standing
and splinters wood. He jumps back startled and his lantern crashes to the
ground...

> TOMBOY'S FATHER: *Jesus Christ!* (he cocks the
> carbine) *They're shootin' at us!*

He swings his rifle up over the top of the log, takes aim and fires: *BOOM!*

The others in his group panic and do likewise: *BOOM! BOOM-BOOM!
BOOM!*

AT THE CAMP
The hobos jump to their feet, confused and frightened. One of the card
players takes the first bullet in his belly and crumples.

ANGLE ON THE ANGRY MAN
He and those with him are startled by the gunfire. They raise their rifles and
let loose with a volley: *BOOM! BOOM! BOOM-BOOM-BOOM!*

AT THE HOBO CAMP, VARIOUS ANGLES
The hail of bullets from two directions tears up the camp. Several hobos drop
where they stand as lead slugs cut through them, blood gushing. Others jump

for cover. The bullets slash through the makeshift tents and bedrolls. Coffee pots fly off campfire embers and wine bottles shatter to bits as slugs pass through them.

There is mass pandemonium and the roar of gunfire is deafening: *BOOM-BOOM! BOOM-BOOM-BOOOM!*

One by one the confused hobos are shot dead as they attempt to escape. Caught in a crossfire, they have little hope of finding cover. One fellow drags himself in agony across the camp by his arms, legs still and unmoving, until a second slug hits him between the shoulder blades. An old wino drops to his knees and falls back, a bullet hole between his eyes and the back of his skull missing. A younger bum screams on the ground, holding his chest as blood gurgles forth, legs kicking futilely.

TRUCKING WITH THE HOBO
But the Hobo who asked for food at Billy Barton's earlier that afternoon makes a mad dash through the hail of bullets for the river. He runs in red wool socks, his shoes left at the campfire. Madly, he leaps across boulders and dives headlong into the swift river as bullets whiz all about him. He surfaces once for a gulp of air, visible briefly in the moonlight, then submerges from sight.

WIDE ANGLE ON THE CAMP
The *BOOM! BOOM! BOOM!* of the rifle fire continues briefly, sporadically, then stops suddenly. There is no movement in the camp.

SLOW DISSOLVE

EXTERIOR, THE HOBO CAMP – DAY
It is early morning but hot already. The camp is crawling with men in blue uniforms and Smokey Bear hats: STATE TROOPERS. They are taking pictures with large cameras and gathering evidence, placing markers around the bodies of the dead hobos where they lay.

EXTERIOR, THE COUNTRY ROAD – DAY
The car that approaches and speeds by with its red light flashing and siren blaring is that of the County Sheriff. We see that he has a passenger with him: young Billy Barton.

INSIDE THE SHERIFF'S CAR
Billy's head is bandaged, his eye swollen, lips puffy. He rides in silence alongside the Sheriff. The Sheriff has had a long night and shows it. His face is haggard; his eyes droop. He lights a cigarette and studies Billy from the corner of his eye.

> SHERIFF: *You know what finger prints are, son?*

Billy doesn't seem too surprised by the question. He nods.

> SHERIFF (continuing) *Whose finger prints you reckon we'll find on that knife?*

Billy thinks about this a moment. He draws a breath to clears his throat.

> BILLY: *The one who kilt my ma.*

The Sheriff nods.

> SHERIFF: *Yes sir. That is correct. That's how we'll know who done it.*

Billy turns his head away and watches the passing scenery from his window.

The Sheriff draws thoughtfully on his cigarette and exhales the blue smoke.

> SHERIFF (continuing): *You've had a pretty tough year, ain't ya, Billy? What with your dad in the accident at the mill, and now your ma.*

Billy does not respond to this.

> SHERIFF (continuing): *She was pretty tough on you, wasn't she?*

Billy turns now and looks at him dully.

> SHERIFF (continuing): *You know your neighbor lady? She told me your ma beat you. That true?*

Billy is horrified that the Sheriff, and others, know this.

> SHERIFF (demanding an answer): ***Huh!?***

Billy studies his hands quietly a moment.

> BILLY (softly): *Yes, sir. Only since Pa died.*

The Sheriff nods, understanding.

EXTERIOR, AT THE SHEEP PASTURE – DAY
The Sheriff brings the cruiser to a halt alongside the two-lane blacktop. There is a line of State Police patrol cars there, black-and-whites, all empty, and he pulls in behind them.

INSIDE THE SHERIFF'S CAR
He turns off the ignition and pulls the parking brake, but does not open the door or move to exit. Instead, the two of them sit silently as the Sheriff shoves the cigarette butt through the wing window and immediately lights another.

> SHERIFF (drawing and blowing smoke): *It's an interesting thing about finger prints, Billy. They smudge real easy, and they wipe clean with a cloth.*

Billy and the Sheriff eye each other a long moment.

> SHERIFF (continuing): *You see, I ain't turned that knife over to the State Police yet.*

Billy is confused and doesn't know how to respond.

> SHERIFF (continuing): *The way I see it, Billy, is this. A bad thing happened last night. Thirteen bums and winos got themselves killed, and so did your ma. You? You got yourself busted up real bad.*

He draws deeply on the cigarette then exhales through his nose.

SHERIFF (continuing): *And a lot of good men, normally law-abiding men, each with families of their own to care for, well, they went off half-cocked and got into a mess of trouble. They may go to prison, Billy, for killin' those hobos – even if they was just bums, tramps and lowlife.*

The Sheriff draws another deep draft on the cigarette, then rolls down his window and chucks it outside.

SHERIFF (continuing): *And, son, you may be goin' to prison too, when they find your prints on that knife what killed your mother.*

This bit of news stuns Billy. His face crumples and he bursts into tears, sobbing heavily.

BILLY (crying, gasping): *I didn't mean it! She was crazy mad – on a drunk! She beat me with that stick, I didn't mean it!*

He sobs with deep despair: *I didn't mean it! I didn't mean it!*

The Sheriff reaches across the car and pulls him to him.

After a moment, he shushes the boy.

SHERIFF: *Now listen to me. There's a way we can fix this mess for ever'body. We got to make them state troopers believe that your neighbors weren't half as nuts as they really was. But you got to tell a story and stick to it.*

Billy looks up at him and wipes the tears from his eyes.

SHERIFF (continuing): *Can you do that, son?*

Billy contemplates the sheriff's question a long moment…

EXTERIOR, THE HOBO CAMP – DAY
The bodies of thirteen dead hobos are lined up side-by-side on the riverbank. STATE POLICE and several NEWSMEN mill about. Some of the newsmen take flash photos of the scene.

The Sheriff and Billy step out of the woods and follow the path into the camp, then make their way towards a group of troopers. The one in charge, a State Police CAPTAIN, spots the Sheriff and Billy.

  CAPTAIN: *Hello, Ed. This the boy?*

  SHERIFF: *Yes sir, it surely is. Pretty game kid. Billy, this is Captain Brown of the State Police.*

Billy looks at him, unsure of himself.

  CAPTAIN: *I know this is tough on you, son.*

Billy nods.

  SHERIFF: *Billy says he won't never forget the men that attacked him and his ma.*

The Captain motions toward the line up of dead winos.

  CAPTAIN: *Go ahead, then. See if you can spot any of them a-lyin' over there.*

Billy hesitates, but makes his way to the gruesome lineup. The Captain and the Sheriff watch him intently.

The youngster starts at one end and steps over the dead men, one by one, pausing to look down at each face. He stops over one of them, pointing.

  BILLY: *This is the one that beat me.*

He continues over two more, then stops again.

BILLY: *This one held my mother down.*

He steps over three more, hovering over the last.

BILLY: *And this one here stabbed my ma. He used a bread knife.*

Billy runs to the river's edge and vomits.

The Captain and the Sheriff glance at each other.

CAPTAIN: *Well, how you like that? We got us a positive ID from a witness at the scene.*

SHERIFF (with a nod and a shrug): *That does it then.* (He eyes the dead hobos.) *What you think'll happen to the ol' boys what done this?*

CAPTAIN (with a chuckle): *Hell, they overreacted some little bit, didn't they!?* (He laughs broadly.) *I dunno, Ed. I reckon no jury is gonna be too harsh on 'em. After all, they got the bastards who hurt this little boy and killed his ma. Right?*

SHERIFF (nods): *That's how I figure it, too.*

He walks over to Billy at the riverside and puts a hand on his shoulder.

The boy wretches some more, vomiting into the river…

DISSOLVE

EXTERIOR, THE COUNTRY ROAD – DAY
The Sheriff's cruiser ambles unhurriedly down the blacktop, heading back to town. There is no siren now. No flashing light.

INSIDE THE SHERIFF'S CAR
The Sheriff smokes in silence. Billy is silent also, staring unseeing out his window. His puffy eyes focus on something far distant…

67

BILLY'S VIEW
In the distance, its image distorted some by the heat of the day, a freight train rumbles along the tracks that slice through a wheat field. The railroad angles across the highway ahead...

AT THE RAILROAD CROSSING
Lights flash, a bell dings. The big train engine steams slowly over the country highway as the Sheriff's cruiser rolls to a stop to await its passing.

INSIDE THE SHERIFF'S CAR
Billy watches the passing boxcars with disinterest. They rumble by noisily.

BILLY'S VIEW
The last of many boxcars approaches just ahead of the caboose and passes before him. Its huge door is open.

The HOBO who begged for food at Billy's home only yesterday sits in the boxcar's open doorway, feet dangling. He wears no shoes and is shaking dirt from a pair of damp red socks...

The Hobo glances up, sees the sheriff's patrol car, and immediately tenses.

THE HOBO'S VIEW OF THE CRUISER
The young boy watches him through the cruiser's windshield, unblinking.

INSIDE THE SHERIFF'S CAR
Billy stares at the hobo as the train passes, eyebrows raised and his mouth a little "o".

The Sheriff glances at the hobo with the red socks, then studies Billy a long moment. He wonders...?

EXTERIOR, THE RAILROAD CROSSING – DAY
The caboose crosses the highway as the train lumbers onward. The lights stop flashing, the bells ceases to ding. The Sheriff's cruiser grinds into first and eases over the tracks, picking up momentum, shifting through its gears...

CAMERA PULLS BACK SLOWLY TO A LONG SHOT
We watch the cruiser and the freight train go their separate ways... until the images of both distort in the blistering heat.

FADE OUT

Everett

I have a confession to make. It's not very pretty, but it's one I feel I must make public – the airing of an old, festering wound which I've kept buried in the darkest corner of my soul for far too long now.

In the fall where I grew up, autumns were *orange*. I mean bright, vibrant orange with variant hues of yellow and red. And the sky was perpetual blue – that crisp, cloudless blue like a canopy stretched taut from the Coast Range to the Cascades with no mar or imperfection. And the grass at our place was thick because it was too damp with dew to mow that late in the autumn, in the fall.

One such fall in my tenth year, there came a new boy to our grade school. His name was Everett and, for whatever reason children choose to do these things, we other kids didn't like him much. Country kids can be clannish, I suppose, and always a new kid has it rough.

Everett's family was from the south, so he had a cowboy drawl, which we mimicked mercilessly. His clothes were a bit more ragtag than ours, and his shoes were what we termed "clodhoppers." I clearly remember all of us standing along the edge of the baseball diamond, taunting him, tossing dirt clods his direction as he ran from us sobbing tearfully. His crying when we teased him was fuel-to-fire. "Crybaby," we catcalled.

Everett and his family were our neighbors. They lived a quarter mile or so to the north of us. Their home was an old, run-down, faded, yellow farm shack that they had rented just that spring. It wasn't much, an acre or so of land, a corral and some stables attached to the back of the house, an old chicken coop used for storing hay.

Everett's mother was a large woman and he had three, maybe four, younger brothers and sisters. They were poor, they just didn't have much. But Everett had something – *one* thing – that was the envy of all of us at school:

70

a great, sorrel-red show horse with white stockings and a blaze face. Oh! It was a beautiful animal.

Now, the owning of a horse was no big deal. I had a horse, my cousins owned horses; in fact, nearly everybody in our rural school grew up owning horses. But Everett's horse was a *show* horse. It had won trophies and ribbons, which he brought to school one show-and-tell session. Everett even got to ride it at the State Fair, on its big black saddle with silver sequins and a braided lariat.

When I would climb to the top of the old cottonwood on our place, I could see him on late afternoons, after school, riding his sorrel around the corral. Round and round, his prize animal jumped barrels, head held high, mane flowing, tail like a flag raised in tribute.

Afterwards, Everett would curry that big animal, brushing dust and dirt from it, talking to it in confident tones carried to my ear by a gentle breeze. A boy and his best friend. Everett was no crybaby with that sorrel.

I will never forget that Indian summer Saturday when, as the sun was just slipping behind Mary's Peak and the western sky began to glow, and we neighborhood kids were playing in our front yard near the weeping willow. We all of a sudden heard Everett's screams and saw him running toward us up the highway from his home. The back of his shirt was black and smoking. He threw himself into the cool grass at our feet. "Our house is afire!" he cried. "Our house is afire! We don't have no phone; call the fire trucks!"

We were stunned. We looked at him, and then at his home. Bright orange flames were licking out the windows and black smoke snaked from the doorway.

The rural fire department responded quickly, but it was mostly too late. They saved what they could of the farmhouse, but the stables in back burned to the ground. My father and brother and I wandered over as the firemen were finishing up. We went between the fire trucks to see what we could see in the dusk. There, where the stables had stood, I saw Everett's sorrel on its side, black with soot. It was burnt, bloated and split like an over-broiled sausage. Its proud tail was gone, nothing left but a charred twig, and its eyelids were burned away. It stared, and I stared horrified, too long. The image and stench of that animal is with me today, I can see it this moment.

Our teacher told us later what happened.

They were painting the inside of that old farmhouse when the turpentine used for cleaning the brushes had flashed against a heater. Everett was severely injured. He was to be in the hospital for some time, we were told, his back badly burned.

Here, I guess, is where my confession begins. I was waiting for the school bus one morning and there, up the highway, came Everett! I hadn't seen him since the fire and he *never* rode the bus. He always walked the mile or so to school.

I watched him as he approached and determined in my mind that I would say I was sorry to Everett, about his red sorrel and about his home burning down. I decided that I would apologize for teasing him and then ask him to play with us at recess.

But when he came near, I couldn't. He stood stiffly and looked across the highway at sheep in the pasture there. He didn't look at me and I couldn't speak. I wanted to tell him that I had watched him ride the sorrel from the top of the cottonwood, and I wanted to tell him that I was sorry we teased him, and I wanted to ask him to play with us at recess. I wanted to tell him all those things but, God forgive me, when he came near I smelled smoke on his clothes and I couldn't speak.

Not one word came from my lips.

Soon, the school bus arrived and we got on it. We went to separate seats, I to my friends and he to the empty bench in the back. His family moved away a few weeks later and I never got to tell him what I wanted to. I never had another chance.

To this day, when Everett thinks of me, he probably remembers a teasing, unfeeling brat who didn't care enough to even acknowledge his presence, much less his pain and hurt. And in a sense, I confess, he's right. I was! But forever after, even now, the smell of campfires, or of fields burning in August, or a backed up flue, any smoke at all brings to memory the sight of that smoldering red sorrel and the smell of Everett's clothes, and deep in my guts I want to find him and tell him:

"I'm sorry, Everett. I really am."

Muddy Boots

I will put this down just as it happened, no yarn or stretched truth. Just because I am Texan don't mean I can't relate facts without embellishment.

I had celebrated my twenty-first birthday. My folks were dead, killed some ten years earlier, and I had no brothers nor sisters; the only relation I got is Old Uncle Billy, my pa's elder brother. Billy is a name that fits him as he is an old goat who lives alone in a little stone house he built himself, in West Texas, near a natural spring on the outskirts of Midland. He is tender toward me so I try to get by to see him once or twice a year, as my travels let me, for although I am poor I travel light and get around some little bit.

By trade I am a drover – that is, I make my living on the back of a horse. I work for hire where I can, at two or three different ranches up along the Red River. I am not inexperienced, despite my young age, and have made the drive along the Chisholm Trail to Kansas and back twice. I am not displeased with my wages, they are enough for a single fellow like me to live as I please, but my pa died owing money and until I have paid all of his debts, I choose to live simply. I learned early to enjoy jerky and soda biscuits. Strangers remark that I am a healthy-looking fellow, for I have broad shoulders and a barrel for a chest. Quite natural, I suppose, given the years I've spent wrestling longhorn steers to the ground.

I was hoping that Uncle Billy would invite me to spend Christmas with him. I was broke on account of the fact that I had paid off one of Pa's creditors. This made the gentleman very happy, indeed, for he told me he never expected to see his money. But it left me with nothing in my pockets. I was feeling restless and was wondering how I would get through the season when a wire from Billy found me in Amarillo. "COME HITHER 4 X-MAS," it said, signed *Billy*, and that was enough. I packed my saddlebags and was off at dawn the next morning.

It can rain, hail and even snow in North Texas at Christmas time, and I saw it all as I traveled. But by the time I reached Midland, it warmed considerable, which brought a thaw and the awful misery of mud. Those last two miles from Midland to Uncle Billy's nearly wasted my old mare – I was forced to stop every hundred yards or so and scrape the mud from her hooves. When at last I crossed the little ridge and came upon that familiar stone cabin, I was quite pleased to see Uncle Billy in a rocker on the porch, bundled against the cold, a slip of smoke curling from his pipe. "It's been nasty," he called out when he saw me. "The ice caved me in." He made a motion with his pipe.

I surveyed his place from atop my mare and could see what he meant. The roof of the cabin had given way on the south end, buckled, and let rain inside. The south end was a spare room where I bunked in past visits. "Reckon we'll bunk together till Aaron Hadley gets my lumber order ready."

I told Uncle Billy that any dry place was good enough for me, that his company was all I sought for Christmas, but I recollected how the old goat snorted and belched in his sleep and the thought of our bunking together did not particularly please me.

Billy rocked himself out of his chair. "Stable your horse, boy, and I will kettle us some beans."

At the stable, just downstream from the cabin, I fed and curried the mare. She had worked up a sweat fighting the mud, and so I curry combed the dirt from her hide. I then hunkered down to the task of thoroughly scraping the pasty earth from her hooves. This was no small task and unpleasant work. I was stooped at an awkward angle and the odor of mud and dung wafted in my nostrils. But it was necessary work and when I finished I had that happy feeling one gets when a dirty job is done. And the mare seemed to appreciate it.

Night fell and we stayed up very late jawing about various adventures. Billy was the only one who remembered anything at all about my ma and pa, so naturally I encouraged him to tell me tales about them. I remembered my folks, of course, but had so many adventures of my own since their departure that my personal memories had faded some. I needed Billy's tales to supplant and fortify my own. They were righteous people, he told me, honest grocers and general goods keepers, who had been the victims of unlawful violence. They had been gunned down, I was reminded, by a one-eyed giant. Billy told me, again, (for he had told it to me many times over the years), how a one-eyed giant had burst in upon them at closing one day, gunning first my mother, then my pa, with no sympathy or apparent remorse. He then rifled their register and took what items he pleased from their shelves. And he gut shot another man, too, who came running to investigate the pistol shots. This fellow lived to provide a firsthand account of what he had witnessed, and the description of the one-eyed giant. People thought the man delusional, regardless his testimony, because no such miscreant was known in those parts.

"All that happened many years ago and far away from here," Uncle Billy muttered, and drifted off to sleep with the telling. I fell asleep, too, on the floor before the fireplace with my saddle for a pillow.

I slept soundly as one might expect, for I was exhausted from my twelve-day journey, and this was the first roof I had had over my head since Amarillo. I remember waking once to the raucous hee-hawing of Uncle Billy's slumbering serenade, but I adjusted my posture and dropped off again. I had a fanciful dream. I dreamed I had hired on at a ranch run by, of all things, giants. The biggest giant paid me twenty dollars a week, ten times my standard pay, and provided a feather bunk to sleep in. The job was an easy one. My only chore was to kill scorpions – any and all that may appear in the presence of this large giant. In my dream I hooted, shouting something like this: "This is a job I shall enjoy, for I surely do despise scorpions!"

Fact is, that I should say something like that (even in a dream) is remarkable because I do *not* despise scorpions – they are, after all, God's creatures same as you and me. I was bit by a scorpion once, and I cannot say it was pleasant, but as a rule I avoid killing anything I cannot eat or make some use of unless, of course, I am physically threatened by it. Oddly enough, when I awoke I rose to splash water on my face at the basin. Lo and behold, at the bottom of the basin and trapped there by its porcelain surface, and mad as hell, was the orneriest looking scorpion I ever met up with.

I jumped back three feet and must have yelped because the next thing I knew Uncle Billy was at my side peering in at the creature with me. "Never seen a scorpion this late in winter," he said. "Reckon it rode in with you, in your saddle bags or on your person." This made us both shudder, at the thought of carrying such a nasty fellow on one's person, in a shirt pocket or such. I lifted the basin to the front door and chucked the critter into the cold air.

The lumber came in that morning on Aaron Hadley's buckboard. The driver and I unloaded it onto Billy's porch. The repairs weren't anything that Billy and I couldn't handle ourselves, and keep warm in the process, so we set right to it. Billy had a crosscut saw and so after we tore out the rotted roofing timbers we spent most of the afternoon cutting two-by-fours to fit. I ran up and down the ladder all afternoon, taking measurements. My hands began to stiffen by day's end.

Come nightfall I was plenty pooped once again, but tired as I was I was none to anxious to go to sleep. Billy and I played cards and shared some whiskey from a bottle he'd bought knowing I was coming, and so we talked as we played and drank. He retold the stories I had already heard many times over of his younger days, stories that included tales of my pa as a boy, the two of them growing up in the panhandle, climbing trees, swimming in fast water, and the like. I desired to know all I could about those days, feeling that somehow they might help me understand my own self better. Billy had no hand in raising me after my ma and pa was killed; I was raised an orphan by strangers and shifted from one family to another. I hunted Billy up only after I ran off once and for all to be on my own.

At last sleep overcame us and Billy crawled into his bunk and I lay down, once again, before the fire with my head resting in the seat of my saddle, staring upwards at the rooftop beams of the cabin.

The moment my eyes shut I began to dream.

I dreamed I was perched up in those beams somehow and was looking down on the scene below. I saw myself sacked out before the fire, the embers spitting and sizzling crimson as the flames died down. I saw Uncle Billy, too, asleep in his bed. Then icy terror struck my heart, for out of the embers copper-colored snakes began to appear. *Rattlesnakes.* They slithered from the coals as if awakened from slumber by the heat and rested on the hearth of the great fireplace. One, two, then four, six, ten and more – I counted twenty-four in all, writhing on the hearth, their forked tongues darting in and out, and each one taking a keen interest in my resting soul. All at once their tails rattled and they opened gaping mouths, jagged fangs extending, dripping, dripping, dripping poison....

Billy shook me awake. I had been screaming. He was sitting on top of me, frightened by my fear. I threw him off me, jumped to my feet and leaped upon his bunk. Slowly I regained my senses and was relieved to see that there were no snakes. I recounted the nightmare to my uncle. He blamed it on the whiskey, but I was not convinced of it as I had drunk far more in dusty towns along the Chisholm without such terrible visions. Uncle Billy fell back asleep, but I was awake all night.

The next day was crystal blue and icy cold. We got much accomplished on the roof of the damaged cabin. It began to take shape once again. By noon we had accomplished the framing, and by sunset we had replaced all of the cedar shakes on the windward side. All that was left for the morrow was to re-shingle the other half and then we could declare the job finished. Just in time for Christmas, too, for the job would be completed on Christmas Day, 1891. Tonight was Christmas Eve. I reckoned my labor would have to do as a gift for Uncle Billy, because I had none other.

Through the day I took notice of my hands. They grew stiff. This was not a familiar sensation to me; I am too young for rheumatism and have never broken my bones. Still, as I said, my fingers became increasingly difficult to bend. Not painful, mind, just inflexible. And cold to the touch, like cold iron. I passed it off in my mind as the result of swinging a hammer the whole day.

After supper it began to rain. It had warmed up considerable through the day, becoming almost spring-like, and now the rain beat down steadily. Billy wished aloud that we'd finished the roofing, but I promised him we'd take care of it first thing in the morning, rain or shine, and that cheered him somewhat. As a gift to me, he offered to clean my boots. They were caked in the same awful mud that I had scraped from the hooves of my mare. Billy had some good saddle soap, which he applied liberally to the leather, then rinsed them off on the porch with rainwater from the roof. After, he smeared bear grease into them, which made them soft and impenetrable to water. He set them by the fire to dry. "Good as new," he chirped, and they were indeed.

While Billy worked on my boots, I sat before the fire with hands outstretched, trying to warm them, forcing the stiff joints to open and close. As I said, they weren't painful, just cold and stiff. An incident came to mind, one that occurred a few years after my folks were gone. I was perhaps thirteen. I'd been taken in as a helper by a man with a terrible temper. He was a smith and worked with iron. Most of his trade was in horseshoes, but every once in awhile he was called upon to make some other implement. One bitter winter day he sent me out behind his shop to retrieve raw iron rods, stacked in a barrel that had filled with freezing rain. I chipped away the ice in the barrel and withdrew a single iron bar – it was all I could do to carry it – and made my way back into the shop. The skin of my fingers froze to the iron and ripped when I dropped the bar at the smithy's feet. He barked at me and ordered more, so I made several trips carrying frozen iron.

I recalled then how the iron had felt, cold to touch but somehow burning, like fire. That was how my own stiffened fingers felt just now.

Billy found the whiskey again, and was determined to celebrate the holiday. It was, after all, Christmas Eve. We passed the bottle back and forth, and for every three gulps Billy took I took care to swallow just one – because I feared a repeat of that dreadful dream I'd had the night before. As we celebrated, Billy's thoughts returned to my father, only this time he told stories that were new to me. For example, though I knew my father had served in the war, I was unaware of his heroism. Billy recounted several tales of frontline skirmishes that he and his younger brother faced together, fighting side by side, and in each of these skirmishes my pa had behaved bravely. He took a bullet on one occasion and rescued the flag of the *Fighting 107th* on another. And after the war, when folks in Texas were unfairly taxed and lost their property to evil carpetbaggers from the North, my pa married his childhood sweetheart and worked hard at odd jobs to make a living. He always shared what he had with those less fortunate. (I had the distinct feeling that he had helped Billy out a time or two.) He even saved a little from his meager earnings and opened his first store just after I was born. Ma worked at his side. It burnt down twice, but they pressed on undaunted.

"Your pa," Billy said with the bullish emphasis of a man three sheets to the wind, "had more gumption than any *six* men. He was a man of honor, a Texan and proud of it. And he loved your ma as she rightly deserved, for she was the sweetest rose in these parts, or any other. And he loved you," he said to me with a jab of his finger, eyes momentarily focusing, "more than I have words to tell."

This talk made me sad, for as I have said, I possessed only a few memories of my parents and I longed to know them better.

"I reckon," Billy muttered, "that your father rests none too well in his grave this Christmas." His words were spoken in a tone so low that I wasn't sure I understood him.

"What, Uncle Billy? How's that?" I asked.

The old goat drew a long swallow on the bottle and finished the last of the liquor. He wiped his grizzled face. "Boy, don't you know? It was Christmas Eve! Ten years ago *this very night* that one-eyed giant bastard burst in upon your ma and pa and shot them dead away."

I did not know. Or, if I had known, I had long since forgotten.

I rested my head upon the saddle and stared at the beams overhead. Billy muttered a few additional incoherent thoughts then closed his eyes. He soon was sawing logs, hunched over in the corner with the empty bottle cradled in his arms like the baby Jesus.

I fell fast asleep. I dreamed that I arose and opened the cabin's door. A fog of damp mist blew in around me. For some time I peered into the darkness, watching the rain fall steadily. I felt my hands stiffen again and looked at them. I discovered that they had hardened into iron. Or, perhaps, steel. My forefingers took the color and shape of the eight-inch barrels on twin Colt .45s. My thumbs became hammers, cocked and ready to fire, and my remaining digits took the form of revolver cylinders. From the weight at the end of my forearms I concluded that the six chambers in these blue steel appendages were most certainly loaded with cartridges. In my dream none of this struck me as unusual, it seemed quite natural to exchange pistols for fists, to have cold steel where flesh and sinew had been before. I scratched my chin with them. I waved them about the room and pointed them at Billy, peering first over one then the other, drawing a bead on my slumbering uncle. I got a sudden urge to go for a walk and made an effort to pull on my boots, but that was awkward with six-guns for hands. I stamped them into place as best I could.

Next I was marching, tramping through the soggy night. The rain subsided. There was no moon, but I followed along a muddy highway that was unfamiliar to me. I had no thought of direction, no intention or will, no destination in mind. I merely walked. The cold steel dangled at my sides. I counted my breaths, which appeared in cloudbursts of moisture, and stopped at one hundred. Then I counted the buildings that appeared before me, and stopped at the seventh.

I stood before a tall house in the middle of a town. In my dream this town was dark and desolate. But a window in this house, on the second floor, was lit with a cheery red glow. I knocked at the door. No one responded, so I knocked again, louder, banging the blue steel of my pointed fingers on the door. A face appeared in the window above me, a woman's face. "Go away!" she said. "It's Christmas Eve, for Christ's sake."

I said, "Come down here and talk, or I'll break in your door."

I repeated this two or three times and was ready to make good my pledge when the door opened a few inches. The woman spoke to me from inside. "Please go away, Cowboy," she said. "It's Christmas Eve and I'm closed for the holiday."

I pointed the tips of my blue steel hands in her face and pushed the door open. "Let me in to dry myself," I said. "I'm soaked to the bone."

She jumped back and her eyes widened. She did not look at me, only at the black holes in the ends those twin .45s. "Go home and sleep it off," she said bravely. "Come back tomorrow and I will give you your Christmas gift."

But I laughed and pushed past her.

She wore very little; I could see a cotton robe tied with a sash at her waist. I continued to point my fingers in her direction but lowered them a bit. She breathed easier, seemed to resign herself as if to an unwanted task, and closed the door behind her. "I see that you will not wait for Santy Claus to climb down your chimney. I reckon you wish to unwrap your presents early."

She pushed me into a chair and loosed her hair. It fell to her shoulders. Then she loosed her sash. Her breasts peered out at me.

But a very loud thump made us both jump, and she snatched shut her robe. "Jesus," she muttered and turned to the door. The thump occurred again, shaking dust from the doorframe, then twice again in quick succession.

"Who's there?" she shouted. "Another damn drunk on Christmas Eve?"

"Open up, Lil," a muffled voice called from outside. "It's me. Ned."

The woman froze a moment. It was clear she recognized that voice. She turned slowly and studied me wryly. "If that truly is Ned, Cowboy," she said, "you better run."

But I did not move from where I sat. I looked instead at my steel hands. They grew suddenly colder.

She marched to the door and opened it. A man stepped inside. He stooped to enter, for he barely fit through the door. He was a giant.

"Happy Christmas, Lil," he said. "I brung ya a present." He held a gaily-wrapped parcel in his hand.

She stepped aside and looked in my direction, and the giant followed her gaze.

He looked at me curiously, a frown creasing his brow. He had but one good eye. It stared, unblinking.

I raised my hands, pointed my fingers, and emptied the chambers. The room filled with smoke. And the giant fell. And the woman screamed.

And I awoke. It was Christmas morning. Light filtered through the window. The fire had gone out. My head ached. I heard Uncle Billy stirring.

We rekindled the fire and made hot coffee, then we had some little cakes that Billy had stored away for the occasion. The joy of the holiday warmed our spirits. Billy set about to make us a breakfast of eggs and ham and flapjacks, all the while whistling a happy Christmas tune. We were both glad to see that the rain had let up. I was anxious to get back up on the roof to finish the job I had started and make good on my Christmas promise.

I washed the sleep from my eyes in the porcelain basin and the cool water felt good. It cleared my head. Bit by bit my dream from the night before came to me, giving me pause to wonder about it; it seemed strange and amazing. I studied my hands. The stiffness had left them completely.

Over breakfast I recounted the dream to Billy. He listened in awe and took in every detail. "I know that place!" he said excitedly. "It's Lil's place." But of course I had never been there, had no idea it even existed, or where it was, and yet from my description he recognized it. I laughed and he laughed, for it all seemed so strange and fantastic.

And now, well fed, satisfied, I was ready to tackle those shingles atop old Uncle Billy's roof. I reached for my boots by the fire but pulled up short. The boots were where I had left them, but they were muddy.

At first I hardly recognized them. Perhaps these were Billy's boots, I thought. But Billy was wearing his. Yes. They were my boots, all right, left by the fire the night before, sturdy leather boots that I had worn on many a long trail. I bought them myself in Abilene some time ago.

But last night Billy had given his Christmas gift to me, and his gift was to clean those boots so thoroughly they looked good as new. Now they were scuffed, torn as if from a long hike through rocky soil, and covered in mud.

And I remembered in my dream how I had stamped those boots into place because I could not pull them up with blue steel fingers.

I suddenly felt sick to my stomach and the room spun about me. I lifted the muddy boots and held them out so Billy could see. He looked at them, then looked again. His happy whistle ceased, and he was as confused and confounded as was I.

I had an instant understanding of what had transpired, a revelation of sorts, a word of knowledge that flooded my being. I perceived with some clarity a brave and honorable man who had waited patiently to avenge a deep injustice, who had longed for opportunity and means to right a wrong and to eradicate the vermin that had cut his own life short, as well as the life of his dearest loved one, his sweetheart, and who had cruelly stolen from his only child the opportunity to be lovingly raised in the warm and pleasant presence of his own parents. In my vision I saw this honorable man return in spirit – freed from the limitations of his own grave – to this stone cabin; I saw him brought to life by the memories of those who knew him, who loved him, strengthened by the retelling of his heroic deeds, empowered by connections of flesh and blood to possess the living and to repay – once and for all – an old debt. This vision came and passed quickly. I sat on a stool, shook my head, and pulled on my muddy boots. "This is nuts," I told myself.

But climbing the ladder to Uncle Billy's roof I glanced down, and there on my feet were those muddy boots.

And it surprised neither Billy nor me when we heard news from town that a one-eyed giant had been gunned down by a stranger on Christmas Eve at Lil's.

The Blue Pencil
(a film play)

FADE IN

EXTERIOR, A DECAYING METROPOLIS AT DAWN
Long blue shadows cast by ghetto-like buildings. We hear a *tap-tap-tapping...*

EXTREME CLOSE UP; A TYPEWRITER CARRIAGE
It is an older, manual typewriter, its ribbon frayed from overuse. Its keys strike paper somewhat haphazardly, *tap-tap-tapping*. Words appear one letter at a time, as follows...

> "...holding her tightly at long last,
> their passion for each other having
> overcome all obstacles..."

The typing ceases suddenly.

CLOSE UP, A MAN'S EYES AND FURROWED BROW
He reads what he has just typed, eyes jumping from word to word. There is hope in these eyes, but they blink twice, and bitter realization glazes them. The eyes sadden, lids drooping as hope passes from them. The owner of the eyes draws a deep breath and sighs....

INTERIOR, STEPHEN'S APPARTMENT – DAWN
Thirty-year-old STEPHEN drops his forehead into the palm of his hand and studies the typewritten page before him. He is sitting at a small desk near an

open window. Yellow light from a just-rising sun filters past curtains that billow in a gentle breeze. He is dressed in jockey shorts and a cotton t-shirt. His cigarette smolders nearby amongst the crushed butts of previous smokes.

Absently, Stephen draws the tobacco to his lips and takes a long hit of nicotine like an addict, holding it deep in his lungs. After a moment he blows grey-blue smoke from his nostrils and rips the page from the carriage in one simultaneous, coordinated motion. He is not happy with what he has written.

He shuffles the page along with thirty others then drops the whole lot into a waste basket.

CAMERA PANS past a rotating electric fan to a double bed in the corner of the room. In it is SARAH, twenty-four, asleep nude with a single sheet for cover. Even that is apparently too much on a sultry summer night – one leg dangles exposed half out of bed. She stirs, her eyes open sleepily....

    SARAH: *Stephen...?*

He turns in his chair and studies her thoughtfully.

    STEPHEN: *Hmmh?*

    SARAH (half asleep): *What time is it? Are you finished?*

Stephen crushes the cigarette in the tray, then rises. He pulls a pair of Levis from the bed post and slips into them, glancing out the window to the empty street two stories below.

    STEPHEN: *I'm goin' for a walk.*

He looks at Sarah, but she has already turned in her bed and returned to her slumber.

INTERIOR, THE APARTMENT AT ITS ENTRANCE – DAWN
Stephen shuffles down the steps to the entryway, past a bank of letterboxes and out the front door.

EXTERIOR, THE APARTMENT AT THE PORCH – DAWN
It is an inner-city dwelling, a turn-of-the-century home divided into rental units, a large structure with character. Stephen pauses at the top of the porch to light another cigarette. The street is empty at this early hour except for an overweight JOGGER who runs past, huffing.

Stephen watches him absently, then skips down the steps. His attitude seems somewhat improved, freshened by the morning air. He makes his way down the sidewalk with hands thrust deeply in his pockets.

WITH STEPHEN ON ANOTHER STREET
Stephen walks along the city boulevard past several sleeping WINOS who stretch out on the sidewalk. He hardly notices them because they are a part of the surroundings, like garbage and fire hydrants. His mind is elsewhere anyway – lost in some short story, some plot intrigue or perhaps some brief character sketch.

Stephen passes before an old woman, haggard and dressed in rags. She wears black, opaque glasses and carries a thin white cane. The woman rests against a building clutching a grimy, near-empty shoe box labeled, "Pencils – 25 cents." She is the PENCIL LADY.

The old woman hears Stephen pass by…

     PENCIL LADY: *You there. Tell an old woman something….*

He stops.

     STEPHEN: *What?*

     PENCIL LADY: *Is the sun up?*

     STEPHEN: *Just barely. It's gonna be a scorcher. No clouds.*

     PENCIL LADY: *Always a cloud over me, boy. Buy a pencil? Four for a dollar.*

Stephen pulls his hands from his pockets, turning out the empty linings as if to show her.

STEPHEN: *Sorry, lady. No money.*

He turns and walks a few paces, head down, but stops short. His eyes spot something in the gutter.

HIS VIEW
A shiny new quarter glistens against the dirt and grime.

STEPHEN (retrieving the quarter): *I'll be damned....*

He turns back to the old woman.

STEPHEN: *Here.*

He sails the coin into the box and turns to leave.

PENCIL LADY: *Take a pencil.*

STEPHEN: *Don't need a pencil.*

She whips her cane up abruptly like a sword, cutting off his advance.

PENCIL LADY: *Take a pencil. A **blue** one.*

Perturbed, Stephen looks in the box thrust before him. There are two dozen or so pencils there, in a variety of colors, each new and sharpened to a fine point.

STEPHEN: *Only a couple blue ones left.*

She grins a toothless, broken smile at him.

PENCIL LADY: *Take one.*

He draws one from the box, examines it, and smiles back.

STEPHEN: *Alright. Thanks.*

She continues her toothless grin and bobs her head repeatedly. Her cane rises like a railroad crossing guard and Stephen continues on his way. He slips the pencil behind his ear as he approaches a corner.

AT THE CORNER
Without warning a huge truck roars wildly around the corner, its tire jumping the curb at Stephen's feet. He leaps back....

STEPHEN: *Hey!*

The truck rumbles noisily past him, heading down the street towards where the old woman stands at curbside. She *tap-tap-taps* at the street with her cane, testing the depth of the step down, oblivious to the onrushing truck. She meanders into the street.

STEPHEN'S VIEW, THE TRUCK AND PENCIL LADY
Stephen watches, horrified, as the truck bears down on the Pencil Lady. She proceeds unaware...

STEPHEN (shouting): *Stop!* **Hey!**

He waves his hands, moving towards her...

The Pencil Lady steps directly into the path of the truck...

Stephen flinches, anticipating the impact...

STEPHEN'S VIEW
The truck rumbles forward with a deafening roar – the Pencil Lady in its path – but there is no impact. No crunch of bones, no flying body. The woman simply vanishes. The truck rounds the far corner and rumbles out of sight.

Stephen dashes to the point where the old woman stood, sliding to a halt. He spins looking this way and that but the street is inexplicably empty. There is no Pencil Lady.

Stephen is confused. His eyes dart. He twists his head; we see his ear: the *blue pencil* is lodged there.

DISSOLVE

INTERIOR, STEPHEN'S APARTMENT – MORNING
The door opens and Stephen enters, still a bit dazed. He is surprised and a little perturbed to see Sarah at his desk.

She is dressed now, in a smart business skirt and blazer, ready to leave for work. Sipping her morning coffee, she reads Stephen's typed manuscript – the one he discarded.

Stephen is not pleased to see her reading it. He folds his arms and frowns.

> STEPHEN: *You'll be late for work, Sarah.*

She gestures with a raised hand to silence him.

INTERIOR, THE KITCHEN
Stephen enters the small KITCHEN, opens the refrigerator and withdraws a jar of orange juice. He twists off its lid and drinks from the jar....

Sarah follows him into the kitchen, depositing the manuscript on the counter without a word. Her silence says a lot to Stephen. She opens her purse and checks its contents.

Stephen forces a response form her.

> STEPHEN: *What'd you think?*

Sarah gives him a look that tells him she thought the story was hokey, trite and silly. And completely unworthy of his effort.

> SARAH: *You were up all night for that?*

Stephen shrugs, but concurs.

> STEPHEN: *That's why I round-filed it.*

Sarah checks her watch.

SARAH: *I'm gonna miss my bus. Be glad you got that teaching job to go back to this fall.*

He nods. She leaves, but pauses at the door before closing it…

SARAH: *Get some sleep. Then try again.*

Stephen smiles as the door closes….

INTERIOR, A MOVING CITY BUS – MORNING
Sarah sits on the overloaded bus trying her best to read the morning paper. She is jostled by commuters as the bus lurches. One man bumps her roughly and she looks up, angered…

JOGGER (still in running clothes): *Pardon me, miss.*

She responds with a shrug and returns to her reading…

INTERIOR, STEPHEN'S APARTMENT – MID DAY
Stephen lies in shorts atop the bed, hands laced behind his head. The room is brightly lit from sunshine though the curtain is drawn. A warm breeze stirs it slightly. The sound of heavy traffic pours through the open window, a police siren wails in the distance.

Stephen's eyes are wide open, glazed by deep thought. He is staring blankly at the ceiling.

EXTREME CLOSE UP, STEPHEN'S EYES
They twitch once.

WIDER
In a swift motion Stephen swings up from the bed and slips into the chair at his desk. He grabs the blue pencil and a spiral notebook.

He presses pencil to paper abruptly – and at once the tip breaks.

Stephen jams the broken point of the blue pencil into the sharpener and cranks the handle furiously.

Examining it at eye-level, Stephen runs his thumb over the finely honed point.

Stephen presses the pencil to paper with renewed vigor and inspiration. He looks at the typewriter a moment, hesitating, but shoves it out of his way.

MONTAGE, STEPHEN WRITING
Various angles of Stephen as he scribbles almost frantically, blue pencil to paper; he paces, writing with the pencil as he walks; he rips a completed page from the notebook; he reads, then laughs at what he's written; he chews on the pencil's eraser; he sharpens the dulled pencil again. The pencil grows smaller....

DISSOLVE

INTERIOR, STEPHEN'S APARTMENT – NIGHT
In cutoff Levis and a pullover cotton top, Sarah sits with her legs tucked beneath her on the couch. She is reading, with great intensity, 35 pencil-written pages torn from the spiral notebook. Her jaw is clamped tightly, eyes riveted to the short story. Those eyes are moist. They blink twice, holding back tears.

Across the room, Stephen watches her intently. He grips the sides of his chair and smokes.

Turning over the last loose leaf of the manuscript, Sarah finishes reading. Slowly her eyes rise from the pages and focus on Stephen. Swallowing hard, she seems almost unable to speak. Her head drops into the crook of her forearm and she weeps....

Stephen is startled by her reaction. Rising, he moves to her, hesitates, then slips into the couch beside her. He draws her to him.

She continues to weep, head now resting on his chest.

> SARAH (between sobs): *It's... so... **sad**. And beautiful. Oh, Stephen. It's wonderful.*

He holds her tenderly.

>SARAH (continuing): *You've never... written anything like it.*

He nods, knowing. Sarah sniffles, recovers, and sits up.

>SARAH (continuing): *The old man in the story... he was so*
>***real***. *When his grandson died I thought, "How sad!" But the*
>*twist you gave at the end....*

Sarah shakes her head sadly, eyes tearing...

>SARAH (continuing): *The old man taking his own life!*

She begins to sob again and buries her head in Stephen's shoulder for a good, solid cry. He strokes her hair lovingly.

Stephen's eyes brighten. He knows he has a winner in this story.

Sarah pulls away, recoiling abruptly from Stephen. She seems almost frightened for a brief moment, frightened of *him*. But then her eyes lock onto his and they embrace.

SLOW DISSOLVE

STEPHEN AND SARAH IN BED TOGETHER
The two make love slowly, passionately, beneath the thin bed sheet. Their bodies glisten in the heat and humidity.

CAMERA PULLS BACK SLOWLY, PANNING
We see: a whirring fan; a Big Ben clock tick tocks on the bedstead; the pencil sharpener screwed down on Stephen's desk; and finally (as the image focuses), *the blue pencil*. Its point is dulled from so much writing. It is reduced in size to half its original length.

FADE TO BLACK

FADE IN

INTERIOR, THE APARTMENT ENTRYWAY – DAY
Stephen opens his letterbox with a small key. He sorts through a series of bills, but drops them all when he finds a certain letter – one he's been waiting for. He opens the envelope nervously and then reads the letter with growing excitement. A broad grin stretches across his face. Then, he begins to dance about....

> STEPHEN (singing): *They bought it! They bought it!* (kicking his heels) *Wah-hoo!!!*

Another tenant in the building, a HEAVYSET WOMAN, comes down the steps and freezes momentarily at the sight of dancing Stephen – she watches the madman boogey a jig with a suspicious look in her eyes. Stephen spots her, grabs her puffy hands and spins her round in a doe-see-doe. The woman gets into it, joins him in the jig, and giggles hysterically....

DISSOLVE

INTERIOR, STEPHEN'S APARTMENT – NIGHT
Sarah enters, just arriving home from work. She clutches her purse and a newspaper. Her features are somewhat troubled, but they brighten when they see Stephen.

CLOSE UP, STEPHEN WITH THUMBS ON A CORK
With a *POP!* champagne shoots from its bottle. Stephen grins impishly at Sarah.

Sarah studies him a moment, confused, then returns his curious grin with an expression that asks: *Did you sell it?!*

Stephen nods enthusiastically: *Yes I did!*

With a squeal of delight Sarah rushes across the room into Stephen's arms. The champagne spills as they spin together triumphantly.

> SARAH (laughing, singing): *You sold it! You sold it!*

They embrace, squeeze each other and fall into the couch. The champagne spills some more but they don't care. This is a moment of triumph that has been long in coming.

Stephen pours champagne into two plastic cups, and they hoist them to toast....

STEPHEN: *To us!*

SARAH: *No, sir. To **you**! The world's next Hemingway! Long live the King! The King of Suspense!*

Sarah drinks but Stephen hesitates...

STEPHEN (protesting mildly): *Please, one published story!*

SARAH: *Oh, Stephen. The first of many!*

They drink. Then embrace.

But the troubled look we saw on Sarah's face at the door returns to her. She eyes the newspaper she was carrying, picks it up and thrusts it into Stephen's hands.

A small article has been circled in red.

SARAH: *Look.*

INSERT, NEWSPAPER HEADLINE. It reads:

GRANDFATHER COMMITS
SUICIDE FOLLOWING DEATH
OF GRANDSON

Stephen is shocked as he reads the article...

SARAH: *It's... it's just like your story.*

Stephen dry swallows and motions her to be quiet. Reading intently, he finishes the article.

> STEPHEN (shocked): *Incredible....*

Sarah nods.

> STEPHEN: *Thank God the names aren't even similar.*

> SARAH: *But look! He was a shoemaker, too. Just like in your story!*

The two study each other a long moment, then laugh nervously.

> STEPHEN (truly amazed): *A shoemaker!*

He reaches behind him to the desk and retrieves a new stack of about sixty pencil-written pages.

> STEPHEN: *I was so inspired by the good news today I wrote another story. This afternoon.*

He plops the handwritten manuscript into Sarah's lap.

> SARAH: *Wow! Is it any good?*

> STEPHEN (shrugs): *You tell me.*

Sarah lifts the manuscript and examines it....

> SARAH: *In pencil? Again?*

> STEPHEN (with a grin): *Hey! That blue pencil I bought brought me luck!*

He holds the blue pencil up for her to see. It's down to about two inches now, and its eraser is gone to bare metal.

DISSOLVE

INTERIOR, THE BATHROOM SHOWER – NIGHT
Stephen stands with his head bowed. The shower shoots a steady stream of water over him.

Unseen by Stephen, blurred by the shower curtain, the bathroom door opens silently. A shadowy figure enters, pauses briefly, then approaches him. The blurry figure's hand rises slowly, overhead, then – with a SLASH! – grabs the curtain and parts it. The movement is so sudden that Stephen is startled....

Sarah, standing nude before him, grins.

SARAH: *Boo!*

Stephen recovers, growls at her playfully, then pulls her into the shower with him. They lock in an embrace.

SARAH (flinching in the water): *Brrr! The water's cold!*

Stephen kisses her neck, nibbling.

STEPHEN: *Feels good in this heat. Did you finish it?*

Sarah nods, biting her lower lip noncommittally.

STEPHEN: **Well?**

SARAH: *Well, it was... What can I say?*

STEPHEN (concerned): *No good?*

SARAH: *Stephen, that was the **scariest** thing I've ever read.*

She shudders and adds for emphasis...

SARAH: ***Ooh!***

Stephen looks at her incredulously. Then he throws back his head and laughs insanely.

STEPHEN: *You silly bitch! It was **supposed** to be scary!*

They laugh together and embrace.

REVERSE ANGLE
Behind the curtain we watch the couple in the shower as water spills over them. Sarah throws her legs up about Stephen's hips; they almost crash down into the tub...

DISSOLVE

INTERIOR, STEPHEN'S APARTMENT – NIGHT
Sarah and Stephen lie in bed, nude under a sheet, quietly resting in each others' arms. Their hair is still wet, hers wrapped in a towel. Stephen smokes thoughtfully. The electric fan whirs on the headboard.

Sarah seems puzzled.

SARAH: *How? Stephen, how did you come up with it?*

STEPHEN: *Hmmh?*

SARAH: *This new story. It is so horrible. Frightening. A train wreck in the Andes, for God's sake. When were you ever in the Andes?*

STEPHEN (shrugs): *A mountain's a mountain, Sarah.*

SARAH: *But you described them in such detail. And the people. It's as if you know them personally.*

She shudders with a grisly thought.

SARAH (continuing): *But, Stephen. The whole idea. **Cannibalism**. People eating each other. **Yech!!***

Stephen's brow furls. He still isn't sure.

STEPHEN: *But... it was **good**, right?*

SARAH: *Well. I couldn't put it down.*

He studies her a long moment. Then his cigarette glows as he draws the nicotine into his lungs.

DISSOLVE

INTERIOR, STEPHEN'S APARTMENT – DAY
The apartment door bursts open as we hear a YELP! of joy. Stephen spins gracefully into the apartment, kicking the door closed as he pirouettes like a ballerina. He clutches yet another opened envelop to his chest. The smile on his face can mean only one thing...

The PHONE rings. Stephen dances over to it and answers dramatically...

STEPHEN: *Hee-Yellow! You've reached the residence of the world famous author of two, count 'em, two soon-to be-published short stories...!*

Sarah is at the other end of the telephone line. Her voice is frightened.

SARAH (on phone): *Stephen!*

STEPHEN (rapidly): *Sarah! My love! I sold another one! **Playboy** bought the story of the train wreck!!! I got a check right here!*

There is a tense moment of silence.

STEPHEN: *Sarah...?*

SARAH (on phone): *Stephen, I'm at lunch. There's a TV here, in the cafeteria.*

Another tense moment follows.

STEPHEN: *Sarah! What the hell is it?*

SARAH (on the phone): *Turn on the television. **Now!***

Stephen moves to the small black-and-white TV and flicks it on. It hums, then brightens....

ANGLE ON TELEVISION

The NEWSCASTER'S VOICE comes up before the TV IMAGE does, but when it appears we see a snowy mountain, the scene of a disaster: *a derailed passenger train.* Several of the train cars are crushed or broken in two, but others lay on their side in the icy terrain...

> NEWSCASTER: *...at the site of the derailment in the Swiss Alps. Government officials have now confirmed that survivors of this disaster resorted to cannibalism in the mistaken belief that rescuers would be unable to reach them. After six days and nights of sub-zero temperatures several of the passengers....*

Stephen watches the flickering broadcast with horror and repulsion. His features contort, eyes sweeping across the room....

STEPHEN'S VIEW
The blue pencil, a mere stub now, rests on his desk where he left it. Its point is dull.

We hear Sarah's voice over the phone...

> SARAH (on phone): *Stephen, how did you know? **How?!***

Stephen mechanically drops the receiver into the cradle.

Stephen's fingers rotate the TV's switch to "off." It silences. Then he crosses the room in a daze.

He slips into his chair behind the desk and studies the stubby blue pencil a long moment, then picks it up. He jams the dull point into the pencil sharpener and cranks furiously.

Finished with its sharpening, Stephen holds the blue pencil to eye level. Not much of it left. He runs his thumb across the sharpened point.

As if in a trance, Stephen opens the spiral notebook and begins at once to write....

DISSOLVE

CLOSE UP, THE ROTATING ELECTRIC FAN
It whirs.

INTERIOR, STEPHEN'S APARTMENT – NIGHT
Stephen is asleep in bed from apparent exhaustion, his head back awkwardly. There is a sound of shuffling papers. He jerks awake with a start, crying out....

CAMERA PULLS BACK

Sarah sits at Stephen's desk reading his latest pencil-written manuscript. Terror is in her eyes.

She turns to Stephen accusingly...

SARAH: *Stephen!* ***Are you crazy?*** *Why did you write this?!*

Stephen shakes his head, his senses still dulled.

STEPHEN (sleepily): *Is it good, Sarah?*

She thrust the manuscript at him...

SARAH: *How could you write this!?*

STEPHEN (shrugs): *It's just a **story**, Sarah. A story.*

Sarah jumps to her feet.

>SARAH: A *story!? A **story!?** About a writer in love with a girl being stalked by a rapist? A murderer!? A – a – a **butcher!?***

Stephen shakes his head again to clear it.

>STEPHEN: *I don't know – is it good?*

Sarah becomes hysterical.

>SARAH: *Good!? **Good!?** Oh, my God! You wrote about me! **Me!!!** Don't you get it!?*

Realization begins to sink into Stephen's features. His face contorts and he leaps to his feet.

>STEPHEN: *I didn't finish it!*

Sarah searches through the pages frantically looking for the last one....

>SARAH: *How does it end? Stephen, **how does it end!?***

>STEPHEN: *I... I... I dunno... I....*

>SARAH: ***HOW DOES IT END!***

Frantic, Stephen nervously paces, runs his hands through his hair. He blinks back his own worst fears....

>STEPHEN: *I dunno! The pencil... it's, it's gone. I couldn't finish!*

He holds up what remains of the blue pencil: it is reduced to a worn nub with a metal band that once held an eraser.

A thought occurs to Stephen and he stops pacing. He dashes madly across the room and flings open the door.

STEPHEN: *I'll get another.*

The door slams as he runs out. Sarah folds in on herself, frightened to hysterics and crying fitfully.

EXTERIOR, STEPHEN'S APARTMENT – NIGHT
Stephen takes the porch steps three at a time and nearly crashes headlong into the overweight JOGGER, passing by on a late night run, huffing. Stephen stumbles past him, apologizing, legs barely keeping up with his own momentum. He dashes crazily down the street.

The Jogger stops. He is perturbed by Stephen's mad, careless dash into and almost right over the top of him. He shakes it off though.

Stephen rounds the corner and disappears out of sight.

The Jogger pauses a moment, watching. Then he looks up at the second story window of Stephen's apartment…

The Jogger steps back, receding into an inky shadow.

EXTERIOR, A CITY STREET
Stephen careens madly down the deserted street, legs pumping. His eyes dart back and forth, peering into the shadows, searching. He begins to gasp for air harshly, short-winded from too many cigarettes.

The city street is dark and deserted – the Pencil Lady is nowhere in sight.

ANOTHER ANGLE, ANOTHER STREET
Stephen slides around the corner and trips over the curb. He tumbles onto the pavement but comes up in a sprint.

Frustrated, Stephen nearly stumbles to a stop dead center in the intersection of two vacant boulevards. He doubles over clutching his belly, gasping, winded, sobbing and angry. He raises his fists to the sky and screams…

STEPHEN: *GOD HELP ME!!!*

A white cane *tap-tap-taps* at the curb behind him. Stephen turns, startled.

HIS VIEW
The toothless, blind old woman grins at him.

PENCIL LADY: *Buy a pencil, boy?*

Stephen rushes upon her furiously, enraged…

STEPHEN: *A blue one!* **Gimme a blue one!**

He rips the box from her hands – the pencils spill wildly into the street. The old woman stumbles back and falls. Her dark glasses fly off her face – her eyes are white with no pupils. She cries out angrily, but then begins to cackle insanely…

PENCIL LADY (laughing madly): *I knew you'd be back!*

Crawling on his hands and knees on the pavement, Stephen searches desperately in the dim light of the boulevard street lamps. He picks up one pencil, discards it frantically, then another…

STEPHEN: *A blue one. Goddamn it,* **a blue one!**

EXTREME CLOSE UP, A BLUE PENCIL
Stephen's hand falls upon it and he lifts it to eye level. He examines it in the street light, running his thumb over its sharp point.

Jumping to his feet, Stephen dashes madly back toward home. The Pencil Lady sits crumpled in the street, laughing, cackling, waving her thin, white cane overhead in broad swipes….

INTERIOR, STEPHEN'S APARTMENT – NIGHT
Sarah sits where Stephen left her, still sobbing quietly as tears stream down her cheeks. Her back is toward the doorway.

Behind her, out of focus, the apartment's door opens slowly and without sound. The Jogger steps inside. We see a streak of light as the blade of a SILVER STILETTO flashes in his hand. He pauses a moment to study her and to check out the room.

Sarah does not see him.

The Jogger approaches from behind, quietly. We hear only her sobs, gradually subsiding. He stops behind her, hovering. His gloved hands rise slowly above her head, the sharp blade of the stiletto sliding into view.

In one swift motion the Jogger clamps his elbow around Sarah's throat. He jerks her upward over the top of the couch and onto her feet. Her body contorts in a spasm of fear, but his grip is unshakable.

The Jogger passes the steel blade of the stiletto before Sarah's eyes, tauntingly...

      JOGGER (rasping): *I've been watching you...!*

Using his great bulk the Jogger drags Sarah toward the bed. The electric fan rotates with a whir. She struggles, kicking, upsetting a small table, and the two slam into the bed.

The electric fan is jarred from the headboard and falls to the floor. Its blade stops suddenly.

The Jogger tosses Sarah like a rag doll onto the bed but his grip loosens. Immediately, she draws a deep breath and screams to curdle blood.

The high-pitched shout stuns the Jogger. He jerks upright stiffly. Then, swiftly, he lifts the stiletto high overhead....

Stephen crashes through the doorway into the room.

      STEPHEN: *NO!!!*

The Jogger jerks, glancing at Stephen, distracted, and then plunges the stiletto's blade downward towards Sarah.

Sarah lurches reflexively, twisting her torso. The steel blade slashes into the bed, missing her by centimeters, piercing the mattress to its hilt.

Briefly, the Jogger struggles to free the blade as it entangles with the torn bed sheet. Sarah backs away from him....

Stephen lurches forward as the Jogger spins wildly, swiping the knife in a broad arc. With a flash the stiletto slices across Stephen's shirt and cuts a long gash in his chest. Blood spurts and Stephen cries out....

Enraged, sensing a kill, the Jogger rushes Stephen with his blade raised high.

Falling back, Stephen lashes out blindly. His right hand, fist clenched tightly, swings out in a backhanded motion at the Jogger....

There is a sickening THWACK!

Everything – all action – ceases momentarily. The Jogger's face contorts; a strange look of surprise fills his eyes.

Stephen lowers his outstretched hand revealing the blue pencil. Its sharpened point passes through the Jogger's throat and extends gruesomely from one side of his neck out the other.

The Jogger is clearly surprised – and physically stunned – by the blow. He attempts to draw a breath but finds it difficult.

He begins to choke – his airway is blocked. The stiletto slips from the Jogger's fingers as he grasps at the blue pencil.

He tugs on it and pulls it from his throat to fling it to the floor.

The Jogger now stumbles about the room, a wounded animal, knocking over a lamp and then the television. He careens off the desk. He makes sickening gasping noises and spits blood.

Stephen watches numbly; he is out of breath and severely wounded. Sarah is terrified, hunched in a corner on the bed.

The Jogger stumbles and nearly trips drunkenly, staggering toward the billowing curtains of the open window. He steadies himself, resting his weight on Stephen's desk....

Stephen shakes his head, drawing upon his last bit of strength. With a scream of desperation and a headlong dive, he throws himself into the Jogger. The impact sends the Jogger through the window. His feet disappear over the edge as Stephen flops to the floor.

EXTERIOR, STEPHEN'S APARTMENT – NIGHT
The Jogger crashes through the window amidst bits of wood and shattered glass, falling to the pavement below.

INTERIOR, STEPHEN'S APARTMENT – NIGHT
The room is in shambles. Stephen shudders fitfully on the floor, the blood flowing from his wound and forming a crimson pool. Sarah cries his name and rushes to his side....

They cling to each other as she takes action to stem the flow from Stephen's wound.

ANGLE AT STEPHEN'S DESK
A breeze through the shattered window billows the curtains gently. The wind catches the pages of Stephen's pencil-written manuscript, stacked on the desk where Sarah had been reading them. One by one they flutter to the floor....

CAMERA FOLLOWS A FALLING PAGE TO A CLOSE UP OF THE BLUE PENCIL
It lies on the floor where it fell when pulled from the Jogger's throat. Blood droplets cling to its sharp point.

We hear sounds of the city through the shattered window, a distant police siren, a bus grinding its gears, a freight train whistling in the dark... and a soft *tap-tap-tapping*.

FADE OUT

Alpha-Beta Critical Discourse: *Education*

Active, boisterous children do experience failing grades. Happily, it jolts kind, loving mothers. Now ordinary parents, quietly reassuring supportive teachers, urge venerable wisdom – x-raying youthful zeal. Zestful Y-chromosomes, X-chromosomes, wondrous variations undisciplined, trigger surprising responses....

Quickly producing organized networks, minds linking, kinfolk join in harmony, graciously forgetting extreme differences, creating binding alliances. After building confidence, daringly exposing falsehood, gently hammering indifference, juvenile knowledge largely matures. Never once proud, quitting rude scorn, tutors, ultimately victorious, win.

"X" young zeros! Zip!

Yet, xylophones won't vocalize unstruck. Tumultuous symphonies resonate quixotically. Primitive orchestrations need melodies, loosely keyed, jingles indelicately harmonized, going flat, evoking drama, composed beautifully. *Aria!*

Active, boisterous children *dare* experience failing grades? Honestly, it's jazz! Keep loving mirth – nourish obnoxious play! Quirky rhapsodies signal talent; uniformity vanquishes wonderment.

Xylophones? Yes! Zing!

T-Bird Travels

excerpt from a travelogue, Tuesday, June 19th, 2002

With a fresh beer in hand I decided to take a look under the Thunderbird's hood to see if I could identify what was binding in the steering mechanism.

Almost at once I saw the problem.

The Thunderbird's "slide-away" steering wheel was the source of the binding. This is similar to mechanisms in modern cars that allow the steering wheel to tilt up, only the T-bird's steering wheel slides inward about ten inches to allow the driver easy access in and out of the automobile. It pivots on a single point attached by a bracket to the frame of the automobile, next to the firewall.

Apparently, along the way somewhere, I'd hit a bump and caused the bracket to slip down a quarter-inch or so. Because of this, I could see, the "flexible steering joint" (also referred to as the "rag-joint") was bumping up against the pivot bracket when the brakes were applied.

As a temporary measure, and since I couldn't kick it (which is my usual method of fixing frustrating problems) I tried gripping it with my fingers and lifting. Amazingly, that raised the steering mechanism high enough to allow the rag-joint to clear the pivot – and the problem was resolved, at least for the moment.

I felt confident the Thunderbird would now get me home in one piece.

New problem: I was coated in grease and soaked to the skin with perspiration! It was hot in Kingman, Arizona!

I checked out the "pool." It was a cement hole, actually, filled with water from a garden hose. I dipped my hand in it. Though maybe not the cleanest pool in the world, at least the water was icy cold!

Back in my room, I washed off as much of the grease I could and changed into a swimsuit. I then returned to the pool and took a dip.

After, relaxing in a plastic recliner, I took a closer look at my home-away-from-home-for-the-evening. Probably built in the 'thirties, I guessed, and once a very fine roadside motel. I'd backed my Thunderbird up before my little bungalow's doorway, as did most of the guests there. About every other room was occupied – but I began to conclude that they were not really travelers like me. These folks were residents, more or less permanent ones, who lived in this place. And why not for the $100 per week rent the owners were charging?

Many of the people residing here had moved chairs to the little patch of cement they called a porch in front of their rooms. This enabled them to remain cool and to visit with one another. They all seemed quite friendly with one another.

I toweled myself dry and went back to my room, determined to also sit outside on my little porch. I put on some shorts and pulled my one-and-only chair outside. Seated there just behind my Thunderbird, I opened another brewsky.

Everyone at the Arcadia was quite chatty. They conversed with me like a long lost brother!

I answered many questions about the car, about my trip from Oregon (they saw the Oregon license plates) and about me.

There was a biker couple in the room above mine on the second floor. Both man and lady had significant tattoos and a variety of pierced body parts. The man called down to me, "Is that a '68?"

"No," I answered. "A '64. The '68s were the ones with four doors."

"I remember that," the biker lady said. "Didn't they have suicide doors and pop-up headlights?"

"They sure did."

"Wish I had me one of them!" she said.

"All it takes is time and money," I responded and laughed.

"I got neither!" her man said, and guffawed.

There was a fellow down at the far end of the motel with a blue shirt and "plumber pants." (You know, the kind of pants that smile at you whenever whoever is wearing them bends over.) For some reason he was meticulously washing the windows of a filthy 1990 Toyota, using a spray bottle of Windex. Inside and outside. I asked myself this question: *Why bother?* Why would anyone carefully wash the inside and the outside of every window on a car that was covered in mud?

Go figure!

I finished that beer and twisted the cap off another.

Then there was a young man, probably still a teenager, doing "cannonballs" repeatedly into the pool. It gave him great pleasure! I called out a compliment to him on his technique: he gave a sort of twist to his body in mid-air before curling into a ball and dropping into the pool. He thanked me for the compliment and said he'd been practicing.

Eventually this young kid finished that and climbed out of the pool. He'd parked his motorcycle in front of his motel room, just two down from mine, and I watched as he began to remove the handlebars.

"Something wrong with the bike?" I asked him.

He looked a little flustered. "Oh, not really. A sticking clutch."

But after awhile I saw him gather together some of the others in a huddle. He conversed with them in hushed tones.

One of them, a pretty lady named Ada, said loudly, "Well, then. Let's just park it for the night in the laundry room. We can lock it up there." And so they began to struggle with the motorcycle, trying to maneuver it through the narrow doors of the laundry room.

I rose from my chair, walked over to them and lent a hand. We had to lift the bike physically, up two steps, and guide it into the laundry room.

"Just curious," I said. "But why are you putting your motorcycle in the laundry room?"

Ada said (I learned she was "Ada," the motel maid, who lived there for free in exchange for cleaning the rooms), "He lost his job and missed a payment. Now they've threatened to repossess it, and he needs this bike to look for work."

"Oh," I said.

Back on my little perch I opened *another* beer. By now I was greatly enjoying myself, carrying on several conversations simultaneously with multiple "neighbors" as they passed by.

I watched over the activity with a great interest and a growing sense of curiosity.

For example, there was a Mexican girl using the pay phone hung on a pole down by the sidewalk. Not the enclosed kind of pay phone that affords privacy, but a pay phone in the open attached to a blue box. The girl was chattering away into the phone, speaking a mixture of Spanish and English.

I could see from her body language that she was growing increasingly upset as she talked. "Don't do that!" she cried several times, making a fist and stomping her foot. "No, please, don't do that!" She spoke like that for a long time, crying openly, wailing and twisting the strands of her long black hair.

In the end she hung up, wiped her eyes and folded her arms across her chest. She marched angrily back to her room.

About 7 p.m. Ada the motel maid came out to join several others by the pool. She was dressed in a yellow bikini. Three kids were there, all under six, calling her "Momma." Regardless, she looked very fine in that swimsuit.

The young man with the endangered motorcycle rejoined them in the pool, showing off his cannonball technique, as did a pregnant girl who could not have been more than 16. The pregnant girl was at least seven months along but that did not stop her from leaping headlong into the pool. She'd stand precariously on the bars of the pool's stepladder, one foot on each handhold, shouting, "Hey you guys, watch this!" Then she'd dive head first into the water. Remarkable!

The only black person I saw was a tall, thin fellow who walked by with his blonde, leggy girlfriend trailing behind. She wore very short shorts. As they passed the three of us exchanged hellos, and they meandered on down to their bungalow at the far end of the motel.

A half hour later the blonde returned. She was carrying a camera.

"Listen," she said to me, "I wonder if you can help me by buying this camera?"

I looked at her and the camera. She appeared to be very shaky; her fingers trembled. I thought perhaps she was nervous to be approaching me. I smiled at her, but she averted her eyes. It occurred to me that the woman was very thin.

I took the camera to look at it more closely.

"I'm all out of cigarettes and stuff," she said. "And I really could use some cash right now."

"How much did you want for your camera?" I asked.

"Oh, anything at all. Five or ten dollars. Whatever you think is fair." She wouldn't look at me as she spoke. "I'm all out of cigarettes and stuff," she said again.

I thought about it a moment, turning the camera over in my hand, then pulled a twenty from my pocket.

"I really don't need your camera, thanks." I handed it back to her and gave her the $20. "But take this for your cigarettes."

She took it without hesitation, spun on her heel and walked away. A few minutes later she and her boyfriend passed through the bushes to the street below.

After that I drank one more beer and watched the sun set. Then I called it a night. I hit the sack at 10 p.m. and slept like a baby.

Not That Kind of Girl

She is my high school sweetheart, the love of my youth, and I watch her as she lies quietly, eyes closed. I calculate the numbers in my mind, foggy from lack of sleep.

I haven't slept. Can't sleep. Should sleep. But I do the math.

Thirty-three years. I've known her that long. I was fourteen when I climbed the big cottonwood in our backyard and watched her dad unload boxes from a rented trailer to carry them into the house next door, and she stood on the porch watching her baby sisters. They were twins and rambunctious, but she cared for them with a stern hand. Her mother was gone already, I think. She died young. I don't remember her mother at all.

At sixteen I pinned her shoulders against the wall of the gymnasium and kissed her the first time. Her lips tasted of banana. Lunch. And to say she kissed back would be an exaggeration. She let me kiss *her*. "Understand, Miles," she said quietly, "I'm not that kind of girl."

In the dark now I look at those sleeping lips, pursed together, silent. Her face is in shadow, but a shaft of light illumines her. They glow, her lips, as if lit from within. They are still kissable, I think. Although we haven't kissed much in recent years. Marriage does that, you know. You stop kissing.

We first had sex in college, once before marriage, in her dorm room. We'd broken up after high school and stopped dating to go to separate universities but promised to remain friends. I càme for a visit after our schools' intercollegiate football game. It was homecoming. There was a party, I remember; we had a few beers. Then it happened. She took me to her room and her shirt came off and I found her breasts. We fondled each other to frenzy and by the time we remembered we weren't dating we were doing it. Her roommate arrived in the middle of it, locked out of the room, banging with her fist, calling. We hurriedly dressed. I remember glancing at her breasts as she pulled her shirt over, and grabbing for them. "Miles," she said pulling away, "I'm not that kind of girl." To hell you're not, I thought then.

I can see the outline of her breasts now, just barely, in the darkness. My eyes linger on them. They are soft and still. Her hands are folded neatly, just under them. After children her breasts expanded, permanently with her waistline. They grew heavy, hanging. She trapped them in huge white cotton cups with wire support that, oh sure, held them up but also set off alarms when checking into airports.

Even so, I never tired of them, those breasts. They are old friends, comforting, and mine to hold. I have an urge to squeeze them now, but I might disturb her. She sleeps.

Tears spring to my eyes as I study her quietly in the darkness. From the wet tracks I know there are tears, but I can't move my hands to wipe them away. Someone speaks as if in another room, far away. A muffled droning. And there is music. Organ music.

I close my eyes and shake my head once, to clear it. Honestly, I should sleep. I need sleep.

But there is no sleep. My mind is active, remembering.

What a fool I was! I wanted more. Over the years, you see, it became routine. *Sex* became routine, Saturday morning whether we felt like it or not. It was boring.

"Some women like to do other things," I said to her. "They don't always just lie still, for example. They move around. They get on top. I've read about it in magazines. Some women like that."

But she said, "I'm not that kind of girl."

So I was unfaithful to her. It's a cliché. She was suddenly unattractive to me. *She cares for our children but not her looks*, I told myself. She quit work, stayed home, and took up baking as a pastime. Cakes and French pastries.

The other woman was ten years younger and a snappy dresser. She gave me sex in all the ways I'd read about in those magazines. It went on for months.

"Do you want children some day?" I asked this younger woman once in the shower.

"No," she said. "I'm not that kind of girl."

That was years ago. I forget her name. But sometimes, I must admit, I still remember the sex.

The room brightens and the muffled speaking ends. The organ music grows louder. I come out of reverie and blink my eyes like a badger emerging from a hole.

People in their Sunday clothes rise and file past her. She is the love of my youth, and they peer at her. She is on display in her slumber. Her sisters pass by, the twins. Old now with fat, round bottoms, and never married. They shake their heads in unison, clucking.

Morbid curiosity. That is why they look. It really is a stupid custom.

Our children, teenagers, sit beside me, and my daughter reaches into her purse. I watch her from the corner of my eye. She produces a handkerchief and dries my wet cheeks.

"Mom wouldn't care to see you crying for her, Dad."

I agree, and nod. Though my throat is dry I manage to croak, "She wasn't that kind of girl."

The Best Man
(a film play)

FADE IN

A COUNTRY MEADOW UNDER GIANT OAKS – DAY
Several dozen COUNTRY FOLK mill about uncomfortably, seeking shelter
from a blistering, midday sun in the shade of these magnificent oak trees.
Their dress defines the era, late nineteenth century, with men in leather boots
and broad-brimmed hats and women in long skirts and bonnets. Children play
crack-the-whip.

A variety of horse-drawn carts and horses are tethered nearby. The horses'
tails slap lazily at flies.

One of the women in the crowd, a girl really, age 17 or so, is obviously
pregnant. Her stomach protrudes way out and she appears to be in her eighth
or ninth month. Her name is LOUISE.

She is rather plain, and pouts. She looks across the meadow at two strapping
young men: HENRY and EUGENE.

The two young men stare back at her rather sheepishly, hands in pockets and
feet stirring the dirt.

There is a sound of approaching hoof beats, a galloping horse that catches
everyone's attention. They turn and look, some pointing…

VOICE IN THE CROWD: *There's the Sheriff!*

THEIR VIEW
Tall in the saddle and broad-shouldered, the SHERIFF rides into view. He reins his horse to a hard stop and jumps to the ground. He tethers the heavy-breathing animal to a wagon and approaches Louise.

>   LOUISE: *Howdy, Sheriff.*

He pauses before her, eyeing her condition judgmentally. He then turns to eyeball Henry and Eugene.

>   SHERIFF (to Louise): *You sure you don't know which is the one?*

Louise shrugs and shakes her head.

>   LOUISE: *Could be either... given the circumstances.*

The Sheriff looks a moment at Louise and furls his brow.

>   LOUISE (defensively): *Well, they was both my beaus.*

The Sheriff draws a deep breath, then crosses the meadow to the two young men.

>   SHERIFF: *Alright, fellahs. I reckon this is as fair a way as any to settle this.*

Henry and Eugene study each other briefly, snarling, then remove their shirts.

The crowd begins forming a circle around the two young men.

>   EUGENE (to Louise): *Louise, please! Can't you just choose between us?*

>   HENRY: *Shut up, Eugene. Let's git down to it.*

>   SHERIFF: *Preacher, you want to say anythin' before we commence?*

A man in black, THE PREACHER, steps forward and bows his head.

PREACHER (piously): *Let us pray....*

All bow their heads reverently; the men in the crowd remove their hats.

PREACHER (continuing): *Oh, Lord! Bless these here proceedings. And giveth strength unto the proper man so that he may reign victorious. Amen.*

The crowd responds in unison: *Amen!*

The preacher steps back to his spot in the circle and the hats go back onto the heads of the men.

Henry and Eugene, stripped to the waist, begin to bounce around, warming up their bodies. They are both strong, good-looking men in their late teens or early twenties. The Sheriff calls them together.

SHERIFF: *Listen here. No punches below the belt and no bitin'. Keep it honest. And may the best man win.*

The two men raise their fists and square off. The crowd that encircles them is silent at the moment, except for one who offers a quiet word of encouragement.

2ND VOICE IN THE CROWD: *Go git him, Henry.*

Someone else balances this by whispering...

3RD VOICE IN CROWD: *You can take him, Eugene.*

Slowly, the two men rotate around one another while orbiting their fists menacingly. Henry seems much more intense than Eugene, who furtively glances at Louise. During one of these quick glances, while Eugene's eyes are off his opponent, Henry lashes out swiftly and drives a hard fist into his jaw. The crowd *"Oohs!"* in unison.

Eugene stumbles backward and spits blood.

EUGENE: *Dammit, Henry!*

Henry moves in swiftly, attacking....

HENRY: *All's fair in love and war, Eugene....*

He flails several blows, but Eugene deftly defends himself. Eugene ducks low, driving his shoulder into Henry's mid-section while pulling at his knees. The two crash into the dirt as the crowd responds with spattered cheers and clapping.

Henry pounds his fist into Eugene's backside and manages to wrangle free. As he does he backhands his opponent fiercely. The two rise to their feet, pause briefly to catch their wind, then lunge towards each other.

VARIOUS ANGLES ON THE CROWD
The on-lookers are warming up to things now, getting into the spirit of a good fight, and they begin call out enthusiastically. They seem about evenly divided, with some supporting Henry and others supporting Eugene. Even the preacher gets into the thrill of the moment, smashing his fist into his palm. But he catches himself in the act. Sheepishly, he tries to regain his composure.

The two young men trade blows furiously, doing their best to beat each other's brains in. Their faces and eyes quickly discolor and swell, and blood mingled with dirt smears across their chests as they embrace in the sweaty battle.

The crowd excites progressively, whooping and shouting now for their respective favorites. Spatters of blood spray upon their shoes and, with a swift uppercut by one of the fighters, a streak of crimson flies across the women's dresses.

The two fighting men pound at each other, trading blows with feet planted, one after the other. They are both tiring. The grueling battle seems to sway in favor first to Henry, then back to Eugene.

Gradually, the two weaken and their punches flail meekly. Blood flows from cut lips, smashed noses and eyes so swollen one wonders how either man sees at all.

Henry's eyes flutter and his knees quiver. Sensing opportunity, Eugene quickly seizes the upper hand. He moves in with renewed vigor, arms windmilling. He fires repeated blows to Henry's chest and mid-section. Then, mercilessly, with one final, rock-hard punch Eugene decks his opponent.

Henry falls with a heavy thud, spread-eagled in the dirt. He lies unmoving.

The crowd cheers, hats fly into the air, and they rush the victor Eugene. They pound his back with hearty congratulations then hoist him onto shoulders.

Though exhausted he warms to his praise and grins broadly.

TIGHT ON HENRY
The Sheriff leans over poor Henry, flat on his back in the dust and grime. He is oblivious to all that is going on around him.

The Sheriff gives an authoritative nod to a MAN WITH A BUCKET. With one SWOOSH he empties the bucket's contents of cold spring-water onto Henry's face and chest. At once the young man sputters to life, sitting upright.

The crowd silences, lowers Eugene to the ground, and turns its attention to the Sheriff. He hauls Henry to his feet.

    SHERIFF: *You fought hard, Son. But ya lost, fair an' square.*

Henry's bloodied countenance falls dramatically.

    HENRY: *Aw, shucks!* (a realization comes to him) *No!* ***Oh, no!***

    SHERIFF (with a nod): *Yup.*

The Sheriff dusts the young man off but keeps a firm hand on his shoulder. Henry struggles a bit.

Eugene grins broadly, although his lip is split and bleeding. He steps forward.

The Sheriff turns to Louise.

> SHERIFF: *You ready to get hitched, girl?*

She, too, grins broadly and nods. She also steps forward, and someone places a bouquet of hand-picked flowers in her hand.

> SHERIFF: *Where's the preacher, then?*

Officiously, the preacher steps forward. He opens his Bible.

> PREACHER: *Righ' cheer, Sheriff!*

Louise marches forward and laces her arm through Henry's. The young man is still semi-dazed from the beating he took, but he is lucid enough to understand what is going on. He groans miserably....

> SHERIFF: *No sense puttin' this off, Henry.* (eyeing Louise's belly) *You two done waited to the last hour as it is.*

> HENRY(one last protest): *But, **Share-riff!***

> SHERIFF: *Hush. It was a fair fight, and you lost. Eugene here, why, he's the **best** man.*

The Sheriff gives a firm nod to the preacher and the crowd closes in around the young couple.

> PREACHER: *Dearly beloved, we are gathered here together in the presence of Almighty God...*

CAMERA PULLS BACK TO A LONG SHOT
The crowd gathers in tightly to witness the ceremony. Henry grimaces, but Eugene is all smiles-and-grins. Louise, the blushing bride, looks at her husband-to-be with loving and prideful eyes....

FADE OUT

Ozone

"An odd thought popped into my head, for some unknown reason," my old pal Al said, and tilted his beer back to drain it. He tossed the bottle to the floor beside the other empties, then strummed his guitar slowly. A melancholy chord. E-minor, perhaps.

"What?" I prompted, but didn't need to. Odd thoughts were perfectly acceptable between us, almost expected. Certainly encouraged. I found the chord on my own guitar and without speaking we hammered out a riff together, about 16 bars.

Al stopped suddenly, put his guitar aside, shook his wispy hair from his eyes, and twisted the top off another Heineken. Then he smoked and said to me:

I remember what I told actor C__ E____ one night at the Dog's Breath, that tavern he used to own up in Carmel. I'd shown him how to eject a single cartridge from a .45 and catch it in the cuff of his pants, and he thought he could maybe use that trick in one of his pictures. (This was... oh, I don't know, after his "dirty cop" films but before that monkey-movie crap.) Anyway we got to talking about some of his stuff and I told him I felt his onscreen depiction of human suffering did a good job showing pain's ability to warp the human spirit, detaching it in a sense, resulting in a cold aloofness. Like that renegade cop character of his, for instance. I told him I thought he was dead-on with that.

He replied by saying that he just played the part as written. Then he launched into a discourse fueled by the brews he'd downed. (Good God you wouldn't guess that a guy who hardly ever strung more than six words together in his films could be so windy!) C__ E____ suggested that people related to that particular character because the renegade cop did things everyone *wanted*

120

to do, that is, react with vengeance against iniquity, but he himself felt no one actually *would* do such things even if given the chance.

When I finally got a word in edgewise I said well I beg to differ. I told him about what my buddy Dave did, Dave the college graduate from Ohio, to a VC spy we found in our midst in the summer of '69. One of our fellow soldiers, a lieutenant in the Vietnamese army, a guy we all trusted, who'd got us good dope and always knew where to find booze and women, had betrayed us. One day he passed along our orders to the Viet Cong for cold cash. Like thirty pieces of silver. Subsequently we were ambushed, half the unit went home in body bags, and Dave figured out right away who'd ratted us out. So, to make my point, I detailed for actor C__ E____ *precisely* what the college graduate from Ohio did to the VC spy in our midst that summer of '69. I guess I was too graphic in my recollection, because I had the unique experience of watching an Oscar-winner double over and blow chunks in his own tavern. Now that was a sight.

Six or seven years later I ran into C__ E____ on the set of one of his westerns and I reminded him of the incident. (I was still working as a stunt double in those days.) He said it wasn't the gory of the story that made him ill that day, but bad shellfish. I thought *Yeah right*.

Maybe the reason that memory popped into my head just now is because, well, to be truthful, I've been thinking about human suffering quite a bit lately. And remember, Mitch, old friend, I've been kicked in the teeth, sliced with razors, thrown out of moving vehicles, buried to my neck in human waste by those damn pajama-wearers, and worse, hogtied by LA cops, beaten with flashlights and pummeled with fists until I passed out. In my so-called film career I've had forty-seven broken bones and lost a kidney when I drove a motorcycle into a rolling bus. So I think I have some level of expertise on the subject of human suffering. Expertise? Hell, I've got a friggin' Ph.D. So, when I tell you that the worst form of human suffering has nothing to do with physical pain *whatsoever*, you can take it to the bank.

See, physical pain you can explain. You can get your arms around it. You can also take drugs to make it go away. You can *smoke dope and hope*, as we used to say in 'Nam. Or pray, if you're the sort. Hope and pray that the pain goes away, so as you can *heal*. (That's the kind of pain, by the way, Mitch, people refer to when they say, "If it don't kill you it will make you stronger," which is also crap.)

No, in terms of human suffering there is something far worse than physical pain. A sort of suffering that always warps the human spirit, or else kills it.

Either way, the end result is the same: a coldness, a separateness – an *alone-ness*, if you will, that belies the old fable that no man is an island. The sea of humanity is full of islands, Mitch. In fact, I am of the mind that *every* man and *every* woman is an island. When we humans do things unthinkable, when we are cold, calculating or criminal, and when we are vengeful, we are behaving most naturally.

Let me give you an example.

Back in the early days following World War II there was a young woman, Estelle, a girl, really, the daughter of a high school teacher in Corpus Christi, Texas. You ever been there, Mitch? No? Well, back then it was not much more than a dusty little seaport. It was hot; there were mosquitoes the size of California canaries, and people as a rule always looked forward to the evenings. Because with the sunset the dampness was a little more tolerable and a breeze off the gulf could cool you if you sat real still on your porch. That's what people did back then. They sat real still on porches in the early evenings and talked with one another. And often as they sat they were treated to a lightshow out in the bay, for as you know the Gulf of Mexico produces some spectacular electrical thunderstorms.

A New York Jew named Harvey moved into town to become the owner of Corpus Christi's only radio station, WGUF. "1440 on your AM dial." He lived on the corner of Main and Sam Houston streets, in a big house at the base of the radio station's massive steel tower. He was deathly afraid of those thunderstorms I mentioned, Mitch, I think for very good and obvious reasons. He used to shake his fist at the sky and call upon God to make them go away, saying with his New York accent, *"God in heaven! Send this accursed demon away from me!"* He did this so often and so publicly that the people in town used to mockingly do what they called "the Harvey." Whenever they were even mildly frustrated with something they would shake fists, pinch their noses to achieve the appropriate nasal tonality, and say: *"God in heaven! Send this accursed demon AWAY from me!"* That's what they called "the Harvey." It started with high school kids using it on cops and math teachers, but spread to just about everyone. It always got a big laugh, to imitate Harvey the Jew-radio-owner.

As evenings progressed people moved from their porches into their living rooms to listen to the radio. They didn't have radios in their cars or at work like we do these days. Radio was something you listened to in your home, and most homes had but one radio. And in those days people would tune in the news and they would listen to music during the day, but what they really wanted most in the evening was entertainment. Vaudeville on the airwaves, they called it. The nightmare of war and economic depression was still a fresh memory. People were developing a taste for escapism even then, Mitch, and radio was the medium.

One day Harvey hired this girl Estelle to answer the phone and do other odd jobs around WGUF. The station consisted of two rooms on the ground floor of Harvey's house at the base of the tower. She came in after school, was a steady worker, and was nice to look at as a bonus. Harvey enjoyed talking, which is why he bought a radio station in the first place, and when he wasn't on the air broadcasting he would use Estelle as a sounding board to test his ideas. She always listened to him with great intensity.

"Our radio listeners are *unrefined, unsophisticated, and immature*, Estelle (he used to say). Texans are *hicks*. I give them the New York Philharmonic; they cry for cowboy singers. It's enough to make a man sick."

(This was a common theme for Harvey.)

"I bring them *quality* programming. I bring to the people of this community artists whose performances uplift the spirit and educate the soul. But, Estelle, this is not to their liking. I broadcast Shakespeare; they want the *Lone Ranger*. I interview the famous Mr. William Faulkner, America's finest literary genius living today, by telephone all the way from Los Angeles California, and so what? They call and complain that they missed an episode of *Amos and Andy*. These people! Schmucks! They are burning holes in my stomach! I give them composers from Europe; they seek comedians from Jersey. Hicks! Cowboys! Jalapeno-poppers! They want crude programming. I refuse! I deliver the quintessential; they demand the quiz show. I tell you, Estelle, our listeners are *unrefined, unsophisticated, and immature*."

One day the white clouds lingering over the gulf darkened again and Harvey went outside into the middle of Main Street and shook his fist at them. "*God in heaven!*" he shouted. "Take this accursed demon and *blow it out to sea!*" This was a variation of his customary curse.

Next day, Estelle was horrified to hear her high school classmates adjust "the Harvey" accordingly. They began to call on God to send the vice principal and various other assorted demons *out to sea!*

Day after day Estelle listened to Harvey and took everything he said very seriously. She was embarrassed for the people of Corpus Christi, her hometown, because they were indeed so *very* unsophisticated. She could see that they were unrefined and culturally immature, just as Mr. Harvey made them out to be. Her boss had become a dashing figure to her – not that he was particularly good looking. But he was an educated, successful businessman. Plus, he owned a new Pontiac. Very soon, Estelle lost her head and her heart to the transplanted New Yorker.

Harvey, a slight man approaching thirty with thinning hair and rising temples, who had always considered himself *un*attractive, was surprised to discover his young employee's attraction to him. He was quite naturally drawn to the dark-haired teenager who showed up at work at three every afternoon. But he never suspected that his ranting on about quintessential programming and artistic performances would arouse a deep longing in Estelle's soul for the things he so vociferously praised, for refinement, for sophistication, and for personal maturity. She perceived that Harvey was the man who could give her these things. In her opinion, there was no hope finding it elsewhere in Corpus Christi, Texas, not in 1947.

From Harvey's perspective, Estelle was a sweet, compassionate girl with a large bosom and a slender waist. He had been in love only once before, to an older girl who lived down the street from his home in Brooklyn. He promised to marry her and planned to send for her once he got settled in Texas. But she did not have the curves of this girl, his employee, Estelle. No way.

So they became engaged. Estelle's teacher-father would not hear of her leaving high school. Harvey agreed, so they waited. She had one year to go to graduate. They waited for the legal paperwork but not much else. Estelle was a passionate young woman, with surging hormones, and the nights in Corpus are, as I mentioned before, sultry. She spent every hour not in school with her new fiancé. And when she was with her fiancé, for whatever reason her shirt flew off.

After school they made love in the locked broadcast booth. Late at night they did it under the radio tower and lay on their backs afterwards, smoking cigarettes, watching the red and white lights flash at the very top of it. Harvey was concerned that Estelle might become pregnant, which of course would ruin him (she was still just sixteen), but he could not control himself. And Estelle did not care because she could sense that she was becoming more sophisticated with each and every orgasm Harvey gave her. And, although Estelle did not know it at the time (and Harvey never would), becoming pregnant was not something she could accomplish anyway.

At last Estelle completed her senior year, graduated, and her father consented to the union. She and Harvey were married. They took a train to New York, where they honeymooned and met all of Harvey's relatives. In front of them, in a toast, Harvey said something like this: "Because of you, Estelle, I am the *happiest* and *luckiest* man in the world!" He was only half right.

Their marriage was nothing short of bliss. They were one of those rare couples whose strengths compensated for each other's weaknesses. While Estelle continued to answer the phone at WGUF, she took on other duties as well. Her husband had been no good at selling advertising, the lifeblood of radio. He lived conservatively and operated the station on a shoe string budget. Estelle on the other hand, with her rosy cheeks, bright smile, and ample bosom, proved to be a natural saleswoman.

Friendly and flirtatious banter with her customers, the businessmen in town, came easy to Estelle. She believed in her product and had faith in radio. She told them how brilliant they were to use it to reach people. "Our listener's are your customers," she would say, "and they will buy your products if they know about them." And for the most part the businessmen believed her. They opened their wallets and began to purchase ever-increasing amounts of airtime.

And so the newlyweds prospered. Unfortunately, before long Harvey's newfound success went, as they say, to his head. It encouraged him to be even more adamant about his convictions with regards to the subject of quality programming. He developed fervor akin to that of the traveling evangelists who set up circus tents to preach the word. He began to cut back further on cowboy singers to broadcast more opera, *in Italian!* (Remember, Mitch, this was postwar Texas, bible-and-oil Texas, the Texas of the Deep South.) Harvey interviewed more famous authors, like Tennessee Williams and Earnest Hemingway. He held on-air panel discussions with left wing political candidates who promoted controversial viewpoints. He even involved Estelle's father, the schoolteacher, who hosted a weekly lecture series on, of all things, natural history.

Estelle believed in her husband. *His* mission became *her* mission, to uplift and educate their community, to elevate its sophistication and teach an appreciation for the finer things in life via the medium of radio. Estelle began to read avidly, mostly novels her husband suggested. She learned to think critically. She promoted the arts and disdained popular culture altogether. When the time came, she agreed fully with her husband's decision to eliminate *The Lone Ranger* and *Amos and Andy* from the Saturday evening line up.

She was greatly disappointed in the inevitable letters and telephone calls that resulted from their programming changes. Estelle assumed the duty of responding to them. The people of Corpus Christi requested more popular radio shows, like the ones they heard up in Houston or when visiting in San Antonio. She disparaged them for this. Then Estelle would report to her husband with tears of frustration in her eyes. "We offer them *Brahms* and *Beethoven"* she would say, "and they want *Hope* and *Crosby."*

Over time, like Harvey, Estelle grew to secretly despise the listeners of their radio station. She was disgusted by their lack of good taste, their apathy towards the finer arts and preference for the mundane. When they phoned to complain she began to chastise them. She backed her husband's decision to reserve all of the weekend evening hours for broadcasting intellectual discussions and classical music selections. Harvey appreciated his wife's unfailing support and would sometimes bury his face in her hair, whispering passionately, "One day, my darling, *one day* these cowboy yokels will understand. Then they will appreciate what we Harveys have done for them."

But one day something else happened, altogether. CBS came to town. They built a radio tower across the bay.

The Columbia Broadcasting System people did not care one bit about cultural development. They knew their stuff, however, when it came to running a profitable radio station. They began immediately to broadcast the most popular and entertaining shows available, westerns, detective yarns and quiz shows. *Gunsmoke, The Shadow,* and *What's My Line* held prime time slots in the evenings, and the comedian *Jack Benny* had a lock on Sunday nights. They offered news on the hour, every hour, and played musical selections from crooners like *Sinatra* and *Crosby* and female vocalists, too, *Ethel Merman, Judy Garland* and the like. And of course, the staple of their programming was the popular big band sounds from Tommy Dorsey and Glenn Miller. But being it was Texas, they devoted lots and lots of airtime to *cowboy* music. On Saturday night, live and direct, they broadcast *The Grande Ol' Opry.*

The new CBS station offered no classical music at all. Nothing educational, nothing enlightening and nothing cultural. Just entertainment – pure and simple – for entertainment's sake. And guess what? *Everyone* in Corpus Christi tuned in to listen.

Estelle was indeed a gifted saleswoman, but all of her powers of persuasion could not keep WGUF's advertisers from abandoning them. "We're shifting our promotional dollars to the new station in Corpus Christi, that one across the bay," the businessmen told her. "The radio our customers are listening to, WCBS." And overnight WGUF went broke. Harvey and Estelle fell upon hard times.

Harvey grew very bitter about this. He felt betrayed and unappreciated. Unexpectedly, for it wasn't really in his nature, he began to drink. He became morose. He smoked too much. He and Estelle came to the point where they couldn't meet expenses and failed to pay their bills on time.

Now when the thunderstorms rolled in from the gulf Harvey would step into the street, shake his fist and shout, "Well, *Goddamn it!* Go ahead then! Strike my *Goddamn* tower with your *Goddamn* electrical demons! Burn the place to the ground! See if I care! *Ha!*"

Needless to say, Estelle was worried sick about him.

One dark and rainy day she went to seek counsel from the new pastor at First Baptist, a fellow named Roberts. People said good things about him. He was a young man, a recent graduate of seminary. He was said to be wise beyond his years, an excellent counselor, and counsel was what Estelle needed just then.

Pastor Roberts' hair was black as coal and he combed it straight back with no part at all. Good looking and unmarried, his arrival in town had made him instantly the most eligible bachelor in Corpus Christi. He was an outstanding Bible-thumper who preached hellfire and brimstone to the unsaved. He also taught the evils of alcohol and cigarettes, railed against both and partook in neither. Estelle came to this young preacher to ask his counsel in helping her deal with her husband's growing alcohol and cigarette addiction. Frankly, she expected condemnation. To her surprise, he listened patiently then told her that since his arrival he had become a fan of their radio station. He tuned in virtually every day. He greatly enjoyed classical music, he said, and drew inspiration from it. And he supported their decisions to minimize popular programming, which he felt glorified base human nature.

"Since you listen to our broadcasts you've heard for yourself, Pastor," Estelle said to him, "and can appreciate how much my husband has done for this community. It has been his mission to educate and uplift the people of Corpus Christi. But now all is lost and hopeless." She explained their predicament, including the details of their worsening financial situation, and began to cry.

The preacher was not unmoved by the young woman's plight. "All is not lost," he told her. "And you must place your hope in Jesus." Then he opened his Bible and quoted scripture to her, which strangely was a great comfort. *"For we know that all things work together for the good of them who love God, and are called according to His righteousness."* He closed the book and looked the young woman squarely in her eyes. "Estelle, God has a plan for your life."

At that moment a blinding flash lit the room, followed by a tremendous *KER-WUMP!* The lights flickered momentarily and went dark. The windows rattled in their frames. The noise was very much like an explosion, and just overhead. Pastor Roberts jumped from his chair and looked at the ceiling. "What in heaven was that?" he cried. But Estelle, who had lived in Corpus Christi all of her life, knew at once what in heaven made that noise. She ran out of the office.

It was as if the black clouds overhead had been ripped asunder. Rain poured down like water spilt from a bucket, turning the streets to rivers. The church was just a few blocks from the radio station. Estelle, forgetting that she had driven the Pontiac, shot out the front door and sprinted fast as she could down Main Street. At once she was soaked to the skin. Her cotton dress clung to her legs, slowing her considerably until she gathered up its hem and held it high. She pumped her feet and splashed down the middle of the street, leaping the rising puddles. Another brilliant flash with its nearly instantaneous roar thundered directly overhead as she rounded the corner at Sam Houston, gasping for air. What she beheld there stopped her cold in her tracks.

Black smoke billowed from the shattered windows of the radio station. The steel of the broadcast tower was scorched, twisted and smoldering.

And there was an intense odor of ozone.

Harvey had been on the air when his accursed demon finally struck. He was broadcasting, of all things, a weather report. The coroner later said that the electrical charge, which struck the tower, had traveled through its steel and down its copper wires into the studio, exploding vacuum tubes and fusing circuits. It then passed through the radio dials into Harvey's fingers, shot through his body to his feet where it burned through the soles of his leather shoes to arc into the iron rich soil below the floor. The blast melted Harvey's watch and blew a hole beneath the building six feet in diameter.

Harvey never heard the *KER-WUMP*. He never saw the flash.

His body was returned to family in New York. For Estelle's sake there was a memorial service at First Baptist. She sobbed loudly, mourning the loss of the man who had brought sophistication to her life. The preacher delivered a message of comfort and hope, but ended the service early.

"It's a tragedy," the good people of Corpus Christi said. "Such a young man, Mr. Harvey. And to leave behind such a pretty wife!" The newspaper printed a tribute to Harvey and noted his many contributions to the community.

Fortunately, Estelle was not left destitute for Harvey was a believer in insurance and the radio station – though completely destroyed – was fully covered for such a loss. Plus the Pontiac was paid for. But Estelle was inconsolable. Around town she was never seen wearing anything but black.

Until the following spring. On Easter Sunday morning, Estelle finally put away her black dress and put on a pink one to attend the sunrise service at First Baptist. Afterwards the new young preacher invited the new young widow to stay for potluck hosted by the church choir. She agreed. Later, he walked her home.

"Everything happens in accord with God's will, with His plan for our lives," Pastor Roberts consoled Estelle as they walked. His voice was tender and compassionate. He spoke with sincerity and empathy. "So when God calls our loved ones home it is our duty to press on in our service to Him," he said. "When the Lord closes a door, He always opens a window."

After he left Estelle pondered the sentiment Pastor Roberts expressed in his profound words to her. The tenderness of his voice resounded in her ears, comforting her, and she came to realize that she was very attracted to him. For his part, the young preacher was similarly impressed with Estelle. They began a courtship.

At once they were an item. They were first seen together at the church picnic, then again walking arm in arm along the beach, and later sharing a soda at the pharmacy. And when the women of the church organized a Vacation Bible School for children, Estelle was invited to teach crafts. She later joined the church. Soon after that the church's Superintendent of Sunday School asked her if she'd care to teach preschool children on Sunday mornings. She agreed.

The children adored their new Sunday School teacher Estelle. She adored them, too, and secretly wished for a child of her own.

Everyone else at First Baptist grew to love her, as well. Over time Pastor Roberts' and Estelle's fondness for each other blossomed, and folks began to speculate about the potential for a wedding. All agreed that they were an ideal couple, the good-looking young preacher and the adorable young widow. No one was surprised, then, when the Pastor announced their engagement. They were wed three months later. It was the fall of 1951.

Pastor Roberts and Estelle served the Lord with gladness.

In those days, Mitch, there was a general feeling of prosperity in this country. The GIs who'd returned from fighting the Second World War were now finishing up their government-paid college education. They got new jobs and bought homes, cars and television sets. And like many of them, Estelle and her new husband looked forward to starting a family and joining the baby boom.

The two were heavily involved in the operation of the church, of course. Back then if you hired a preacher you got the service of his wife for free. Estelle happily took on many unpaid duties, working as church secretary beside her husband. Customarily they worked until around three in the afternoon then crossed the street to their home in the parsonage to make love. After, Estelle would busy herself preparing dinner while her husband returned to the church to make a few telephone calls. This routine worked well on two counts. First, they were confident that their efforts would make a baby sooner or later and second, as a result of their activity the pastor was strangely empowered to build God's church. His late afternoon phone calls began to yield much fruit.

"Understand you are new to the area," Pastor Roberts would say into the telephone, his voice relaxed, warm and sincere. "Our church is ideal for young families like yours… We've got Sunday School classes for the kids and lots of opportunities for you and your wife to fellowship with other young parents. Why don't you come visit our services this Sunday?" His invitation was always open, honest and genuine. And people responded to it.

It is understandable, I think, that this approach resulted in a growing membership at First Baptist Church. The pastor and his wife were attractive, personable and caring. People loved them. The church flourished.

But Estelle did *not* get pregnant. After a year or so of trying she saw doctors. They performed tests. She learned she would never have children. She was barren, the doctors said.

Disappointed, the couple redoubled their efforts in growing the church. The membership doubled, then tripled. It grew so dynamically that it became apparent that a new, larger church must be built. A committee was formed. The young pastor and his board met with architects and bankers. Plans were drawn, new land on the outskirts of town was purchased, and contracts were signed. The blessings were enormous. There was a great deal of excitement in the community in those days. The air was full of electricity.

Pastor Roberts had a vision. He insisted that the new sanctuary include a great, glass walled baptistery. Like all Baptist churches, the congregation of First Baptist believed in the ordinance of water immersion as testimony to the power of Jesus' death, burial and resurrection. The young preacher envisioned a large tank situated high above the choir loft with an outer wall made of glass so that those sitting in the pews could clearly see the newly saved being baptized.

Back then, Mitch, it was generally felt that a good Baptist preacher ought to be able to raise the rafters and call down fire and brimstone under the power of his own two lungs. But Pastor Roberts had mellowed considerably since his marriage. Estelle had influenced him significantly. He was now convinced that the Word of God should be more lovingly preached, not shouted by a red-faced preacher. He found that his message of a compassionate Christ was better delivered in a soft voice, one that turns away wrath. Consequently he felt appropriate sound amplification was a necessity.

His board of deacons fully agreed. So, the plans for the new church called for both a glass walled baptistery *and* sound amplification that included a chrome microphone, a large amplifier and big speakers.

Estelle, meanwhile, had not given up on having a child of her own. She prayed daily for conception but found no little baby knit in her womb. At night her dreams were of motherhood, of blue and pink booties, of cribs in a nursery. She secretly purchased cotton diapers and pastel blankets when she found them on sale. She was banking on a miracle. And sometimes she awoke at night, breasts full and nipples aching. Sadness would overwhelm her. She prayed harder.

Her husband also prayed, but he was more pragmatic. "Perhaps it is not God's will for us to be parents," he said.

Some nights Estelle would have unpleasant dreams. They were nightmares of doctors examining her with strange instruments, performing various tests. They consulted one another in whispered conversations, looking over their shoulders, scratching their chins and frowning. In these dreams she would find herself in a sort of court of law, with medical specialists in white jackets seated at the jury box. A cruel-looking judge would pound a gavel and pronounce: "You will *never* bear children!" It was horrible, and from these dreams she would awake in tears.

So, as the young pastor busied himself with the construction of the new church Estelle began, ever so gradually, to lose hope. Her faith in God was sorely tested. She grew depressed and, at times, even physically ill. She and her husband stopped having sex in the afternoon.

Then one fine day the new church was completed. It was a grand structure, with a tall tower and a white cross that was lit at night. There was a ceremony, the church was blessed and dedicated, and the whole town was caught up in the excitement at First Baptist. A final service was held in the old church. The following Sunday would mark the official opening of the new church and everyone freely and openly admitted it was the result of God's blessing and the hard work and unfailing devotion of the young pastor and his lovely wife.

It was the first Sunday in May 1954.

What better way to celebrate the opening of a new Baptist church then to do so with the joy of baptizing new converts into the faith? No one disagreed with this. So, on that first Sunday a dozen new members of the First Baptist Church of Corpus Christi met Pastor Roberts, one by one, in the waist high waters of the glass walled baptistery.

The baptistery was lit with a brilliant light overhead and was situated high above the choir. The young pastor rejoiced as he lowered each new Christian into the waters, saying, "I baptize you in the name of Jesus Christ. *Amen!*" And the congregation, watching from the pews, solemnly echoed *"Amen!"* in response. It was a glorious experience for everyone.

Estelle Roberts watched proudly from the front pew. She was happy for her husband.

Finally Pastor Roberts baptized the last of them. Turning to face his congregation, his robe swirling in the waters of the baptistery, Pastor Roberts smiled broadly and raised his hands in praise and in triumph. (Later, everyone said that this was his finest hour.)

He announced, *"Hallelujah! Let us pray!"* and bowed his head. Instinctively he reached for the chrome microphone to draw it near…

There followed a loud *POP*, a sizzling noise, and a brilliant flash of light.

The congregation raised their bowed heads, startled. They beheld their young pastor grimacing, teeth chattering, eyes curled upward so only the whites were showing. His right hand gripped the gleaming chrome neck of the microphone. His left hand fluttered spastically overhead looking all the world like a dove descending. Electricity danced up and down the preacher's white-robed body, visible through the glass wall of the baptistery. It emitted an eerie, bluish hue as it raced through the water, circling his torso like a hula-hoop sent from hell itself. Pastor Roberts jerked three times and then stood rigid, his back arching. For a moment time froze, then the church's new fuses blew and all the lights in the sanctuary went dark. The blue hue of the electrical charge faded. He fell backward with a splash and slipped under the water.

Estelle Roberts rose in the front pew. Her jaw worked but no sound emerged. She wore a dull expression and clutched the Bible in her hands. Then she wobbled, her knees buckled and she fainted dead away.

Later what people most remembered was the intense odor of ozone.

(No, Mitch, legal charges were never brought, though a board of inquiry did determine that the electrician who had wired the sound system had botched the job. No proper ground, they said. Now days there would have been a lawsuit and a major settlement for wrongful death, but in the 'fifties people didn't think that way. What happened was an accident, pure and simple. As Pastor Roberts himself would have said, God had a plan for his life and apparently that plan ended abruptly that first Sunday in May. It is true that God works in mysterious ways.)

Estelle Roberts had a nervous breakdown. She was deathly ill for several months but, being young, there was never any real doubt that she would bounce back eventually. The good folks in Corpus Christi prayed for her. She was one of their own and twice widowed before her twenty-fifth birthday.

When Estelle's health returned she eventually was asked to move out of the church-owned parsonage, to make room for the new pastor. She took an apartment down by the docks. She liked the salty air on the bay, and took up painting. She had no need to earn a living because in addition to the insurance money from the radio she now received a monthly stipend from a pension paid to the widows of Baptist preachers.

She discovered she was a gifted artist, though untrained. She liked bright colors and had an eye for perspective. Estelle would sketch what she observed down on the waterfront and then paint from her drawings in her apartment. Actually, she preferred to paint on the apartment's back porch. It faced the gulf and there was plenty of light and fresh air. She painted beach scenes, mostly, the colorful buildings and characters one finds in coastal towns like Corpus Christi.

One day, as Estelle painted on her back porch, a little fellow of no more than three or four crawled upon the wooden fence that separated her porch from that of her neighbor. He straddled the fence and placed one foot each on the rails on either side, balancing himself there.

"Hello," Estelle said to this little fence-sitter.

"Hello," he responded.

She continued to paint and he watched her. He was most interested in what she was doing. She was just finishing a view of the marina that included many sailboats, and the boy pointed at one of them – a bright blue one with a tall mast – and said, "That's my daddy's boat."

Estelle looked at him and smiled. It seemed unlikely that anyone living in these apartments would own a sailboat like this one because the boat was quite expensive and was moored at one of the better marinas. But she was happy to engage the little fellow in conversation.

"Your father has a boat like this one?"

"Yes," he said. "And he takes me fishing in it."

The boy's father stepped out on the back porch just then and, seeing his son was visiting the neighbor, peered over the fence. "Oh, hello. I hope he's not being a bother."

Estelle shook her head. "Not at all. He's a bright boy, isn't he?"

"Look, Daddy," the youngster said, pointing again. "Our boat."

The man squinted and took a closer look. "By God, that *is* my boat!"

Estelle checked to see if he was joking, saw that he was not, then looked back at the painting in surprise. Her mouth fell open.

"How is it that you are painting *my* boat?" the man asked with a rather suspicious tone of voice.

"I had no idea I was painting your boat!" Estelle responded defensively. The man looked at her doubtfully. "Now look here," she said. "I paint scenes from all over the marina. How was I to know that one of these boats was yours?"

The man rubbed his chin and shrugged his shoulders. "A coincidence," he said. He stuck his hand over the fence and extended it to Estelle. "But a happy one. I've been looking for an excuse to introduce myself to you since you moved in. I'm your neighbor, Allen Greggor."

Estelle stepped to the fence and shook the man's hand. "Very nice to meet you, Mr. Greggor. And who is this fence-sitter you have next to you?"

Greggor smiled and put his arm around the boy.

"This is my son, who is somewhat of a rascal. He is known as Little Ally, or sometimes Ally Oop because he does like to climb on things."

"Like fences?"

Greggor nodded. "Like fences. He's a bit of a daredevil."

She rubbed Little Ally's tummy and looked into his eyes affectionately. "Well, Little Ally, you may call me Estelle."

"Okay," the boy said.

"Does that privilege extend to his father, as well?" Greggor spoke wryly and leaned against the fence. The tweed jacket he wore fell open. Estelle's eyes focused upon a pistol holstered there, under his arm. Instinctively she stepped back.

Her movement did not escape the notice of Allen Greggor. He followed her glance to see with his own eyes what hers saw, his Colt .45. "I am sorry," he said pulling his jacket closed and buttoning it. "Let me explain, please. I am a policeman. Here, look…"

And with that Allen Greggor withdrew his wallet to display his identification.

Greggor, it turns out, was a homicide detective with the Corpus Christi police force. He had lived and worked in Corpus Christi since the war, in which he'd served in the Navy as a military policeman. His wife, the mother of Little Ally, had left them both a little over a year before. She'd abandoned them.

Within a few weeks Estelle knew that she had fallen in love with both Allen and Little Ally. Allen was a dashing figure of a man, an Irish Catholic with sandy hair and a square jaw. Unlike either of her previous husbands he was robust and strong, an outdoorsman who loved to fish in his sailboat and hike along the gulf shores. And because he was a policeman, and kept very odd hours, he desperately needed someone he could trust to watch after his son. Estelle fit that bill nicely.

As you might guess, Little Ally quickly became the child Estelle had so desperately longed for. He was bright and curious, adored Estelle and loved to paint with his own watercolors alongside her as she worked at her easel. And he was indeed a bit of a daredevil. Little Ally loved to climb things and was more or less fearless. He gave Estelle many heart-wrenching moments, as she often would discover he'd gone missing only to find him on rooftops or hanging from the highest branches of pecan trees.

Many nights Little Ally stayed over at Estelle's while his father worked, and she would read to him until he fell asleep in her arms. Then, fearing he might awaken, she would remain perfectly still until her body ached from holding him. She loved the smell of him, loved his crooked little smile and the way his eyebrows sometimes seemed to work independent of each other, and loved his wispy, straw-colored hair.

And Little Ally loved her. He no longer remembered his mother so Estelle became the only mother he knew.

Estelle and Allen Greggor's physical relationship began after several months living next door to one another. He came late from work one evening, knocking softly on Estelle's apartment door. She'd fallen asleep next to Little Ally, on the couch. When she opened the door to Allen Greggor she felt her heart jump, a curious feeling she hadn't had in some time. She was hungry for him, and he was hungry for her. She put her arms around his neck and he slipped a hand under her blouse.

They made love that night on the porch, with a warm gulf breeze carrying sounds of the ocean to their ears.

After that, they more or less lived together. They kept separate apartments but exchanged keys. Never before had Estelle experienced a more complete and satisfying existence. Never before had she been as happy or felt more fulfilled. Though she and Greggor did not marry, Estelle functioned for the first time in her life as a true wife and mother.

For five years they lived this way, the three of them together. She was able to help both Greggors in her life, the young one *and* the old one, to grow, develop and mature. Estelle taught Allen Greggor many things, for although she was still young she was a very mature soul. She taught him to enjoy a good book and to listen critically to good music. And she taught Little Ally the things every good mother teaches a child. She taught him to read and write long before he entered school, and how to play the piano. And she taught him bible lessons, about Jesus, about how God loves us.

And Estelle grew, too. She learned to sail, because that was Greggor's passion. He taught her how to fire a weapon, how to defend herself and Little Ally in an emergency. And from Little Ally Estelle learned how to fix booboos, because he certainly had his share of them.

The elder Greggor never spoke much about Little Ally's mother. Estelle gathered that it had ended suddenly, with the woman departing for parts unknown. She didn't much care, frankly.

Eventually, Little Ally came to think of Estelle as his natural mother. She did not correct him when first he called her *momma*. She liked the sound of it too much to put an end to it. She did sense a pang of guilt, but Allen Greggor did not seem to mind and the word seemed so very delicious to her, coming from Little Ally's mouth and directed to her in his sweet tone of voice. He was already a son to her, as far as she was concerned, and the only one she would likely ever know. Then after *momma* came *Mommy*. And on his ninth birthday, after blowing out all of his candles, Little Ally declared to Estelle and to Allen and to all of his little friends who had been gathered to celebrate the occasion: "Only sissies call their mothers *Mommy*."

Estelle felt her heart shrinking, and looked to Allen for support. Instinctively the policeman placed his hands on his son's shoulders and looked him square in the eyes. He said, "Well, old sport, you're certainly no sissy. What exactly would you like to call her?"

The boy looked at Estelle and grinned. "I'm gonna call her *Mother.* What else?"

His father smiled and Estelle breathed a great sigh of relief. "What else, indeed, Ally," she said to him, and kissed him.

But one afternoon not long after that birthday party a woman appeared at Estelle's door. She was very beautiful, with golden hair that flowed over her shoulders and penciled eyebrows that arched in perfect half-moons.

"My name is Connie Greggor," she announced. She smelled of gin. "And I believe you have something that belongs to me."

Estelle did not reply. She simply closed the door and locked it, then checked on Little Ally. For once he was safe in the back room, playing. Then she called Allen at work.

She told him about the woman at the door. There was a long moment of silence at his end of the line. Finally Greggor sighed deeply and muttered, "I told her to stay away from you."

Estelle was shocked. "Told her? You mean you *knew* she was in town?"

"Yes," Greggor told her. "She's been staying in the sailboat."

"The sailboat?" Estelle was stunned by this. And confused. "For how long?"

Greggor hesitated. "Three weeks."

Estelle's pulse began to pound in her ears. *Three weeks!* Her throat was instantly dry and the room began to swirl about her. She swallowed twice to compose herself. "What should I do?" she croaked.

"Nothing. We'll talk about it tonight." He hung up the phone.

Something in his voice frightened her, and she worried about it all afternoon. She did not know what to think. She wondered what it was Allen would say to her when he got home.

But Allen Greggor did not come home that night. At first Estelle assumed that he'd gotten caught up in a case he was working, because that sometimes happened. But after ten o'clock she knew otherwise. He'd always called before when he was running late.

At midnight, with Little Ally asleep in her bedroom, she called the station and checked on Allen's whereabouts, but no one knew. He'd left work early, actually, they said.

She waited another hour. He did not show up.

At two in the morning Estelle locked the apartment and walked to her car. The Pontiac was now twelve years old, older than Little Ally, but it ran perfectly. She drove it to the marina. Greggor's car was there, and she parked next to it. She placed a hand on its hood. The engine was cold. She could see the sailboat tied to its mooring. Quietly, she walked down to the dock. It was very dark – there was no lighting at all, no moon. She groped her way along in the darkness, nearly tripping over ropes and other things on the pier, until she came up alongside Greggor's boat. It was unlit inside. The water lapped gently against its side.

As far as she could see there was no one there. She looked anxiously about her, peering into the dark, but there was nothing.

She considered climbing over the railing and entering the cabin, but knew that in the darkness she'd probably slip and wind up in the water.

She moved to a porthole, leaning close to peer inside. It was black. There was no sound.

This is getting me nowhere, she reasoned to herself, *and I've left Little Ally alone.* She decided to return to her apartment.

But as she turned the sound of a match being struck stopped her cold. Through the porthole, from the corner of her eye, Estelle saw its glow. She pivoted her head slowly to watch. Inside the cabin slender hands cupped the burning match and held it to the tip of a cigarette. It glowed like a tiny red beacon as the tobacco ignited. In its dim light Estelle saw the golden hair and arched eyebrows of Connie Greggor as she drew a long drag on the cigarette then blew out the match with a puff. The woman lay nude just opposite the porthole atop the V-shaped bunk wedged in the forward hull of the cabin.

A second match was struck, this one just under the porthole. Estelle leaned forward to look, her brow nearly resting on the glass. This second match lit a cigarette clenched between the teeth of Allen Greggor. He rested on one elbow and lay next to Connie.

Estelle gasped, but did not cry out. She felt the air depart her lungs and her eyes flooded, but she fought to maintain control of herself. She needed time to think things through. She blinked rapidly to clear her eyes, then stepped slowly back from the dim light of the porthole. Placing one foot toe-to-heal behind the other she quietly moved back.

When she got clear of the boat she turned and made her way to the Pontiac. Once inside, its door closed, she let loose and bitter tears streamed down her cheeks. Estelle sat there, in the dark, sobbing for half an hour. She needed a plan.

Greggor phoned her the next morning from work. He told her he'd gotten pulled in on a stakeout at the last minute and apologized for not calling.

There was no time, he said. But he told her he'd see her that evening, and that they needed to talk. Estelle couldn't tell from the tone of his voice what he meant by that. She said she would have dinner waiting for him.

It occurred to Estelle that if she was going to keep hold of the light of her life she was going to have to fight, and hard. So she sat down and penciled out a plan. She had lived with Allen Greggor for five years. That was in her favor, she knew, because she was aware of all his favorite things. She jumped in the Pontiac and drove to the store with her plan in hand. She purchased two large steaks, two dozen jumbo shrimp fresh from the gulf, and a bottle of Allen's favorite burgundy.

That afternoon, before Ally got home from school, Estelle shelled pecans and baked her man's favorite pie. She determined that if she had to lose Allen Greggor he would at the very least go out with a full stomach and a clear notion of what he had given up. Then, she called the mother of one of Ally's playmates and asked if he could spend the night with them. This was to be a very special night, she told her, and Estelle needed the time alone with Ally's father.

When Allen Greggor arrived home that evening he could smell the fragrance of his favorite meal as he stepped from the car. Estelle had the grill fired up and the shrimp and steaks were sizzling.

She met him at the door with a kiss. She wore that red dress he'd bought for her, the one cut low in front.

And before he could say anything she had him seated at the table. The meal was served.

"We have to talk, Estelle," he told her.

"I know, Allen," she said. "That's why I asked if Ally could spend the night with his little friend. But let's enjoy this meal together first. Then we'll talk."

Greggor hesitated, unsure of himself.

"*Please*, Allen," Estelle prompted him. "I went to all this trouble and I made your favorite meal." She reached across the table and held his hands in hers.

He studied those hands a moment, knowing that the task ahead would be difficult.

"All right," he said quietly. "We'll eat first."

She poured the burgundy in his glass but did not drink any of it.

At midnight Estelle stepped into Allen's slacks and cinched them tight about her waist with a narrow leather belt. She slipped her arms into Allen's coat and pulled his hat over her head, shoving the locks of her long black hair up under its brim. She studied herself in the mirror.

Estelle had thought she would be nervous, or frightened perhaps. But she felt nothing save a cold aloofness. She was detached from the rest of humanity. She was an island.

She walked to the living room where Allen lay slumbering on the couch in his underwear. The sleeping pills she'd crushed and mixed in the wine had done their stuff. He was out cold. Estelle slipped on a pair of gloves she'd gotten from his apartment and then withdrew the Colt .45 from its holster.

After dinner, she had plied him with more of his favorite burgundy and the two of them talked. As she'd expected, Allen told her he was returning to his wife. They had never divorced, he told her. He could never bring himself to go through with it. She was the love of his life and was also, after all, the *mother of his child*. Now that Connie was back he wanted to work things out with her.

As Allen Greggor said these things his eyes grew heavy. Estelle encouraged him to lie on the couch and rest awhile. After he'd passed out she removed his pants.

This time she drove *his* car down to the marina. She parked it and checked the pistol's safety by the soft glow of the running lights before killing the engine. Then she walked down to the sailboat with a flashlight in her gloved hand.

Estelle climbed into the sailboat and opened the door to the cabin. She shined the beam of the flashlight in Mrs. Greggor's eyes as she sat up in the bed in the hull of the boat.

"Allen?" Connie said.

Estelle pulled the trigger three times. She didn't miss, not once.

Then she gathered up the spent cartridges, tossed them over the edge of the boat, and clamored back onto the dock.

At his trial Estelle testified that, to the best of her knowledge, Allen Greggor had spent the night and had never left her apartment. Connie Greggor had come to town and threatened to take Little Ally away from them, she told the court. But Allen had assured her he would not let that happen. After all, Ally was the light of her life. Allen would never let someone take him from her.

But the evidence was against him. Someone in another boat had seen him walk the dock that night, hurriedly away from his boat, after the gunshots.

He entered his car and drove away. Others reported that Greggor had been down to the marina many times those weeks before the shootings. He'd been keeping a woman there. And the police recovered the spent shell casing from the water where he'd tossed them. Attempting to hide evidence was proof that this was no murder borne of passion, in the spur of the moment. And of course, the striations on the bullets removed from Connie's body proved they'd been fired from Greggor's police-issued pistol. This was murder in the first, the prosecutor declared, coldly calculated, planned and executed.

Three years passed. Estelle went to Huntsville. She wasn't exactly family but she had the prisoner's permission to observe the proceedings. Permission? Hell, Mitch, Allen Greggor wanted Estelle there to see what she'd done to him. So she watched as they strapped him into the chair called *Ol' Sparky*. He had exhausted all of his appeals and had come to grips with what was happening to him. And Estelle watched as the condemned murderer stated once again, for the record, that he was an innocent man. They threw the switch. A fifteen second blast of electrical current entered his body through the metal cap strapped to his head, coursed through his robust frame and blasted out through his fingers and toes, shorting all brain waves in the process.

One newspaperman reporting the execution mentioned an intense odor of ozone.

He died on November 15th, 1963. Just seven days before John F. Kennedy was assassinated in Dallas.

With that my old pal stopped talking and polished off the last of the Heineken. No doubt it was warm by then.

He packed up his guitar and I walked him to his shiny black Corvette, parked in my driveway. The sun was rising; we'd been up all night. I knew it would be sometime before I saw him again and I had questions that wouldn't wait. I leaned against the open window of his car.

"Al, ol' pal," I said to him, "that was some tale you told tonight. Was it the beer, or was any of it true?"

He laughed, rolled his shoulders and lit a cigarette.

"Every word of it."

I thought about that a moment. "Someone got away with murder."

He turned the key and the car's engine rumbled to life. "Yes, Mitch, that's true. Someone did get away with murder, and double murder if you count the job the State of Texas done for her in Huntsville. Both Connie and Allen Greggor."

"But whatever happened to the boy?"

"Estelle raised him," he said. "They took her maiden name and moved out west."

I shook my head in disbelief and asked: "Who told you that story?"

Al drew a long drag on the cigarette and let the smoke slip out through his nostrils. His eyes looked very sad, just at that moment, his thoughts far distant. But he focused and looked at me.

"My mother," he said. "Just before she passed away last spring."

And I saw then why my old friend Al had been so morose this evening. Little Ally! Imagine hearing such a tale from the lips of the woman he'd called 'Mother' since his ninth birthday.

At the Wedding

"He's insane," Bill said, and he may have been.
I shook my head. "Of course, she *is* a ten."
"Maybe, but to give up so much…" He sighed.
"I wouldn't do it," I lied.

In fact, I knew I would.
Any woman, to look that good!
For heaven sakes, what a shape,
She passes by and men gape.

All in white, coming down the aisle.
Getting hitched, at last, after a long while.
My old best girl! Who'd a thought!
Tying the knot.

And my former best friend, up by the priest.
Tuxedo, white tie, pants creased.
What a monkey suit, I thought with disgust.
Like a turkey at dinner, trussed.

"You ever stop to think," I scratched my chin,
Just what some men will do to stick it in?"
Bill whispered, "They give up freedom, take a wife.
Live their days in endless strife."

I nodded, agreeing fully.
"Chain themselves to emotional bullies."
Bill laughed and shook his head,
"All that to spend *less* time in bed."

We looked at each other and said out loud,
"Not us!" We were shushed by the crowd,
Then seated ourselves in the hardwood pews.
"We are gathered here today…" Yawn, some news.

But cynical as I am, and doubting success,
My old girl did look fine in that white dress.
And my former best friend looked, well, happy.
(All right, with that goofy grin, call it *sappy*.)

But if anyone can make it, I hope it's them.
I wish you well, my old best girl and former friend.
But at the reception, I'll toast with glee,
"Old Girl, Old Friend: *Better you than me!*"

A Man's Personal Philosophy

I once knew a man who worked hard all his life until he was eventually promoted to a position of authority. He became a manager of others. He determined early on not to become one of those bosses he hated, those men and women whose only interest was self-aggrandizement and personal career advancement. Of course, not all of his managers were of this ilk, but those who adopted the worldly-wise philosophy, *"Look out for Number One,"* easily outnumbered those who followed the biblical model, *"Do unto others as you would have them do unto you."*

He took this "golden rule" to mean that one should a) Look *up* for Number One (seeking direction from God in Heaven), b) Look *out* for interests of others, and, c) Look *in* at one's self to do *always* that which is right and honorable.

One day during his long commute between home and office, when he had an hour behind the wheel of a car to contemplate next steps, strategy and tactics, a flash of insight struck him. It defined for him once and for all, in simple terms, his own personal philosophy. He kept a framed copy of it hanging in his office. It read:

My Personal Philosophy:
Figure out what sucks, and then don't do that.

Forever Yours
(a novella)

ONE

He popped the trunk of the beamer and its lid swung up. The movement caught his eye, and he watched it rise through the rear view mirror. *Life is like that!* he thought, and stepped out of the car.

He grabbed the gym bag from the trunk, checked to make sure his shorts were there, then slammed its lid shut. *Life is like that, too,* he mused, and shrugged his shoulders. He crossed the lot to the little footbridge that spanned the alleyway below. He had parked on the third story of the parking structure.

Sometimes an opportunity suddenly opens as if someone somewhere pulled a latch. And just as suddenly sometimes someone somewhere slams the door in your face. He whistled a tune as he thought these thoughts, opened the door at the end of the footbridge, and went inside.

TWO

Th-wack! Howard slapped the ball and sent it sailing across the court. It hit both walls in the right corner pocket two inches from the floor. Howard was a man possessed when it came to this game, but then so were they all. In his middle thirties, with a pronounced paunch developing just north of center, Howard used his bulk to play mostly a power game.

The small door in back court opened, and James stuck his head into court three of the Downtown Athletic Club. "Howard!?" He sounded surprised.

"So I'm told," Howard said, and smacked a second ball.

James entered and the door swung shut behind him. He began at once to stretch.

"What are you doing here? Why didn't you say you scheduled a match with Reggie?"

"I didn't," Howard responded. "Till I found out *you* scheduled one."

James, younger by a few years and sixty-five pounds lighter, slapped his arms up and down doing his spider-like imitation of jumping jacks. Howard looked on, not hiding his disgust.

"Where is he?" he asked.

"Late, per usual. Cutthroat?"

Howard leered. "Uh-huh."

James winced at the thought of taking one of Howard's hard hit fastballs in the buttocks or, worse, in the back of his head. "Great," he said weakly, and ceased jumping. He began an almost ceremonial stretch, separating his lanky limbs and forcing his forehead to his knee.

Howard practiced his serve from the center line. *Th-wack!* The ball bounced off the forward wall and zipped across the service line by inches. "How long we been doin' this, James?" he asked, retrieving the ball.

"Doing what? Racquetball? Ten years, maybe twelve. Why?"

"Yet we're still bullshittin' one another, right?"

James grabbed one of the blue racquetballs from Howard's hand and dropped it. Before it hit the floor his racquet tagged it and sent it to the forward wall. It never rose more than a few inches off the wooden court's surface.

"I bullshit no one, Howard," James noted, then returned his own volley. "I'm up front with everybody."

"You're an attorney, James. You're an *affront* to everybody. That's why you're successful." Howard caught James' ball mid-flight and folded his arms. "I think you're gonna do somethin' stupid," he said, eyeing him coldly.

James was defensive. "I hardly think telling Reggie the truth constitutes stupidity."

"So I'm right. You do intend to tell him."

"I do."

"Why?"

"Why?" James face turned incredulous. *"Why?"* He snatched the ball back from Howard and smacked it with some fury. "Any fool can see *why*."

"Enlighten me."

James let the ball roll at his feet. "You're his brother, Howard. You should be the one telling him. But as Reggie's attorney it's my duty to give him the facts if you don't."

"Facts don't count, James. They have no bearing on reality."

"What!?"

"It's the perception of fact that matters."

"Don't give me that new age crap," James sneered. "Are you lame enough to believe that what Reggie doesn't know won't hurt him?"

"Exactly."

James was utterly disgusted. "Jesus, Howard. What kind of a brother are you? Can't you see that Reggie is an unhappy man?"

"Unhappy!?" Now Howard sneered. "He drives a BMW, drinks J&B and dresses GQ. Oh, yes. He's so unhappy he's alphabetical."

The little door in back court opened again. A balding, bespectacled man in his early forties stepped inside.

James and Howard were both surprised to see him. "Ralph!" they shouted in unison.

"Oh, hello fellahs," Ralph said, adjusting the band on his court glasses. "What are you doing here?"

"Fighting," Howard snorted.

"I see. What about?"

"Reggie. What else?"

James spotted his chance to win support for his argument. "Look, Ralph, since you're here. Did you know that Eleanor is sleeping with Alex Newton?"

Ralph lowered his eyes as he slipped a thin, leather glove over his grip hand. He hesitated. "I'm not one to spread rumors."

Howard and James looked at each other in dismay.

"I suppose everyone knows," Howard lamented.

James looked Ralph in the eyes. "How long have you known?"

Ralph shrugged. "Oh, I dunno. Several months, I guess."

"Several months!"

"We only just found out!" James shook his head. "Of course, I don't want to believe it. I have my doubts."

Howard sneered. "Have your doubts! You smell a divorce, you leech."

"Of course, I'd represent Reggie if he needs me."

Ralph was disappointed with this remark. "You really are a leech, James," he said. He studied Howard a long moment. "You OK, Howard?"

"Yeah, yeah, sure." Howard drove another ball across court with a loud smack. This one sailed high toward the far corner and bounced off three walls before coming back. He turned to Ralph with a pained expression on his face.

"I learned long ago not to trust women, Ralph. They are inherently corrupt. It's their nature and nothing they do surprises me."

"Oh, for Pete's sake," James cried. "Howard is driving me nuts with this new age bullshit. He acts like it is no big deal."

"Of course, it's a big deal!" Howard bellowed. "But Eleanor's a good lookin' woman, she's always been hot. Reggie knew that when he married her. Somethin' like this was bound to happen sooner or later."

James shook his head in disbelief. "Would you listen to this guy?" He put his hands on his hips and squared shoulders with Howard. "Answer me this. Is Reggie your brother or not? Will you stand by and let his wife make a fool of him?"

Howard moved forward threateningly, speaking through clenched teeth. "Look, James, as long as Reggie doesn't find out about it he won't be hurt. Alex Newton is decent enough – a jerk, sure, but a decent jerk. And that's what women want. Decent jerks with tan bodies and little gold chains around their necks. Besides, as long as Eleanor is gonna sleep around it might as well be with someone with lots of money."

James was flabbergasted. He looked at Ralph and shrugged. "Have you ever heard such crap?"

Ralph studied James curiously. "Hold on a minute, James. Am I to understand that you think something should be done about this?"

"Positively."

"And I am positive," Howard inserted, "that the one thing you *ain't* gonna do is tell Reggie."

Ralph was startled at James' attitude. "Is that you intention? To tell Reggie?"

"Well," James said, "perhaps someone should tell him."

Ralph shook his head slowly and walked in a circle. He ran his fingers through the few hairs on his head. "Look, James," he said finally. "It's true, I've known what's been going on for some time now. And, of course, I've been very worried about Reggie…"

James concurred. "Then you see how Eleanor's made him a perfect jackass."

Ralph raised his hand to cut him off. "If men are jackasses because their women are unfaithful, then the world is a barnyard full of braying men and God knows what we're standing in. Maybe my being on the other side of forty gives me a perspective you two don't have. But I can't attach too much significance to these things. They come and they pass. The trick is to live through them. To survive. Eleanor is an attractive career woman. She works hard, she plays hard. She has a whole circle of friends and activities outside her relationship with Reggie. If she has lunch with a business associate, whose crime is that? And if she meets an old friend after work for cocktails, does that make Reggie a jackass?"

James stamped his foot. "Dammit, Ralph! We're not talking about martinis at happy hour."

"I know, I know," Ralph continued. "But listen, it's all a matter of degree. With the doors closed and no one hurt, what is the difference? In the end, who does Eleanor call husband and where does she call home?"

James' mouth fell open, and for once he was speechless. He studied Ralph, then Howard, and then Ralph again, stymied.

"In fact," Ralph added, "it occurs to me that Eleanor must love Reggie very much."

Even Howard was confused by this comment. "Ralph, how can you say she loves Reggie when she's diddlin' Alex?"

"Because," Ralph smiled, taking the ball from Howard. "If she didn't, why would she go to so much effort to keep this little affair from him?"

James drew a deep breath and shook his head. "You do have a point. Clearly there is something in the marriage she wants to hang on to."

Howard nodded thoughtfully.

"Exactly," Ralph said, and smacked the ball across court. *Th-wack!* It bounced back without touching the floor and James caught it.

At that moment Reggie, a rakish smile on his face, tapped on the back glass wall of the court. At thirty-three he still had a laborer's build, but the calluses on his palms had long since passed. His hair was dark, his eyes bright. He grinned at them through the glass, spinning his racquet, then ducked through the door.

"So help me, James," Howard muttered under his breath. *"One word and I'll bury that ball in the back of your skull."*

"Hi, guys!" Reggie said, entering. He knelt to tighten his laces. "Sorry I'm late." Looking up, he studied the three of them a moment, noting their long faces. His grin faded. "Whacha talkin' about so serious?"

James glanced at Howard, then at Ralph.

"We were talking," he said slowly, his eyes turning to Reggie, "about how only a *jackass* would call everyone together for a game and then show up twenty minutes late." Then, with a swift motion, James spun and drove the ball to dead center court for a kill shot. It sputtered and rolled back on the floor.

"Let's play," he said.

THREE

They played hard, these men. To win. With an earnestness befitting gladiators in a duel to the death, they moved across the court scooping up impossible shots with sheer will. All skilled players, they reveled in the power and poetry of the game, when body, mind and soul meld to a harmony only athletes often experience. When the thought to do and the doing become instantaneously one. When the phrase "*be the ball*" has serious implications. They operated separately, of course, but a casual observer might think their movements were choreographed. Theirs was a skill born of passion, a love for the game, and driven by fierce competitive natures. One would spin and, not seeing the ball, strike it in such a way as to drive it to the forward wall only inches from the floor. Then, with a mighty forearm thrust, another would play the ball into the side wall with such force that it would strike the opposite wall before ricocheting into a corner. Or, with a backhanded motion, lob it off the back wall with a precision that would impress military mortar crews. The ball thus hit would arch high, missing the ceiling by mere inches, or even brushing against it just slightly giving it a backward spin, then drop down to the forward wall and off it at surprising, impossible angles. The ball moved at such speeds as to be at times no more than a blur. The racquets whistled as they sliced air. And, often as not, balls returned at impossible angles were managed. If the volleys were endless, the inevitable exhaustion that came upon them was memorable, a physical manifestation of their raw, undiluted *joy.*

FOUR

After the game, at Howard's suggestion, the four men jumped into the club's sauna for a hot sweat. This was a long, narrow room lined with redwood planks and redwood benches. At one end of the room were a heated rock steamer and a bucket of water with a ladle. Reggie liked lots of steam; Howard preferred dry heat. Of course, being brothers, they fought over this. And it was no use looking to their friends for consensus, because Ralph was agreeable to either steam or dry heat while James hated the sauna altogether and refused to vote.

James had another issue on his mind. "What held you up today, Reggie?" he asked, leaning back against the redwood planks.

Reggie gave up bickering with Howard, but managed to splash one last spoonful of water onto the hissing rocks before relinquishing the ladle. "Oh," he said, sitting. "I had a meeting with Alex Newton."

James, Howard and Ralph all exchanged glances.

"In fact," Reggie continued, "he's coming by here in thirty minutes to wrap it up."

Howard put the ladle in the bucket and sat across from Reggie. "Alex is coming *here?*"

Reggie nodded. "Bringing some papers to sign."

"Papers? What papers?" James asked, suspicious. "You have business with Alex Newton I don't know about?"

"Didn't Howard tell you?" Reggie asked, surprised. "They want us to build their new facility."

James turned his eyes upon Howard, who managed only a weak smile in return. "Some would call *me* a leech," he said under his breath, and then, to Reggie, "Wonderful!"

"Sure is," Reggie said, enthused. "This is the biggest project Howard and I have landed since Dad died. And it just fell into our laps, out of the blue. *Jennrette Industries!* Alex's father-in-law put him in charge of developing this new plant of theirs and he remembered Howie and me. Pretty lucky, huh?"

Now both Ralph and James looked upon Howard as if he were a traitor. Howard could only shrug.

"Did you have lunch with him today?" Ralph asked.

Reggie shook his head. "I think he had lunch with his mistress."

James, Howard and Ralph reacted to this statement with a stunned moment of silence. Reggie snickered at their reactions like a kid who just spilled the beans.

"It's true!" he insisted. "Don't ask me how I know but I get the feeling that ol' Alex is stepping out on his wife." Reggie snickered again.

The others, however, did not find this amusing.

James began to speak, caught himself, hesitated, and then after rephrasing, said, "You usually have lunch with Eleanor, don't you Reggie?"

Reggie considered this. "Yeah, but only if she isn't 'doing lunch' with a client, as she calls it."

"Have lunch with her today?" James asked innocently. Ralph and Howard frowned at him sternly.

"Nope. She had an appointment."

"I see. Where? With whom?"

"I dunno, a client I guess. What's with the third degree? I learned a long time ago that husbands ought not ask too many questions."

"Why not?"

"Because," Reggie said slyly, "with a wife, *her* business is her business, and *your* business is her business."

He laughed at that.

FIVE

The four men emerged from the shower room and headed for the courtside refreshment bar, which was their custom after a game. With freshly drawn drafts in hand they collapsed, exhausted, at a table overlooking court number one. Two glass-walled courts adjoined the refreshment bar, numbers one and two, and at this moment number one was occupied by two very healthy looking young women. The two twenty-year-olds were decidedly attractive and wore tight shorts over spandex that seemed contrived for the purpose of broadcasting their sexuality. They were not particularly talented racquetball players, however. Novices.

One of them, a blonde with a large bosom, swung blindly at a returning ball and missed by a mile. The miss upset her, apparently, because she clenched her fist with aggravation and stamped her foot coquettishly. The four men, observing this, responded to her frustration in unison.

"Oh-h-h! Poor baby!" they all said.

"She's having trouble handling those balls," James observed.

"She's gripping the shaft too hard," Howard noted.

"She should rotate her hips," Ralph added.

"You guys!"

The young lady under observation stooped to retrieve the ball before them. Her cleavage flashed. She eyed the male chorus in the gallery behind the glass and smiled at them demurely, then turned and trotted jauntily back to the service line. Everything she owned jiggled as she did so.

"Oh-h-h-h-h-h-h-h-h-h-h-h-h-h-h!" they all said.

Alex Newton, handsome in a movie star way, his collar open and a thin, gold chain around his neck, passed through the street level entryway and surveyed the patrons in the refreshment bar. He spotted Reggie and the others engrossed in the observance of the women in court one and approached them unseen.

"Beautiful, aren't they?" Alex said after a moment.

"Alex!" Reggie said, turning to greet him. The smile left Howard's face when he saw Alex and he began to rise from his chair.

"James and I were just leaving," he said.

"Were we?" James asked, definitely *not* rising.

The blonde in court one tapped on the glass wall behind them and they all turned to look at her. She smiled and waved at Alex.

Alex smiled and waved back.

"You know those girls?" Ralph asked.

Alex nodded. "The chesty one is a secretary at the plant. Heather, I think. And I believe the brunette is our receptionist."

Reggie made introductions at the table. "You know my brother, Howie," he said. "And James Emery, our attorney. And this is Ralph Steiner, my accountant."

"I think I know everybody," Alex said, shaking hands around.

"Good to see you again, Alex," Ralph said warmly.

James noted a flash of gold and studded diamonds on Alex's wrist. "Nice watch, Alex," he said. "New?"

"Yes it is, as a matter of fact," Alex said, holding it up for them to see. "Just got it today."

"Did your mistress give it to you?"

There was a moment of stunned silence as all eyes turned to James. He studied Alex coolly, as if expecting an answer, and the others followed James' gaze back to him. Alex seemed taken aback momentarily, glancing at them nervously, but a smile curled the ends of his lips.

"What makes you think I have a mistress?" he said.

"Reggie told us."

Now all eyes shifted to Reggie, who began stammering. "Well, I, I, I..." He looked at James and shot daggers from his eyes, then turned to Alex and smiled weakly. "I was only speculating. There were some long black hairs on your jacket when you stopped by my office this afternoon. I know your wife is blonde..." He shrugged.

Alex raised his eyebrows and tossed his head casually. "Guess I'll have to be more careful, won't I?" He pulled up a chair and joined them at the table.

"Who is she?" James pressed. "Anybody we know?"

"Don't tell, Alex," Howard interjected.

"Yeah, keep us guessing," Reggie added.

"I didn't realize my affairs were of such interest."

"Affairs are everyone's interest," James stated.

"How is your wife, Alex?" Ralph said. "I haven't seen her in an age."

"Jacqueline? She's fine. Just fine."

"The last time I saw her she was leading a fundraiser for the civic theater," Ralph continued.

"Yes, she's the essence of benevolence, isn't she?"

Ralph scratched his chin thoughtfully. "I've always wondered about this business of having affairs. Keeping up the front and all, sneaking about."

Alex shrugged. "To be truthful, that's the thrill of it."

Ralph was genuinely perplexed. "But aren't you afraid Jacqueline will find out?"

Alex shook his head no. "If she did I doubt she'd believe it, if she held the proof in the palm of her hand."

Reggie grinned and suddenly rose to his feet. "Hey, there's Eleanor!" he said, waving his hand at her across the room. She waved back, smiling brightly. She was dressed in a dark blue skirt and blazer, her jet-black hair spilling over her shoulders. At thirty-two, she was just beginning to ascend the corporate ladder and did her best to look and dress the part. She crossed the room towards them.

"She's been busting her tail at work," Reggie remarked as she approached.

Eleanor came up behind Howard, draped her arms around his shoulders, and kissed him on the cheek. "How's my favorite brother-in-law?" she asked.

"Horny."

"You're always horny, Howard, and it serves you right," she laughed, and sat in a chair they secured for her. "You know, I only married Reggie because his big brother wouldn't have me."

"That isn't the only mistake I've made," Howard mused. "But it's probably the dumbest."

They all laughed at this. Eleanor opened her purse and withdrew a cigarette. She lit it with a gold butane lighter.

The others stared at her a moment.

"Eleanor," Reggie said, "what are you doing?"

She noted their stares. "What?" she demanded.

"You can't smoke in here. It's a *health* club!"

She looked at her cigarette and realized what she had done. "Oh," she said, and snuffed it out. "How silly of me." She looked over her shoulder surreptitiously. "I suppose I'll have the smoke police after me."

James took the lighter from her hand. It looked expensive, was trimmed in black and had her initials engraved: *ERP.*

"New lighter, Eleanor? I thought you quit."

"I have quit, James," she insisted. "It was a gift."

"I see."

"What have you been up to today?" she asked Reggie.

"Among other things, I closed the deal with Alex," he told her. Then, to Alex, "Did you bring the contract?"

"Glad you asked," Alex said, dipping his hand into the inside pocket of his jacket. He produced the document and laid it before Reggie.

"I should probably take a look at that," James offered.

Reggie shrugged, and slid it across the table. "Suit yourself."

"How's business, Alex?" Eleanor asked.

"Great. Sales are up on our new products."

"Amazing," she said, and added, "considering your ad campaign sucks."

"And you can do better?"

"Reggie has a hamster named Chester who could write better copy, Alex," Eleanor said, and laughed.

"Hey!" Reggie interjected, "Chester died last August."

"That's my point."

They all laughed at that. Alex said, "You Porters are after *all* my business!"

"Why don't you join us for dinner tonight, Alex?" Reggie offered.

Alex shook his head. "Thanks, but no. I've had a long day. I'm going right to bed."

"Reggie, that's why I came by," Eleanor said. "To tell you I won't be home until late this evening. "I'm this close to securing that account for the agency and I think I can do it over dinner tonight." She put her thumb and forefinger a quarter inch apart and peered at him through them.

"That close?"

She nodded.

"Damn!"

James passed the contract back to Reggie. "Just a cursory glance, Reggie, but it looks OK," he said, then turned to Reggie's wife. "Eleanor, it's occurred to my legal mind that you've always got the perfect alibi. If ever you want to do anything or go anywhere you can just say you've got an important client and no one can doubt you."

Eleanor bit her lower lip and thought about that a moment. "Men have done it for centuries," she said.

"Don't give her ideas, James," Reggie said as he signed the contract. "Eleanor would never lie to me, would you Sweetheart?"

Eleanor smiled and drew near to her husband. "Never," she said, and kissed him.

Alex folded the freshly signed document and stood to his feet. "I do admire you two," he said to Reggie and Eleanor. "Still in love after... How long have you been married?"

"Twelve years this September," Eleanor said, also rising.

"It only seems like twenty," Reggie snickered. Eleanor punched him playfully.

"Well," Alex said and checked his watch, "it's been nice seeing you all, but I've gotta jet."

"And I've got get back to the office to prepare for my meeting," Eleanor sighed. "Don't wait up for me, Reggie."

Reggie pouted at this and Eleanor, taking pity on him, kissed his forehead. Then she turned to follow Alex out the door. James stopped her.

"Don't forget your lighter, Eleanor," he said, and handed it to her.

She opened her purse. "I'm always putting this thing down and forgetting it," she said, and dropped it inside.

The four men at the table watched Alex and Eleanor depart and then, uniformly adjusting their chairs, they refocused their attention on the two young women in court number one.

The bosomy blonde named Heather was at the center line, crouched for aggressive play. Her opponent, serving from behind, slapped the ball with some force and drove it forward, *Th-wack!* It was probably the hardest hit ball of their game, and it sailed cross court to impact the blonde dead center on her buttocks. The struck young woman jumped with a start, squealed painfully, and rubbed her smarting anatomy.

Reggie, Howard, James and Ralph all gasped.

"Oh-h-h-h-h-h-h-h-h-h-h-h-h-h-h!" they said.

157

SIX

The Porter brothers took over their father's construction business after he had died unexpectedly of a stroke some four years previous. Howard Porter, who had worked on job sites most of his life and had developed an understanding of the practical pressures of the business, managed the construction crews and controlled all functions of the projects once they were begun. Reggie Porter, on the other hand, had continued in college after securing his engineering degree to complete his master studies in architecture and design, which was his passion. Neither of the brothers had been schooled in the business end of things, which in the beginning proved almost fatal to the family business. It had been up to Reggie to develop these skills, partly because Reggie's personality lent itself to acquiring the business and social expertise needed to succeed in business. He was a people person.

Their current project was a new hospital wing, a fourteen story edifice attached to the existing hospital by a series of sky bridges and a parking structure. It was a complex project, and Reggie's creative design (which is what won them the contract) had caused no end of headaches for the construction crews. They were four weeks behind schedule and just beginning phase three of the construction. Phase three normally began after completion of the steel framed skeleton of the structure, but Howard felt it possible to "catch up" by starting phase three on the lower floors while continuing the final stages of phase two in the upper stories. This meant twice as much work for him, but well worth the extra effort if they could avoid the late-completion penalties iterated in their contract.

The construction site was a busy, sometimes confusing place, but Howard reveled in its busy-ness. Huge cranes hoisted giant steel girders, swinging them into place as any number of crew members scurried about below. Torches showered flaming bits of steel, like fireworks. Thundering jack hammers pounded rivets into submission. And overseeing it all, usually from a twelve-inch wide girder some three hundred feet in the air, stood Howard Porter. He loved it there.

It was from just such a location Monday midmorning that Howard happened to glance down to the earth below. A midnight-blue BMW pulled off the highway and entered the construction site, rolling to a stop near Howard's camper which doubled as the site office. It wasn't unusual for Reggie to show up at the construction site but this morning Howard had something on his mind, something he wanted to discuss with his younger brother. He walked across the narrow girder to the wooden platform and removed his safety harness, a quarter-inch steel cable attached to the leather belt strapped to his waist. Then he entered the elevator, closed the steel mesh safety gate, and began his descent.

He found Reggie hunched over the hood of the BMW, a set of blueprints rolled out there. As he approached him Howard turned his sleeves up past the elbow, thinking about how he could broach the topic foremost on his mind with his younger brother.

"Hey, Reg," he said, and Reggie looked up at him.

"Hi, Howie. How's it hangin'?"

"Down and dirty but willing to negotiate. What's up?"

Reggie rolled the blueprints and shoved them into a cylindrical container. "I want to check those new girders against the specs," he said, and struck off across the site. Howard quickstepped after him.

"Here, put this on," he said, presenting a spare hard hat to Reggie. "You're always forgetting your safety stuff. You want to get us fined?"

Reggie took the hat and put it on. The two men ambled across the site together.

"I've been wanting to talk to you about Eleanor," Howard said, screwing up his courage.

"Ely-belly? What about her?"

"I dunno," Howard shrugged. "I just sensed a little tension the other day at the club."

"Oh, that," Reggie dismissed it with a wave of his hand. "I was just a little upset because she had to be out another evening. I sometimes think she works too hard."

Howard thought about that a moment. "You ever jealous of the clients she sees at these business dinners?"

Reggie shook his head no. "She can handle herself should one of them try to take liberties with her."

"The pursuit of liberties is guaranteed in the constitution," Howard observed.

"And anyway I've met some of her clients at parties and such. They're all old and fat – the kind of men who'll spend eighty grand on a Mercedes while bickering with their secretaries about overtime."

They circled around the site to a pile of neatly stacked steel girders. Reggie referred to a computer printout while cross-referencing the numbers stamped into the girders.

"Alex Newton just bought a Mercedes," Howard continued. "Did you see it?"

"Yeah. A convertible. Nice car."

"That Alex has some tan, huh?"

"He's a bit stuck on himself. Eleanor says he's a *him*bo, that's her term for a boy bimbo." Reggie laughed at that.

"Women don't always speak their minds."

"Good thing, or we'd all be damned."

"But Eleanor usually talks straight."

"Sure she does," Reggie exclaimed. "But when she chooses not too, it's my job to get a little deaf. That's what married people who love each other do. They turn a deaf ear. After all, it's hard to hear the truth when you're listening to a lie."

"My wives were *both* pathological liars," Howard said. He sounded depressed.

"C'mon, Howie. Talk like that and you'll never find the right woman."

Howard shrugged. "Maybe."

"Besides, what woman ever told a lie she hadn't heard from a man? Do you really think women are that inventive?" Reggie shook his head emphatically. "When it comes to deceit, their amateurs."

Howard snorted at that remark.

"It's like they've got training wheels, Howard," Reggie elaborated. "They pedal along concocting their little schemes while we men roar around them, Hells Angels on Harleys."

"What about Adam and Eve?" Howard interjected. "Eve told the first lie."

"That the devil whispered in her ear."

Howard considered that and nodded. "I wish we'd had this talk before my second marriage," he said wistfully.

"You're a bright guy, Howard. What do you think?"

Howard shrugged. "Hell, what do I know," he said. "I'm a two-time loser."

"A guy can miss a serve and still win the point."

"I double faulted."

Reggie smiled wryly. "That's because you took your wives too seriously. Women are sweet but it's crazy to take them serious."

Howard studied his brother a long moment until Reggie finally noticed and looked up from the printout.

"You don't love Eleanor anymore, do you?"

"Of course, I do."

Howard drew a deep breath and blew it out slowly, then looked over Reggie's shoulder at the city skyline behind him. He lifted his finger and pointed at a tall, silver structure glistening in the sunlight.

"Hey, look!" he said. "There's Eleanor's office."

SEVEN

Eleanor's office was located on the twenty-second floor of a sleek, mirror surface building downtown. It was a busy office, the largest advertising agency in the region, with affiliated offices in New York, Seattle and Sydney. At that moment Eleanor Porter emerged from her own private office, just two offices down from the sales manager, and paused briefly to check her reflection in a wall of mirrors. She had worked hard to earn that office, and was considered among the best sales executives in the industry. She was proud of that.

She breezed past the receptionist. "I'm out till after lunch, Janice," she said.

"Right, Ms. Porter," the young woman at the front desk responded. She watched her leave, checked the clock on her desk, then turned to the coworker seated next to her.

"Another nooner," she said, and the two of them giggled.

Eleanor rode the elevator to the first floor, then made her way though the lobby of the building. She bustled past numerous other business professionals, most barely acknowledging one another, each absorbed in his or her own pressures of the day.

She did not know – she had no reason to suspect – that she was being observed. He was a tall fellow, silver haired, with broad shoulders and a thin, narrow waist. He wore dark glasses and an overcoat, unbuttoned, and clenched a newspaper with a very large hand. He watched Eleanor over the top of it as she crossed the lobby toward the huge, revolving doors at street level.

When she emerged from the building he was right behind her, passing through the rotating door just moments after. He watched curbside as Eleanor took the first cab in the queue that lined the street, then entered the second. The two cabs departed together, the second shadowing the first.

EIGHT

That evening it was Reggie who worked late. He was all excited about the design he had begun for Alex Newton's father-in-law's new manufacturing plant, and he could not pull himself away from it at quitting time. He called home, left a message for Eleanor, and sat entranced at his computer in the downtown studio office of Porter Engineering, Inc.

He never noticed when his staff left for the evening. He was unaware of the passing of the dinner hour. His mind was focused on one thing: *work*. He was creating a variety of new and inventive design configurations, then testing them against the budget constraints given him by Jennrette Industries. To Reggie Porter, this was nirvana.

He was still at it at seven o'clock, fully absorbed, humming to the tunes of an oldies station, and did not hear the *rap, rap, rap* on the glass door of the studio entrance. After several moments the door swung open and Ralph Steiner stuck his head inside.

"Hello, Reggie."

The voice startled Reggie. He looked up from his computer screen and blinked twice, like a badger emerging from a hole on a bright morning. "Ralph!?" He jumped up and crossed the room to greet his friend. "What are you doing here?"

Ralph let the glass door swing shut behind him and stepped inside. He pulled a manila envelope from a leather brief. "Just came by to drop off this quarterly report," he said.

Reggie took the envelope. "You didn't have to do that, Ralph."

"I know, I know," the accountant said, nodding his head. "Truth is, Reggie, I wanted to talk to you about Eleanor."

The two of them sat down on the plush couch Eleanor had picked out for the studio lobby. "You, too?" Reggie said, puzzled. "Look, if it's about the other day at the club, I was just a little upset because Eleanor's been so wrapped up in her work lately. It's no big deal. If your wife is career oriented you make a few sacrifices."

Ralph leaned back and rested his arms on the back of the couch. He looked at Reggie a bit vacantly, as if he were evaluating his own words carefully before he spoke them.

"Reggie, listen. Take some advice from a man who's been successfully married for twenty-five years. I think you and Eleanor need to spend more time together. Alone."

"We're together every day, Ralph."

"You know I got that place in Maui," Ralph continued. "Very nice. A condo on the beach. Why don't you guys take a month off and vacation there. My treat."

Reggie grinned incredulously. "A month!" he said, and laughed. "I can't afford a month away from the shop!"

"Why not?" Ralph asked. "You could set up a table under a palm – hook your computer to a modem – work a couple hours a day. Fax your stuff back and forth and spend your afternoons chasing Eleanor around the lanai. What could be better?"

Reggie considered this a moment, then scratched his forehead. "It sounds... wonderful! But Ralph, even if I *could* get away, Eleanor never would. We're a two career family. Getting a weekend off together is a miracle, much less a month."

"But it's precisely because you are a two career family that I think you should get away together," Ralph insisted. "To spend some time with only each other to think about, away from your respective careers."

Reggie tried to imagine this in his mind, but shook his head. "It'd never work," he said. "I'm a workaholic and Eleanor eats-and-sleeps advertising. We'd be at each others' throats in forty-eight hours."

Ralph sighed, sensing he was losing the argument. "Won't you at least suggest it to her?"

"I don't think Eleanor will go for it," Reggie said thoughtfully. "It might look like I'm not supportive of her career."

"There's no reason to think a career is threatened by a vacation!"

"You don't know advertising. Out of sight is out of mind in that business." Reggie turned the notion over one more time in his mind, then shook his head. "Besides," he said, "I'm up to my eyebrows in this project for Alex Newton."

This last remark aggravated Ralph. He rose to his feet abruptly and thrust his hands deep into his pockets. He paced forward and back a moment, then gave a lecture. "I think you're making a serious mistake," he said. "You're both making serious mistakes, substituting this love affair with your careers for the real thing. Suppose your career fails you? Is your career going to comfort you in your old age? Is your career going to nurse you back to health when you're ill? Did your career take a vow to love, honor and obey? For crying out loud, I don't understand any of this!" With that he threw his hands up in the air.

Reggie sat with his mouth open, stunned.

Ralph sat again and calmed himself. "Look, Reggie... my friend. It's a damn crazy world we live in and I honestly *don't* understand it. But I want you to know, if you change your mind the condo in Hawaii is open to you." Ralph put his arm around Reggie's shoulders and squeezed the nape of his neck. "Just say the word. OK?"

Reggie didn't know what to say. But he felt he should say something. Finally he simply said, "Thank you, Ralph."

Ralph stood again. "*Anytime*," he repeated, as if it had special meaning.

"I appreciate it, Ralph," Reggie insisted. "I really do. But I doubt that Ely and I will ever take you up on it."

Ralph rolled his eyes and gripped his head with both hands in an exaggerated gesture. "No. Of course not," he said, then looked at his watch. "It's awfully late. Aren't you going home?"

"Sure," Reggie said, rising to his feet. He walked to the door with Ralph. "I just want to finish my preliminary layout for Jenrette Industries tonight."

Ralph hesitated at Reggie's remark as if he were about to say more, but instead simply nodded. He was confounded and more than a little disappointed. He shook Reggie's hand and left him there, alone with his work.

Reggie locked the door and quickly returned to his computer.

NINE

James put the menu down and checked his watch for the third time. It was twenty minutes past noon. This was beginning to be habitual and had it been anybody else he wouldn't put up with it, he told himself. He swirled what was left of his martini and downed it, then looked for the waiter. He really didn't care about ordering anything to eat, but he could – *he would* – have another martini.

Reggie slipped up from behind him and seated himself across the table. "You're late, per usual."

"I know, I'm sorry James," Reggie said. "Have you ordered?"

"No, nothing to eat," James said, and looked around the restaurant for that waiter. "Unless you count the olives." They were seated next to a window with an excellent view of the river. Reggie glanced at his menu while James snapped his fingers at a passing waiter. The fellow ignored him.

"Reggie," James said in his offhand way, "how are things on the home front?"

Reggie peered over the top of his menu curiously. "Just fine, James. Why?"

"I want to speak to you about Eleanor."

Reggie lowered his menu. "Not you too!"

"You know I adore her."

"So do I. She's witty and pretty and likes to do it," Reggie grinned. "That's why I married her, remember?"

"Too well," James admitted. "And you're right, those are admirable attributes in a woman."

"Not necessarily in that order, of course."

"Of course. Still, there are concessions to be made in life," he said. "One has to play the cards one is dealt. Right?"

Reggie shook his head. Had he missed something? "What are you talking about?"

"Nothing," James said. "Everything. Eleanor. *You.*"

"Is this about the other day at the club?"

The waiter who had ignored James approached the table and James looked up at him with a curious expression on his face. "Where is it?" James asked.

The waiter was confused. "Where is what?" he responded.

"Marvelous technology," James said to Reggie. "They're making them so small now they're almost invisible." He returned his gaze to the waiter. "Nevertheless, YOU NEED A NEW BATTERY!" The patrons in the restaurant turned at once to see what the shouting was about. Silence settled over the place as they all looked at James and the waiter.

James gestured at his ear and smiled kindly. "FOR YOUR HEARING AID," he continued, as if talking to an elderly aunt. He spoke very loudly and broke each word into separate syllables. "WHEN I CALLED YOU BEFORE YOU OBVIOUSLY *COULD NOT HEAR ME!*"

Reggie lowered his eyes, put his elbows on the table and his fingertips to his brow. He had seen James in this mood before.

The waiter glanced around the room, straightened his tie and cleared his throat. "I assure you, sir," he said, "my hearing is *not* impaired."

"Oh. My mistake. I'll have another martini."

The waiter nodded coolly and turned to Reggie. Reggie looked up at him. "Nothing from the bar for me." The fellow nodded again and left.

"Really, James."

James continued as though nothing unusual had occurred. "Reggie, if your relationship with Eleanor suddenly went south you would tell me, wouldn't you?" He leaned forward in his chair and spoke with such earnestness that Reggie became concerned.

"Of course," Reggie said. "You are my oldest and best friend, James. Best man at my wedding, and all that."

"Good." James relaxed, leaning back.

"And besides, you're my attorney. Naturally I'd seek your advice."

"It's just that, well…" James stopped abruptly and studied the river through the window. After a moment he continued. "Another client of mine came to me with the news that his wife has been running around on him. He put off talking to me about it because he was embarrassed to have her making a jackass of him."

"Oh," Reggie said, and nodded knowingly. A sly grin curled the ends of his lips. "Who was it?" he asked, flashing his eyes.

James dismissed him. "You know I can't tell you that. Client confidentiality."

"I see. And what sage advice did you give him?"

"I consider myself an authority on the subject of marriage," James said, "having successfully avoided it all these years. Married women are unfaithful to their men for one reason. They find others who are more attentive to their needs. Wives are not inclined to cheat on husbands who pamper them."

"*Cheat,*" Reggie repeated thoughtfully. "There's a word you don't hear much anymore."

"Yes, and here's another," James continued. "*Adultery.*"

"Listen, James, do you mind if I take notes?"

"Don't be dull."

Reggie slapped his pockets. "I need a pen. No really. When a single man starts lecturing on adultery there's bound to be a chuckle or two, and I'm no good with jokes unless I write them down."

James was insulted. "I happen to believe in the sanctity of marriage. That's precisely why I choose to remain single. And, I consider the marital vows sacred. It disgusts me to see them trampled and trivialized, as people are inclined to do these days. Jumping from bed to bed like frogs on hot mud."

"James, you've had more women than I can count!"

"Yes, but one at a time. I'm sequentially monogamous."

The waiter returned with James' martini. James took it and gulped it down.

"Excuse me," Reggie said to the waiter. "I'm supposed to meet a young lady here. A Miss Sally Morgan. If she comes in, would you direct her to me?"

"Certainly, sir. Are you ready to order?"

Reggie shook his head. "I'll wait for her."

"Bring me another of these," James blurted, waving his glass. The waiter lifted his nose, then departed.

"Who is this woman?" James asked. "Shall I buzz off?"

Reggie shook his head. "As a matter of fact, I need your help."

"Is she a client? Looking to erect something?"

Reggie shook his head and grinned slyly. "No, James. Don't you remember? Sally Morgan?"

James thought a moment. Nothing.

"C'mon," Reggie insisted. "You must remember Sally Morgan. We went steady."

"What? In high school?"

"Yes."

"Reggie, you can't expect me to remember all the girls you dated in high school," James stated.

"But I dated Sally longer than any of the others."

"I see," James said, and thought a moment. A light went on in his head. "Long, *tall* Sally?"

Reggie nodded and grinned.

"Built sweet?"

"That'd be the one."

"I do remember her," James said, thinking back. "You were quite serious about her."

"I still think about her from time to time."

James dismissed the notion. "You have Eleanor to think about."

The waiter returned with James' third martini. He placed it at the table and took the empty glasses away.

"Why did you break up?" James asked.

"We were just kids," Reggie said. "She was a year younger than we were. We all went off to college. You remember. That's when I met Eleanor."

James fished the olive out of his drink and chewed it. "You don't suppose this Sally Morgan is still in love with you?"

Reggie shrugged. "After all these years? Not likely."

James studied Reggie a long moment, his eyes narrowing to thin slits. "Don't bullshit me, old pal. Old flames often burn brightest."

Reggie became defensive. "How could she? I haven't seen her since I married Eleanor. She lives in Korea, for crying out loud."

"Korea?"

"She runs a family export business. Something her father started."

"Why is she here? Did you write to her?"

"James, what would I write to someone I haven't seen in fourteen years?" Reggie sat forward in his chair and ran his fingers through his hair. "Boy," he said. "You sure are making this difficult."

James snorted and swirled his martini.

"Look, the other day I got a call from her saying she was in town and wanted to see me, that's all. So I asked her to meet me here today."

"I see," James said. "And what is my role in all this?"

"Well," Reggie said, and produced a pack of cigarettes from his pocket, "she might be different."

"You mean she might be married?"

"Oh, I don't think so. She didn't mention a husband. No I mean, years can take a toll on a woman."

"What are those?" James asked, referring to the cigarettes.

"Winstons."

"I can see that," James said, irritated. "I mean, what are you doing with them? You aren't taking up smoking along with your womanizing, are you?"

"Of course not, James." Reggie said, and opened the pack. "You see, maybe she's gained eighty pounds and sags. Maybe I'll wish I never saw her again. Maybe I won't want to be alone with her at all."

"Maybe, maybe, maybe. I have a feeling there's one more maybe."

Reggie's eyes flashed and he grinned his sly smile. "Then again, *maybe* I will."

James laced his fingers and rested his chin on them a moment. "I'm still not seeing my part in this little scheme."

"You're my fall back position. My plan B."

"I'm to bail you out if this old flame fizzles?"

"Something like that."

"I see. Am I to use my own judgment in this matter?"

"No, listen, that's what the Winstons are for," Reggie held them up and also produced a package of matches. "See, if I think she's hideous we'll just talk about sports."

"Sports?"

Reggie nodded. "After that we'll talk about cars."

"You aim to bore her away?"

"She'll be out of here in a jiffy. Women hate it when men talk about things they know nothing about."

James agreed. "They've never developed the knack of bluffing a poor hand."

"Right," Reggie continued. "On the other hand, if I think she's nice I'll just suavely light up a cigarette and casually place it in this ashtray."

James thought about this a moment but could not make sense of it. "Why?"

Reggie was becoming a little exasperated. "You idiot!" he blurted. "That's your signal to check your watch and say, 'Oh my god, I'm late for an appointment!'"

"Oh," James said. "Now I get it."

Reggie sat up in his chair and his eyes focused across the room. His jaw dropped and his mouth fell open.

James turned to look and his mouth fell open, also. A woman was being directed by the waiter toward their table. She was tall, as they remembered, with blonde hair pulled back in a ponytail. She had an athletic build, with a narrow waist and strong legs that were showcased in the short skirt she wore. A sleeveless, pink mohair sweater accentuated her shapely figure. Visually striking, every male head in the room pivoted on its base as she walked past. James recognized her as Sally Morgan.

She smiled warmly at Reggie, flashing brilliant teeth against her deeply tanned features. The two men rose to their feet in silence as she approached... actually, in more of a *dumb awe.*

Reggie held out his hand but she ignored it. Instead she kissed his cheek and hugged him. "Oh, Reggie," she said. "After all these years!"

"Sally?" Reggie's voice squeaked. He stared at her a bit dumbfounded, then cleared his throat and regained his bearings. "You remember my best friend, James Emery?"

Sally took James' hand and shook it. "Of course I do. But I'll bet he's forgotten me."

"If I did," James said, "I won't be forgetting you again."

They sat, with Sally between them, and at once Reggie tapped out a cigarette from the pack of Winstons.

"So," James began, "would you care for a drink before lunch?"

"No thanks," she said and laughed. "Frankly, I just popped a Prozac."

Reggie placed the cigarette between his lips, then tore a match from the pack and struck it. He lit the cigarette and immediately placed it in the ashtray.

"To steel your nerves before seeing me?" he asked Sally suavely.

"Something like that," she admitted.

"Afraid I'd gone fat and balding?"

"You haven't changed a bit," Sally said and smiled warmly. "But that's not what I was nervous about."

James did not notice the cigarette. "So, tell us. What have you been doing with yourself these last fourteen years?"

Sally drew a breath. "Gosh, has it been that long? Well, I've been in Korea since I graduated high school. I took over my father's business there. Believe it or not, this is my first trip home."

Reggie glanced at James and frowned, gritting his teeth. He slid the ashtray a few inches nearer to his old friend. James was oblivious to this, enraptured as he was with Sally. He sat with his chin in his palm, transfixed by her beauty, his eyes more or less vacant. Frustrated, Reggie tapped out a second cigarette and struck another match. He placed the second smoldering Winston alongside the first in the ashtray.

"Is it difficult being a woman entrepreneur in Korea?" James said, missing the smoke signals.

"Yes it is," Sally responded. "At times it's been impossible." She looked at Reggie, then at the two cigarettes. Her brow furled.

"Does your husband help you?"

"No, James. I'm not married."

"Oh," James sighed. "Reggie said you were married to a certain Korean gentleman."

"I did not!"

"Perhaps I misunderstood."

Sally turned to Reggie and studied him a moment. He was a bit embarrassed by this scrutiny. "You're still married?" she asked at last.

"Oh, yes," Reggie nodded. "Twelve years. My wife is in advertising."

Sally checked her memory. "Don't you have an older brother?"

"Yes I do. We're partners in an engineering firm."

There was an awkward silence. James still had not noticed the cigarettes. In desperation Reggie tapped out a third one and lit it, then placed it beside the others.

"You must be quite fond of the Orient, Sally," James observed, "to have made your home there. I for one have *always* been fascinated by it."

Reggie rolled his eyes at this remark.

"It is wonderful," Sally said, looking out the window. "But this feels like home to me."

Reggie found James' foot under the table and stepped on it, hard.

"Ow!" James said with a start. He looked at Reggie, who directed his eyes to the ashtray. Three cigarettes lay smoldering there.

James' eyebrows shot up. "Oh, my God!" he blurted, sitting up. He looked at his watch. "What time is it?"

"It's later than you think," Reggie said coolly.

"I'm late for an appointment," James said as he rose to his feet. He offered his hand to Sally and she took it. "I hope to see you again, Sally," he said to her.

"I'm sure you will," she said, and smiled. "I'll be here all summer."

James leaned in close to Reggie and said in a loud whisper, "You really *must* do something about that tobacco habit."

Reggie forced a smile and glanced at Sally. She laughed. "So long, James," he said to his friend through clenched teeth. "Sorry you have to run off."

James left and Sally sat quietly a moment while Reggie snuffed out the cigarettes one by one. "I guess I was nervous, too," he admitted.

"What on earth for?"

"I dunno," Reggie said. He scratched his head. "I had the world on a string when I was in high school. Girls were attracted to me. But I've put on a few pounds since then, and I've got crow's-feet and even a few gray hairs already. I suppose I was afraid you might be disappointed in me after all these years."

"Disappointed?"

"When you came in I was watching your face. I was afraid I'd see, 'My-God-he's-disgusting.'"

She sat back in her chair and laughed. Her ponytail hair caught the beam of the sun as it filtered through the restaurant's window and sparkled like gold in Reggie's eyes. He grinned at her and recalled in an instant all the things he loved about her in high school.

"And did you?" she asked, still laughing.

Reggie shook his head no. "You were self-conscious when you came in. You had other things on your mind."

"That's true," Sally said. "Fourteen years ago you were what we girls called a *hunk*. I was worried about meeting your expectations."

"No problem there," Reggie understated.

"Good," she said, and reached across the table to grasp Reggie's hands in hers. "You have matured, Reggie. But frankly you're much more attractive to me now than you were even then."

171

"Really?"

"Don't you believe me?"

Reggie looked down at her hands grasping his, and a flood of warm memories came over him. "We did have some times, didn't we Sally?"

"Yes we did," she said quietly.

"Why haven't you married?" Reggie asked this without looking at her. He couldn't bring himself to look into her eyes as he waited for a response.

"Because, Reggie," she said after a moment, "you were the only person I ever loved that way."

Reggie felt a lump form in his throat as he heard her words. "I'm sure you've broken a few hearts, then, over the years."

Sally shrugged. "Oh, at least a dozen," she said, and smiled. "But you're the only one who has ever broken mine."

Reggie was at a loss for words. He remembered how he had ended it, so long ago, and he remembered that he had not done a particularly good job of saying goodbye. He had ditched her for Eleanor. It was a simple as that.

"You see," she continued, "I've come half way around the world to see if I can't get it mended."

Reggie hesitated as he considered what she had said. "I hope you do," he said after a moment. "It's no good being unhappy about the circumstances we find ourselves in."

Sally did not respond directly to that comment. Instead she leaned forward, rested her chin on her hand, and gazed into Reggie's eyes. "I hope you'll let me see a great deal of you in the short time I'm home," she said. "That would make me very happy."

"Gladly," Reggie said, and gazed back.

"But there is one thing I must say. I've come a long way to say this, and I'll say it just once." Sally sat up straight, pulled her hands back and folded them in her lap. "Reggie, I was hoping that seeing you again would somehow change the way I feel. It hasn't. I'm still in love with you."

Reggie lowered his eyes uncomfortably. He shifted in his chair and started to speak, but Sally stopped him with a gesture.

"I think I will always be in love with you," she continued. "I've learned to live with it. It's always there, a feeling in my heart, like I missed something – something important. Frankly, I've come home to deal with it. But I want you to know that you don't have to worry about me interfering in your marriage. I wouldn't think of coming between you and your wife. That's not my style."

172

Reggie nodded but couldn't look at her.

"I want to be happy, Reggie. But not at someone else's expense."

Again Reggie was at a loss for words. There was an awkward moment of silence.

Sally continued, shifting her eyes out the window to the passing river. "All I ask is to be near you awhile, and if in the end I am still in love with you at least I will know that it is more than just the silly infatuations of a high school girl. Fair enough?"

Reggie thought about that a moment. His gaze followed hers out the window. He smiled to himself as his thoughts drifted along with the river. "Hey," he said softly, "remember when we floated down that river on inner tubes?"

She smiled, too. "I remember the sunburn I got when you made me take my top off."

They giggled, and their eyes connected again. Reggie cleared his throat and nodded. "Fair enough."

At the entrance of the restaurant, unseen by Reggie or Sally, Eleanor stood looking at faces. She was seeking a particular someone but was puzzled when she spotted Reggie. She did not know the blonde who was with him, but that wasn't what concerned her. She was not looking to find Reggie here, at all. For a moment she considered ducking out but changed her mind. She approached her husband's table.

"Reggie?" she said as she came upon them. "What are you doing here?"

"Eleanor!" Reggie wasn't too surprised to run into his wife in this restaurant. He knew she often entertained business clients there. "Do you have an appointment?"

"Do I need one," Eleanor asked, "to see my own husband?"

"No, I meant..." Reggie laughed nervously. "You know what I meant. D'you remember Sally Morgan? From high school?"

Eleanor sat in James' vacated seat. "You forget I didn't go to high school with you, dear."

"Oh, yeah," Reggie said. "I was dating Sally when I met you. Sally, this is my wife, Eleanor."

"Hello," Sally said, and extended her hand across the table. Eleanor shook it. "We met once, years ago. I doubt you remember."

"To be honest I have to admit I don't," Eleanor said, and smiled. "Actually I do recognize you from some old pictures Reggie doesn't know I know about. He keeps them in a little toy safe at his office."

"Never mind that," Reggie said. "Sally has just come home from Korea."

"Korea? You live in Korea?"

"Yes I do."

"Well, then," Eleanor said, and placed her hand on Sally's arm, "we'll have to have you to dinner. Will you?"

Sally looked at Reggie, then back at Eleanor. "I'd love to," she said.

"Good." Eleanor stretched her neck and looked around the room. "I'm supposed to be meeting a client here for lunch, but I'm so late I may have missed him."

"Will you be working late tonight, El?" Reggie asked.

"I almost hate to tell you."

"Not again!"

"I'll do my best to be home by eight," Eleanor said and rose from her seat.

"OK," Reggie said, a bit dejected. "I'll stay at the studio and work. But see you at eight."

Eleanor nodded and kissed him on the cheek. "Good. Then you won't be bored at home." She turned to Sally. "I'll leave it to Reggie to set a date, Sally. We have a wonderful home – you'll love it."

"I'm looking forward to it," Sally said, and extended her hand again. "Thanks for asking."

Eleanor shook it. "Bye-bye for now, then," she said, and departed with her customary quickstep.

Reggie smiled at her as she walked away.

"I can see you two love each other very much," Sally said.

Reggie nodded happily. "As a matter of fact, we do."

TEN

Eleanor emerged from the restaurant with nerves only slightly shaken. She paused outside, drawing a cigarette from her purse, and lit it with her butane lighter. The shadow of a man fell across her.

"Smoking is hazardous to your health," Alex Newton said, and smiled.

Eleanor let the smoke escape through her nose and frowned. "So is what we're doing," she said. "Reggie's in there."

Alex went pale in an instant. "What!?" he said. There was panic in his voice. "Does he know?"

Eleanor shook her head. "Take it easy. It's just a coincidence. He's chatting with an old friend."

"Oh," Alex said, and drew a deep, relaxing breath. "Thank God."

"We'll have to go somewhere else," Eleanor said. A sly smile crossed her lips. "The penthouse?" she suggested.

A *lusty* smile crossed Alex's lips, and he nodded enthusiastically. They crossed the parking lot together and jumped into the new Mercedes.

The Mercedes backed out of its parking space and then squealed out of the lot past an older, dark green Plymouth sedan. Crouched at the wheel sat the tall, silver haired man in dark glasses and an overcoat. As the Mercedes passed he turned the key in the Plymouth's ignition and its engine started. He hesitated a moment, then pulled away from the curb. In a roar of blue smoke he followed after them.

ELEVEN

The days that followed were pleasant ones for Reggie Porter. The best part of being an engineer, in his opinion, the designing and development of a new architectural project, comprised his business activities. And his free time was occupied showing Sally around town, reintroducing her to the community they had both grown up in, checking the haunts of their youth.

One morning Reggie took her to the hospital construction site and caused several near-disasters. Wherever Sally went she had a particular effect on men. They lost their focus, trains of thought got suddenly derailed, and necks turned to rubber as they twisted so eyes could follow her movements. This was never truer than at the work site. At best the workers simply ceased doing whatever they happened to be doing when Sally walked by. At worst they attempted to continue working while ogling her. When one is operating a crane with a three-ton beam attached, or cutting steel with a thousand-degree flame, this is not a good thing.

Reggie wanted to reintroduce Sally to his brother, and he knew just where he would find him. He strapped a hard hat to her head and put one on himself. Then they entered the elevator at the base of the unfinished building and ascended to the top.

The two emerged on the top, open floor. I-beams jutted up, seemingly at random. A sub floor of plywood had been laid, loosely placed over the floor joists. The panoramic view of the city from here was phenomenal, though

175

Sally found it a bit frightening. Howard was there supervising a crew of riveters. They all stopped as Reggie and the blonde vision approached them. A strong wind tugged at Sally's dress. Mouths fell open. One of the men removed his goggles. Another swallowed his gum. Sally noticed none of this. She clung to Reggie, daunted by the altitude.

Howard told his crew to take five. He had heard from Reggie that Sally was back in town, and remembered better than anyone how intense their romance had been so many years ago. He spread his arms wide and grinned at her.

"Good Lord, an angel!"

She laughed.

"Pretty close, Howard. Remember Sally Morgan?"

"How could I ever forget?" He threw his arms around her and gave her a bear hug.

From the top of the building Howard and Reggie showed Sally the sights. They pointed west to the high school they'd all attended. The county court house was visible nestled in some oak trees just south of the building. And looking east they could see the river snaking through the city, ambling gently southward towards the gulf.

Howard chatted amiably with Sally but inside he was quite disturbed. In truth, he loved his little brother more than anything on earth – they were, after all, the only family either of them had any more, since their dad died. Howard could not bear the thought of anything hurting Reggie, or any*one*, for that matter. And given what he knew about Eleanor's current activities he was concerned about Sally's reappearance and what it might mean to his brother's marriage. Howard was determined in his heart to dislike Sally Morgan.

Sally, however, proved to be as charming as she was beautiful. She became a common sight around the Porter home that summer, playing cards on Saturday nights or joining Eleanor and Reggie with their friends for an evening barbeque. Everyone grew to adore her – including Reggie's brother Howard and, yes, including his wife, Eleanor.

Perhaps Eleanor more than any of them. When Sally came for dinner, Reggie was the third party. She and Eleanor found countless things to talk about and enjoyed each others' company immensely. They had similar tastes in nearly everything, books, movies, art and clothes. In fact, they often went shopping together, dragging Reggie along despite his protestations. Both Eleanor and Sally liked to shop seriously, discussing the fashions the saw, dissecting the outfits and arguing over which of them would look better in each one. To prove their point they modeled them for one another. Reggie resigned himself to hours of agony on these shopping trips but secretly enjoyed the fashion show.

Sally also joined them at the many suburban lawn parties that invariably occur in the summer. She was always a welcome addition, though women were often initially jealous of her good looks and shapely figure. Their animosity passed as Sally's unpretentious nature was revealed to them. Of course their men were instantly attracted to her, but found that what initially drew their attention proved to be mere frosting to her charm, wit and pleasant personality.

Sally, Eleanor and Reggie joined Ralph Steiner and his wife at the theater one warm evening. They ran into Alex Newton there, with his wife Jacqueline, during intermission. It was, perhaps, the first awkward moment Reggie had experienced since Sally's arrival. He could tell by her demeanor that she disliked Alex the instant she was introduced. She ignored his rather obvious advances, speaking only a few, polite words to him, and those rather coolly. Jacqueline, a round-faced woman with a cheery personality, did not exhibit the initial jealousy Reggie had observed in other women. She clearly liked Sally right off, putting her arm around her and calling her "dear." Sally and Eleanor were intrigued by a flashy necklace of diamonds that Jacqueline wore, a unique design, and the three of them wandered off to discuss it. Alex was left to fend for himself.

All things considered, it was a remarkable summer for Reggie Porter. The work on the hospital progressed and it now looked as if they would finish on time. His architectural design of the new Jenrette Industries plant had been approved and all related plans were nearing completion. In addition, Reggie often found himself in the company of two of the most beautiful women in the city. And on top of all that, his racquetball serve had improved unexpectedly.

Who could ask for more? he thought. *What could be better than this?*

TWELVE

Reggie cocked back his arm in a way that is similar to the pulling back of a hammer on a revolver, locking it in place, its tension ready to unleash a lethal force. Suddenly, with a snap and a *wish* of air, his arm sprung forward, rotating slightly, the wrist whipping loosely. *Th-wack!* The ball smacked into the forward wall and flashed back just inches over the service line. Ralph Steiner leapt forward, digging it up with the tip of his racquet, sending it forward once again.

Sally watched the two of them play behind the glass, seated in the refreshment bar. She had finished a workout of her own – stair-climbers, the stationary bike and a two mile jog – and was enjoying a Coke while waiting for them to finish up. She chewed her lower lip pensively. A lot was crowding her mind. Summer was nearly over and she had some serious decisions to make. Decisions she dreaded making.

Howard Porter slipped into the chair next to her.

"Well, hello, Howard," she said smiling.

"Hi, Sally. Who's winning?"

"Ralph is having a terrific game, but you know Reggie. He often comes through in the final moments."

Howard nodded. "That's a keen observation." They watched a moment. Ralph regained the serve. Reggie paused to wave at the both of them through the glass.

"Reggie promised me dinner out some place special if I'd wait for him," Sally said. "Want to join us?"

Howard shook his head no. "You been having a *good time* since you've been home, ain't ya?"

Sally sensed an edge to Howard's question which put her on alert. She looked at him, but he continued his gaze into the court. "Yes, I have," she said. "Everyone has been wonderful to me. Especially Eleanor and Reggie."

"You like Eleanor?"

"Very much. She is the sister I never had."

Howard shifted his weight in his chair. "You know," he said, "I remember you from before. From high school."

"Do you? You were Joe College when Reggie and I were dating."

"True. But I was home often enough to hear him talk about you."

"What did he say, I wonder?"

Howard looked at her now. "He didn't talk about you like most teenage boys talk about their girls," he said. "I honestly think he thought the two of you would get married one day."

Sally felt herself tightening and her breathing grew shallow. She tried not to change the tone of her voice. "That was a long time ago," she said lightly. "We were kids and too young to talk of such things."

"Bullshit."

Howard's tone startled her. She looked into his eyes and saw bitterness there. His face was lined and toughened by years of working in the elements. He studied her with an intensity that frightened her.

"I know you two talked about it all the time. You made plans. He was in love with you and you were in love with him. Weren't you?"

Sally returned her gaze to Reggie and Ralph on the court. "You know," she responded coolly, "it's been so long ago I forget."

They were silent for a minute. Reggie regained the serve and fired the ball mercilessly, running Ralph ragged.

Howard said, "I introduced him to Eleanor." He watched her closely for a reaction. "He ever tell you that?"

She swallowed and shook her head.

"I was dating her at the time."

She was blinking back tears now.

"I also advised him to marry *you.*"

Sally turned abruptly and gasped. Her features contorted. "You did? *Why?*"

Howard shrugged. His voice was like gravel. "For one thing, you had bigger tits."

Sally looked away briefly and drew a deep breath. She determined that it was time to drop any pretenses with Howard.

"I still do, Howard," she said to him. "What is your point?"

He shrugged again. "D'you suppose he regrets marrying Eleanor instead of you?"

Sally turned in her chair to look directly at Howard, squaring her shoulders, putting her back to the glass. She stared at Reggie's brother a moment, considering his position. She knew that he loved Reggie. She knew he also loved Eleanor. And she knew he had been kind to her this summer, as well. Despite his hostility toward her, her heart warmed to him. She smiled.

"He's perfectly happy with Eleanor, Howard," she said softly. "You know that."

"Must be frustrating to you."

She shook her head slowly. "Not particularly."

"But you still love him, don't you?"

"Oh, Howard," she said, and sighed deeply. She could feel the emotion that had been accumulating all summer well up inside of her and she was afraid of unleashing it, here and now, in this very public place with Reggie just a few feet away. "Please," she said, "stay out of this."

"Do you get your kicks making trouble for people?"

She shook her head and her eyes closed. Two large tears shot down her cheeks. She drew another deep breath, then spoke with as much control as she could muster. "Howard, I am only here for a few more days. I want to make people happy, not cause them trouble. My friendship with Reggie means a lot to me, more than I can express. I hate the thought of losing it – which certainly would happen if I ever attempted to come between him and Eleanor."

Howard saw her clearly for the first time. He understood, finally, that they were a lot alike. He knew that neither of them could or would do anything, ever, that jeopardized Reggie Porter's happiness. He put his hand on her shoulder and squeezed it.

"Have you stopped to think," he said flatly, "that maybe Reggie wants more from you than just friendship?"

She glanced at Reggie through the glass, slapping the little blue ball across the court, then shook her head no.

"Certainly not," she said. There was a sadness in her voice. "Reggie is devoted to Eleanor and that is that."

A moment passed. There was a *tap-tap-tap* on the wall. Sally quickly wiped her cheeks and then pivoted in her chair to smile at Reggie. He stood there, grinning at the both of them, and held the fingers of both hands in the air. "Ten minutes," he shouted, his voice muffled behind the glass. "I'll shower and be out in ten minutes." Then he and Ralph disappeared through the little door in the corner of the court.

"You know, don't you?" Howard asked her.

She looked at him dully.

Howard nodded. "You *do* know… that Eleanor's having an affair with Alex Newton."

Sally snapped. She glared at Howard and looked as though she could claw his eyes out. "Don't say it, Howard. Don't *ever* say it. It's none of your *Goddamn business.*"

She rose from the table and left him there, knowing he had gone too far.

THIRTEEN

Reggie turned the key to the front entry of the building and opened the door. He pushed it open wide to allow Sally enough room to pass through with the large, flat pizza box in her hands. Reggie followed her inside with two medium root beers cradled in his arm and let the door swing shut behind him.

This was her first visit to Porter Engineering, Inc., and she stood in the office entryway examining it as an art aficionado might admire a Rembrandt or a Picasso. She knew that Reggie had designed it, and that her affection for him certainly could taint her appreciation for the design, but in spite of this she found herself truly impressed with its sleek, flowing look. Somehow it captured the image of another era while simultaneously giving a feeling of ultrahigh technology. This seemed to her, from a marketing perspective, to be exactly what a purchaser of Porter Engineering services would be seeking. It was a masterful blend of past and future, and she loved it.

Reggie stood back quietly and let her take it all in. He had promised her dinner out at a special place and she was expecting a fancy meal in yet another local restaurant. But not tonight. He hoped she wouldn't be disappointed, but he had been putting off showing her his studio office all summer – waiting for just the right moment – and tonight was it. He watched her as she wandered slowly past the foyer into the reception area, turning slowly to see every detail, and then around the corner into his work studio. He was certain she would comprehend the dual functionality of his design, to mix the comfort of the past with the excitement of tomorrow, and he could see that his confidence in her was justified. He closed his eyes a moment and thought about her. They were warm feelings. Then he opened them again and followed her into his studio.

She turned as he entered and smiled at him, that brilliant smile he had become accustomed to. She raised her eyebrows and glanced once again around the room.

"It is magnificent, Reggie."

Her praise for his work meant everything to him. It was the one thing, oddly, that he never got from Eleanor.

"Thanks," he said simply, and the two of them sat down at a small table. "C'mon, let's eat."

They opened the box and pulled stringy cheese slices to their lips. "I hope you like pineapple," Reggie said, referring to the topping he had chosen.

"I love pineapple. It reminds me of Hawaii."

"You like Hawaii?"

Sally nodded, munching and swallowing, peeling cheese from her chin. "Who doesn't? But it has special meaning to me, because my father used to take us there when we were kids. It is probably my favorite place on earth."

"Ralph Steiner thinks I should take Eleanor there."

Sally felt her emotions slipping from her again. After that business with Howard at the club it was all she could do to pull herself together for dinner with Reggie. "Oh," she said simply, and put her pizza down.

Reggie sensed that something was changing between them. He looked at her a moment but she didn't return his gaze. That was very unusual for Sally, he thought. She *always* looked him square in the eye.

"Hey," he said softly. "What's wrong?"

She shrugged and smiled. "Nothing."

"You look funny."

"Thanks loads."

"No, I mean…" Reggie set his pizza aside and leaned across the table to her. He put the palm of his hand on her forehead.

"I can read your thoughts, you know."

"What are they telling you?"

"You're worried about your business."

Sally smiled and shook her head. "No more than usual."

"You miss your loved ones."

"I've never been closer to them."

Reggie was suspicious. "You're not secretly married to a certain Korean gentleman, are you?"

She laughed at this, that warm embracing laugh of hers, and Reggie felt reassured. Still, something was not right.

"Do you know what I would like?" she asked him.

"Your wish is my command," he said, grinning.

"I would very much like to see your secret cache of old photographs Eleanor told me about," she said, and laughed again. "The ones that she knows about but you don't know she knows about."

"Oh, those." Reggie winced but nodded. "All right," he said, and jumped up from his seat. He crossed the studio to a wall of shelves that held a collection of antique toys, a windup space ship, old metal cars and toy soldiers made of lead. Amongst this menagerie, pressed back against the shelf, sat an old toy bank. Reggie retrieved it.

"This was my father's toy bank," he replied, "and he gave it to me when I was a kid." He returned to the table and sat down in the chair next to her, then turned the dial to number nine. "I was nine when I got it, so Dad set the lock to open on number nine. I've never changed it."

He swung open the door and peered inside. There were several old photos there, of James and Reggie in the boy scouts, of Reggie and Howard dressed like chipmunks on Halloween, of a variety of cherished memories. Reggie sifted through them slowly.

He stopped when he came to Sally's high school graduation photograph. It was yellowed and worn, as though it had been carried in a wallet, which it was, for many years before being transferred to this place. Reggie put the other photographs aside and cradled the one of Sally in his palm. She smiled at him in it, that same warm smile of hers, unchanged in a decade and a half.

"Do you remember when you gave me this?"

She nodded. "On our last date."

Reggie looked away.

"Only I didn't know it was our last date."

"I had already met Eleanor," Reggie told her. "I was away at college, feeling tied down by our relationship. I didn't know how to break it off with you. I know I did a lousy job of it. I didn't want to hurt you."

"I know," she said softly. "I've always known."

He sighed. "I hoped you did." He looked up and into Sally's eyes for a long moment. "Do you remember what you wrote on the back?"

She thought briefly, then shook her head. Reggie gave her the photograph and she turned it over.

Forever Yours it said. Nothing more.

Sally looked at it for a long time. She could feel tears welling up inside of her and she was afraid to move, or even breathe, much less speak. She swallowed hard and blinked twice, trying desperately to control herself.

"What were you and Howard talking about at the club tonight?" Reggie asked her quietly.

She swallowed again. "Nothing," she managed.

"Nothing?"

She shrugged. "We reminisced a little."

Reggie fell back into his chair and dropped his hands to his lap. He sat there that way, as if drained, unfocused, and felt himself growing angry with his brother.

They sat for several minutes, not speaking.

"You've made me very happy these last several weeks," Sally said at last.

"I haven't done much."

"Yes you have," she insisted. "You've let me be near you. I am grateful for that."

"Strangers on a plane have that privilege."

183

Sally looked at him, thought a long moment, and then came to a conclusion within herself. The time of reckoning was at hand, she thought. She grabbed a napkin and dabbed the corners of her eyes. Then she drew a deep breath and said, "Reggie, please don't think that because I haven't mentioned it I've stopped loving you."

Reggie heard her words but responded coolly. "We're not in high school anymore, Sally."

She shrugged. "I loved you in high school. But I love you a thousand times more now than I did then."

"Sally, don't…"

"I have to, Reggie," she interrupted him. *"I have to."* She folded her arms and continued. "I've kept my feelings to myself all summer and just this once I'm going to let myself go."

"I wouldn't if I were you."

"Well, you're not me. Just this once I want to tell you how completely devoted I am to you. There's never *ever* been another man in my life."

"Sure there has, Sally. You've broken a few hearts."

Sally shook her head. "Not really. If I've broken hearts it's only because I love you with all my heart. I admire you more than any man I've ever met. I respect you, and the work you do. I'm a damn fool for you. I will do anything to assure your happiness, even if it means destroying my own. I don't know how to say it more simply. I love you. I just want you to *know* that, to fully comprehend it. And if you are ever in trouble, or if you need someone to care for you, I'm here for you."

She sat silently after that, but did not take her eyes off him.

Reggie thought through what she said. Finally his own eyes focused and he looked at Sally. "I don't know what to say."

"Do you believe me?"

Reggie's charming grin returned, and he nodded. "Of course I do."

"I won't say it again."

"I wish you hadn't said it at all."

"Are you mad at me?"

Reggie shook his head.

"I'm mad at Howard," he said.

FOURTEEN

The black, gloved hand of the tall, silver haired man tested the doorknob, then twisted it. He was twenty-eight stories up in a downtown office building. The door opened silently.

It was nearly midnight, the appointed hour. He closed the door behind him and surveyed the room. First class, as he had expected. Plush, burgundy carpets lined the floor, mahogany paneling adorned the walls, except the back wall which was comprised of a single, huge bookshelf filled with leather-bound tomes, each with gold imprinted lettering. Light spilled under a closed door there. The silver haired man checked his watch, just to make certain. That would be him, all right, his client. He crossed the dark room silently.

He had worked this case all summer. It was not unpleasant, all in all, though not exactly something he'd put on his résumé. Still, he was sorry to be done with it. He had stretched it into as long a gig as he dared, and in the end had come through with exactly what the client wanted: clear, indisputable evidence obtained through clandestine surveillance. And best of all, the targets never knew they were under observation. They never had a clue.

He swung open the door and it squeaked on its hinges. James Emery was there, working late, and the noise startled him. Seated at his oversized desk, his work illuminated by an antique lamp with a jade-green shade, James leaned back into his wing backed leather chair. His features disappeared into inky shadows.

The silver haired man stood before him and removed his gloves, then reached into the breast pocket of his jacket. He produced an envelope, sealed, and dropped it onto James' desk.

"That's what you want, Mr. Emery."

James hesitated. Even in the shadows the silver haired man could sense his disappointment, and it confused him. James reached out his narrow hands and slit the envelope with a gold blade, then dumped its contents onto the ink blotter that lined his desktop. They were photographs, 35 millimeter, 36 in number. James spread them apart, thumbing through them. They were of Alex and Eleanor, together, in a variety of locations. James recognized several restaurants, some out-of-town places, a resort at the beach, a chalet in the mountains.

The last dozen photos were the most disturbing of all. They were of the two of them in various stages of undress, including some fully nude shots of them having sex in a bedroom. These were not fuzzy, questionable images, but clear and undeniably explicit.

"How did you get these?" James asked, referring to the last pictures.

"Telephoto lens, fast film," the silver haired man said. "Alex Newton has a penthouse suite atop the St. Gregory downtown, ostensibly for entertaining corporate guests. People who have penthouses have a thing about leaving the windows open. For the view, I guess."

"I see."

"They don't realize that if they have a great view *out*, everyone else has a great view *in*."

James nodded, and his hands began to shake visibly. He opened the desk drawer, removed a banded stack of one hundred dollar bills and handed it to the man before him. Then he rose from his chair and crossed the room to a well stocked liquor cabinet, placed two cubes of ice in a glass and poured vodka over it. He swirled the vodka over the ice to cool it and shot it down.

The silver haired man thumbed through the hundreds quickly, counting his money. "Who is she, Mr. Emery? A lover?"

James didn't respond. He moved to the window, which ran from floor to ceiling, and looked out into the darkness.

"You know, I used to do quite a bit of this sort of thing," the silver haired man said as he pocketed the cash, "back before no-fault divorce."

James wasn't hearing him.

"When they put in no-fault divorce they took a sizable portion of my income and chucked it out the window."

The fellow looked at James a moment, standing silently with his back to him, staring at the city below. It was clear that their conversation was over. *Very strange*, he thought, and left.

James watched the traffic in the near empty streets, his hands clasped behind his back. He had hoped that the rumors were wrong about Alex and Eleanor. Now he knew the truth.

He felt betrayed by one dear friend and feared for the other.

FIFTEEN

Alex Newton stood at the crowded elevator and perspired. He couldn't help it. He always perspired when he was nervous. Today he was squirting. He rode to the twenty-second floor in silence, mopping his brow with his damp, monogrammed handkerchief.

The elevator opened onto a beehive of activity. He had never been to Eleanor's office and was not prepared for the rapid pace that was standard-operational-procedure in the creative environment of the city's largest advertising agency. Three phones were ringing, each with its own electronic pitch. A loud *thump-thumping* track of music was playing in the background, but would stop suddenly and be replaced by a high-pitched squeal as somebody reversed it, and then it would start up again at the same spot. Executives, usually in pairs, were all going somewhere, but each two in separate directions. They were absorbed in animated discussions, sometimes with each other and sometimes on separate cell phones. A young man in tennis shoes ran past him with some artwork under his arm. Three beautiful women sat in the lobby, chatting. Alex thought he recognized one of them from a billboard and the other two seemed familiar. A little girl with curly red hair stood crying next to a stern-looking woman Alex took to be her mother. She was scolding her. Alex shook his head and wondered about Eleanor. How could she survive in this? He was used to the more controlled business environment of manufacturing, and thought all this pure craziness. He approached the receptionist named Janice.

"Hello," he said, "is Eleanor Porter available?"

"I can see," Janice said, and punched in Eleanor's extension.

At that moment a door burst open. Eleanor and two others emerged from a paneled conference room. She stopped short when she saw Alex Newton.

"Alex?" She was surprised and perplexed.

"Ah..." Alex said, and glanced at the receptionist, "Mrs. Porter?" he extended his hand.

The receptionist looked curiously at Eleanor, then at Alex. Eleanor crossed the room and shook Alex's hand. "Yes," she said, her head bobbing. "What can I do for you?"

"Sorry to drop in without an appointment. Can you spare a moment?"

Eleanor put on her best sales executive's smile. "Certainly," she said, and led Alex down the hall toward her office. "How are things at Jenrette Industries?" She spoke just loudly enough to assure that Janice would overhear.

She did. The receptionist watched Eleanor close the door to her office, then turned to the coworker beside her. She rolled her eyes. "Five bucks says Ms. Porter instructs me to hold her calls," she said. "Her in-box is about to be filled." The two of them cackled at this remark.

Eleanor at that moment had her tongue down Alex Newton's throat. She had grabbed him the moment her office door had snapped shut. Normally Alex liked Eleanor's aggressiveness, but not today. He broke away.

"Dammit, Eleanor!"

"What's wrong?"

"It's Jacqueline."

"Jacqueline?" Eleanor crossed her arms. "What about Jacqueline?"

"I think she knows."

"Knows? Knows what?"

Alex mopped his forehead. "About us!"

"Why?"

"She acted funny last night," he said. "After she kissed me good night. I was falling asleep when suddenly she sniffed and asked me what I'd been up to all evening."

"I assume you didn't tell her."

"Of course not." Alex began to pace about the room. Eleanor could see he was distressed, but then she knew he was easily distressed. "I said I'd been working late."

"That was original."

"Then she said she called the office."

"How did you handle that?"

"I got mad and told her I wouldn't have her checking up on me like some parole officer."

Eleanor nodded approval. "A good offense is the best defense," she said.

"She slept with her back to me the whole night."

"Is that all?"

"She wouldn't say goodbye to me this morning," Alex said, and ran his fingers through his hair. "She pretended to be asleep."

"Maybe she was asleep."

Alex shook his head. "She always gives me a kiss when I leave in the morning. It's a ritual with her."

Eleanor thought about this a moment, leaning back on the top of her desk. "Well, I think you're making too much of it," she said flatly.

Alex drew a breath. "Maybe. My nerves are shot."

"Alex, you've got to stay cool."

"You don't know Jacqueline the way I do," he said. "Little things count to her."

"You mean little things like marriage vows and so forth? Or your little thing?"

"Very funny," Alex snorted. "I mean details. She has an eye for details."

"Well," Eleanor said again, and shrugged. She thought a moment. "There's a big difference between suspicion and solid proof."

"Oh, she couldn't prove anything, but she could sure stir things up with Reggie."

Eleanor considered that possibility. "Reggie can handle it," she said. "The best tactic with Reggie is to tell him everything and beg him to forgive me."

Alex nearly choked on that statement. "Great idea, Eleanor. He'd forgive you and come after me with a nine iron."

Eleanor laughed at that and shook her head. "Not Reggie. He's above that."

Alex stepped in close to Eleanor and slipped his arm around her waist. "Damn," he said. "If I didn't know better I'd be jealous of the way you talk about your husband."

She laced her fingers around his neck and pulled him into her, and they embraced. "Feel better?"

"I'm beginning to feel something."

"Getting your nerve back?"

He shrugged. "Talking to you it doesn't sound so bad."

"I'm sure it was nothing."

"It's just that I've risked everything for you. Jacqueline's father would finish whatever Reggie might leave undone."

They kissed again, and suddenly Eleanor was breathing rather hotly. She unbuttoned her blouse and leaned back on her desk, pushing clutter to the floor.

"Here?" Alex said, surprised.

Eleanor calmed herself and reached for the phone. "Janice," she said into it, "hold my calls."

SIXTEEN

Reggie worked his thumbs back and forth, millimeter by millimeter, until the gasses exerting pressure inside the bottle overcame the resistance provided by the swollen cork against the glass. *POP!* The cork shot straight up into the ceiling, smacked the plaster there and rebounded to the patio floor. A half-second later the foamy liquid erupted, spilling onto the deck as Reggie vainly attempted to direct its flow into the long-stemmed crystal glasses in the hands of the revelers. They cheered at the champagne's uncorking, a resounding *Hurrah!* to welcome its release after nearly forty years of bottled captivity.

A banner hung from the rafters. *BON VOYAGE SALLY !!!* it proclaimed. Sally, the guest of honor, looking radiant as always, stood in the midst of all the friends she had learned to love these last few summer months. They were Reggie's friends, she knew, and that made them all the more precious to her. Her eyes drifted from face to face as they crowded around Reggie, holding their glasses like the beaks of young birds looking to be fed.

James was there, as persnickety as ever, complaining first about the humidity and then about the mosquitoes. There, too, stood burly Howard, his huge forearms crossed and graveled voice booming laughter. Howard had been especially sweet and kind to her since she had announced her pending return to Korea. The incident at the club was never mentioned between them. She knew he had only Reggie's best interests at heart when he said those things, which made any action he undertook, even those hurtful to herself, acceptable to her. And Ralph, loveable, thoughtful Ralph, maneuvered his way into the fray of upraised glasses with surprising agility. Ralph's gentle nature and kind words of wisdom had been a refuge to her on more than one occasion this summer, and she knew Reggie often found insight and solace there, as well. And Eleanor, *Mrs. Porter,* she forced herself to remember, who had virtually adopted her from the moment Sally had come to town, elbowed Howard and then James in the ribs. Eleanor had become Sally's sibling, for she had none by natural means, and her best friend, as well (other than Reggie.) Despite the fact that she knew of Eleanor's deception Sally could not judge her too harshly. She believed that Eleanor was the perfect wife for Reggie, beautiful, witty, successful – and she also believed that one day soon the woman would wake up to realize just what a fool she had been to risk it all.

And there in the middle of them all, spilling champagne on each of them, stood Reggie. *Her Reggie.* Naïve, trusting, unsuspecting, loveable Reggie. Ever grinning, ever joking, ever boyish Reggie. She had traveled thousands of miles, halfway around the world in fact, to find him again. And now that she had found him she discovered the truth in what she had presumed all along, that the two of them could *never* be together. They must always be apart. That was certain because circumstances had conspired against them.

James began to raise his voice above the din of the friendly chatter. "A toast, a toast!" he said.

"Wait a minute," Reggie said, grabbing the last glass, "let me get some." He poured his own glass to the brim and set the bottle aside.

James raised his glass to Sally and the others followed suit. "Here's to Sally," he said. "Hard evidence that beauty and brains are *not* mutually exclusive, and living proof that earthly pleasures are often wrapped in heavenly packages!"

"Here, here!" they all agreed, and drank.

"OK, lemme, lemme!" Howard shouted, his voice rumbling. He lifted his glass again and the others did likewise. "To Sally Morgan," he bellowed, "a real *head twister.* No man alive would call her mister! Narrow waist and fair of face, not much upstairs but *what a staircase!*"

There followed a groan and laughter, a wolf whistle and more laughter. They tipped their glasses and drained them.

They called for refills and Reggie took the champagne bottle by the neck and ran it over the glasses again. Then Ralph Steiner hoisted his crystal glass high and, his gentle voice rising above the din, said: "*Now* it is my turn!" All of them hushed to hear what he would say, lifting their glasses.

"Sally," he said and smiled broadly, "may you *never* forget the friends you have here. Mind your liabilities, my dear, and leave it to guys like us to keep an eye on your assets."

"Here, here!" they shouted, laughing and drinking. Reggie whistled shrilly. Sally threw back her head and laughed at Ralph's uncharacteristic remark, and then kissed his cheek to show her appreciation.

"All right, all right," Eleanor shouted, "let a woman show you how it's done." She threw an arm around Howard's neck to support herself, hoisting her glass. The others did likewise. "Sally, girlfriend," she said, "may *three things* be long in you life: your days, your financial statements, and most importantly, your *men!*"

Again there was a groan of laughter and loud whistles, and they all drained their glasses. Reggie refilled them and they began to press him for his contribution. He declined at first but they insisted until, at last, he raised his glass and smiled at Sally.

There was a long pause. They stood there quietly, glasses raised, Reggie's eyes locked on to Sally's. He shook his head and grinned, "I'm no good at this," he said but they pressed him. He drew a breath and cleared his throat. "Sally," he said...

From the street there came a loud *SCREECH!* as four tires locked up on dry pavement. It sounded as though it should be followed by a loud crash, but none came. Almost instantly the smell of burnt rubber wafted over them, carried by a summer evening's breeze.

"What was that?" Reggie asked.

They all shrugged. Reggie put his champagne glass down and hurried through the patio door, the others close at his heels. They crossed the living room to the entryway and Reggie threw open the door.

Jacqueline Newton stood there, looking like hell. Her eyes were reddened, hair in disarray, and mascara ran in streaks down her cheeks. The Mercedes sat idling where it had come to rest in the street, its tires still smoking.

She looked at Reggie a moment. "I must speak to you," she said simply, and slipped past him through the open door.

Eleanor Porter, at the precise moment she heard Jacqueline's voice, fished her cigarettes from her purse and tapped one out of the pack. James watched her. She sat down on the couch and showed no reaction. She felt around the inside of the purse grasping for her lighter.

A second car squealed around the corner and roared up the residential street, then slid to a halt behind the Mercedes. It was a Jaguar, with Alex Newton at the wheel. He jumped from the car and ran to the porch. He was panic-stricken.

"My wife," he said to Reggie at the door. "Is she…?" He peered over Reggie's shoulder.

Reggie Porter stepped before Alex at the entryway of his home and spoke in a very low voice. His words were in the form of a command, not a request. "Keep your mouth *shut*, Alex. Let me handle this."

Alex seemed more than willing to obey. Relieved, in fact. Reggie turned and he followed him inside.

"What's this about, Jacqueline?" Reggie asked.

She looked at Eleanor, seated on the couch, with fury in her eyes. Eleanor took the unlit cigarette from her mouth, gave up looking for her lighter, and returned her gaze. Then Jacqueline turned back to Reggie, oblivious of the others.

"I thought you should know that your wife is screwing my husband," she said, seething.

"Jackie!" Alex shouted.

Reggie shot a sharp look at Alex which silenced him, then turned back to Jacqueline. "What gives you that idea?" he asked her.

Jacqueline unclenched her fist and lifted her palm. She held a gold and black butane lighter. It was engraved with the initials *ERP*.

"Does this look familiar?" she said. "I found it in their love nest, on a pillow."

There was a moment of stunned silence in the room. All eyes rested on the lighter. Then, gradually, they shifted to Reggie.

"Oh, terrific," he said, and grinned. "I've been looking all over for this thing." He took it from her hand. "Thanks."

The wind seemed to escape her lungs as if someone had punched her. She looked at him suspiciously. "It isn't yours."

"It most certainly is."

"I went to the penthouse suite downtown," Jacqueline said. "The one father always used for business. They've been using it for noontime trysts. I found *that* in the bedroom."

"Oh, that's where it was," Reggie said. He looked at her and shrugged. "I met Alex at the St. Gregory to review the designs I've been working on for the new plant. We rolled the blueprints out on the bed and I guess I left my lighter there." Reggie flipped it in the air, caught it in his palm, and slipped it into his shirt pocket. "I'm always putting this thing down and forgetting it," he said, and smiled at Jacqueline.

"But it has Eleanor's initials on it," she protested.

Reggie shook his head. "Not Eleanor's, Jacqueline," he said softly. "Mine. I was named after my father, Eugene Reginald Porter. Around the house they called me little Reggie, and it stuck." He shrugged. "I can see how you could make a mistake."

Jacqueline's face twisted with anger. "How naïve do you think I am?!" she shouted.

"It's easy enough to prove," Reggie said. "Should I hunt up my birth certificate? Or will my driver's license be enough?"

The anger left her face and was replaced with a dull, lifeless stare. She studied him a long, quiet moment, not blinking, then glanced at the others around the room.

"Eleanor," Reggie said to his wife. "Grab my wallet, will you? I left it in the kitchen."

Eleanor nodded and rose to her feet.

Jacqueline raised her hand and shook her head. "No," she said. "Don't do that." She swallowed twice, then looked again at Reggie. "I fear I've made an ass of myself."

"I tried to stop you, Jackie," Alex said.

She nodded listlessly.

"You've made an appalling allegation against Alex and my wife, Jacqueline," Reggie said quietly. "Was there anything else?"

James' hand instinctively felt the pocket of his blazer. The photographs were there. He thought about it but dismissed the notion and dropped his hand back to his side.

193

Jacqueline shook her head. "Just my suspicions. Until the lighter. I found it. I thought..." She began to sob uncontrollably.

"A suspicious mind is a nasty thing, Jacqueline," Reggie said to her, and took her into his arms. "It'll eat you alive."

"I've always trusted Alex," she said between sobs. "I feel like a fool!" She turned to Alex and looked at him pitifully. "I'm sorry, darling!"

"Don't talk to me," Alex said, looking away.

Jacqueline turned to Eleanor. "Can you forgive me?"

Eleanor shrugged. "You've insulted me in front of all my friends. And you've ruined a perfectly good party."

Alex turned his back on Jacqueline and crossed his arms. "After seven years of total devotion," he pronounced. "How could you *ever* doubt my love for you?"

Jacqueline was stunned by this proclamation. She began gasping for air and turned very pale. Her head spun about the room, looking into every face, until at last she stumbled toward the door. She opened it and looked back at them once again.

"Please forgive me!" she cried, and left.

For a moment no one took a breath.

Finally Sally turned to the others, disgusted. She studied Reggie's wife briefly, until Eleanor cocked her head and gave a little shrug. Then Sally faced Reggie and looked into his eyes. "Are you OK?" she asked tenderly.

He nodded. "Drive her home."

Sally agreed and hurried after Jacqueline.

Eleanor sat down on the couch again. "I need a cigarette," she said, and retrieved the one she had before. Reggie tossed the butane lighter to her across the room and she lit up.

"I'll never forget this, *Eu*-gene," she said, blowing smoke. "You were incredible."

"I've never seen anything like it," Alex said, bewildered. "Reggie, I..." He looked around the room, embarrassed. "We didn't mean it to happen."

"Oh? Which time?"

Eleanor said what they were all thinking. "You knew all along, didn't you?"

Reggie crossed the room and pulled his jacket from the closet.

"You've been laughing at me all the time," Eleanor said, drawing deeply on the cigarette. "You smug little bastard."

Reggie slipped his arms into the jacket. "Forgive me for depriving you of letting you think you deceived me," he said.

"Where are you going?"

Reggie looked around the room at the others. "The party's over."

"It would've been awkward if Jacqueline had insisted on seeing your driver's license," Eleanor blurted.

"I knew she wouldn't."

Alex was perplexed. "How?"

Reggie looked at him. "I could see in her eyes she was no more interested in the truth than I was."

"Do you think so, Reggie?"

Reggie nodded. "Here's what you do, Alex. Don't talk to her. Never let her defend what she's done here tonight. Make her cry and feel stupid. Say you're leaving and pack your bag, but let her stop you before you do it. Make her beg you not to go. And after a month of so when you've nearly ruined her health, when she's heartbroken and weak and crushed and despondent, then and only then, tell her she's the only woman you ever loved and that you'd like to start over."

Alex considered that a moment and his face brightened. "By God, that'll do it all right, won't it?" He glanced around the room at the others, checking for their reaction.

"One other thing," Reggie said. "Don't go home tonight."

"Right," Alex nodded. "Good point. I'll stay at the St. Gregory."

James cleared his throat. "I'd suggest you draw the curtains," he said dryly.

"Huh?"

James looked at him blankly. "Nothing."

Alex left.

James turned to Reggie and considered the photographs once again. Then to Eleanor he said, "You may not want to hear what I have to say."

"I suppose you are about to shred me," she said, and lit another cigarette. "I can take it."

"Fine. Reggie, I can't imagine why you spared that sleaze ball," James began. "Maybe for Eleanor's sake, or maybe to avoid looking foolish yourself..."

Ralph interrupted him. "James, before you go on, let me say something. Reggie, I beg you not to make any rash decisions. Take your time to think things through. Your marriage to Eleanor has been a good one all these years..."

"What a crock!" Howard snorted. "Don't you get it, Ralph? Their marriage has been a sham. A big con the two of 'em have played on the rest of us."

195

"SHUT UP!"

The outburst from Reggie startled them all. He zipped up his jacket and put his hands in the pockets, then looked at each of them a moment. He shook his head. "I'm gone," he said, and left.

They could hear the sound of the beamer starting up, and of Reggie backing it out of the driveway. The three men turned their attention back to Eleanor, each hoping she would jump up and run after him, begging for reconciliation. Of course they knew better.

She finished the second cigarette and snubbed it out in a tray, then looked up at them. "He's a big boy," she said. "He'll get over it."

"I'm sure he will," Ralph agreed.

Howard nodded. "You're right."

James drew the envelope from his pocket and dropped it beside Eleanor on the couch. "Some snaps for the family album," he said.

And the three of them left.

Eleanor, alone now, smoked another cigarette and then went to bed.

SEVENTEEN

The unfinished hospital's skeleton-like frame stood in silhouette against a pale sky. It was just after five, and although the sun had not yet risen the horizon was already pink. It had been a cloudless night, and the crispness of the air was an indicator that fall was not far off.

Howard eased his four-wheel-drive pickup over the curb into the lot. The construction site was empty. There was no sign of activity. He pulled further in, curving slowly around the site's office. The pickup's tires crunched the soft gravel as Howard locked them up suddenly. *There he is,* Howard thought, relieved. Reggie's BMW, its windows fogged from condensation, sat parked near the camper. Howard pulled his truck next to the beamer and jumped out.

When Reggie hadn't come home by three Eleanor began to worry about him. It simply wasn't in his nature to be out all night. She called Howard and it worried him, too. He set out to find him.

He looked first at the studio, and could tell that Reggie had been there – there was a missing bottle of scotch and the oldies station was blaring – and then down by the river. As kids the river had been their favorite hiding place and they had spent many a night camping out there. He also drove up on old

Spyglass, on a hunch, where they used to take girls after the movies. Nothing. Howard had driven by the work site twice, but the camper's lights were dark and the place looked deserted. Now he wished he had looked closer the first time. It would've saved him a heap of driving around.

He peered though the BMW's fogged windows. It was empty. He felt the hood. Cold. Reggie didn't have a key to the camper, but Howard rattled the door anyway. "Reggie?" he called. There was no response.

Howard turned and put his hands in his pockets, perplexed. *Where could he be?* He looked up at the new hospital. The first pink rays of the morning light were visible through its frame. A thought occurred to Howard, and a sinking feeling came upon him. He tilted his head and peered up at the top floor.

It was a bit eerie riding in the caged elevator in the black of night. Howard worked the controls while studying the city below him. It was still slumbering. In an hour or so traffic would begin to fill the streets, shops would open and life would go on. That's how it always is. Life goes on.

At the top floor the elevator ground to a halt. Howard pulled the steel mesh doors apart and stepped between them. The sub flooring had been completed, which was a good thing, he thought, because if Reggie was up here at least he wouldn't be slipping through a black hole in the floor. He walked across the area. It looked deserted. *Where in hell is he?* He thought that thought as his eyes drifted upward, then caught his breath in a quick gasp.

Howard hadn't spotted Reggie at first because he still wasn't looking high enough. His eyes focused on an extension ladder that someone had leaned against a steel girder. It rested on the crossbeam of an H-shaped structure on the eastern corner. There, seated at the edge some twenty feet above the unfinished top floor of the building, was his baby brother. Reggie sat there with his back against the steel support beam, his head turned toward the rising sun. One foot dangled over the edge, the other was tucked up under him. A bottle of J&B scotch whiskey rested under his arm.

Howard felt his stomach knot. He had seen what a fall from this height does to a body, and the image flashed in his mind. He drew a deep breath and calmed himself, then approached Reggie.

"Yo there, little brother," he called softly.

Reggie threw his head around loosely and grinned down at his brother. His eyes focused. "Hi, Howie," he said. "Whacha doin' up so early?"

Howard shrugged. "Lookin' for you."

"Oh," Reggie said, and returned his gaze to the eastern horizon.

"Eleanor sent me."

Reggie didn't respond to that, but thought a moment. "Remember when we were kids, Howie?" he said. "How we'd crawl out on the roof at night and watch the stars till the sun came up?"

"Sure," Howard said, and smiled to himself. "I remember."

"Well, lemme tell ya somthin'," Reggie said and waved his hand broadly across the horizon. "*This* has got *that* beat all to hell!"

He drew a long swig from the bottle.

In spite of himself, Howard laughed. "Why don't you come down and we'll watch it together."

Reggie considered this, then tossed the bottle to Howard. "Have a drink," he said.

Howard caught it and held it up against the pink light. It was nearly empty. "You didn't leave much."

"I know," Reggie said, and laughed.

The sun broke just then over the eastern plains and a warm, brilliant yellow beam engulfed them.

"Eleanor's worried about you," Howard said to him.

Reggie sniffed and drew his sleeve across his nose. "Our marriage isn't a sham, Howard," he said after a moment.

"I know that."

"You shouldn't have said it."

"Yeah. You two have always been good for each other."

Reggie sniffed again. "Yeah."

"I just can't figure out why you didn't do somethin' about it when you first found out."

Reggie shrugged. "To tell you the truth, Howie, I didn't think it was any of my business."

"But she's your *wife*, for Christ's sake."

"Yep," Reggie said, and looked into the sun. "The little woman. My bride. The ball-and-chain. My significant other. My domestic partner. My spouse, my associate, my companion, my wife." Reggie drew a deep breath and yawned broadly. "You know, Howard," he continued, "Eleanor and I are two very lucky people. For twelve years now we've been absolutely crazy about each other. *Twelve years!* That's longer than most couples have if you think about it."

Reggie rose stiffly to his feet, his toes hanging over the edge of the narrow girder, and stretched. He wobbled and grasped the I-beam next to him.

Howard swallowed hard as he watched him. "Come on down now, Reggie," he said sternly. "I mean it."

Reggie nodded. "OK," he said. He took two steps toward the ladder, then stopped. "But don't be too hard on Eleanor, Howie," he said. "Of course she's to blame. "She's been very, very naughty. But women are women and hell they can't help themselves."

With that, Reggie took one more step toward the ladder but his foot missed the girder. He flipped forward, falling into the sun, and dropped like a brick out of sight.

Howard watched, the empty bottle of scotch slipping from his fingers. For the first time in his life, he screamed.

"REGGIE!"

Howard dashed to the edge – nearly slipping over himself – catching a hand on the vertical beam. He swung out as far as his arm would let him and peered down, terrorized.

The shadowy rooftops of other buildings were visible far below, the light of day having not yet reached them. The cottonwoods and maples were just beginning turn color, and their leaves fluttered gently in the morning breeze. A silent jogger ran through the hospital grounds, her golden retriever at her side. And there, swinging crazily at the end of a thirty-foot length of quarter-inch cable, was Reggie. The cable was attached to the wide leather safety harness fastened around his waist. He looked up dizzily at Howard.

"Wow!" he said, his arms flailing at empty air. "Good thing I remembered my safety stuff, huh!?"

Howard was white as a sheet. He gripped the I-beam to steady himself. *"Damn you, Reggie!"* he shouted.

Reggie spun slowly at the end of the cable, like a disabled Spider-Man.

"Howie," he said weakly. "I think I am going to be sick."

EIGHTEEN

Sally Morgan stood hunched over, peering at Reggie through the tiny window in the little corner door of court number three at the Downtown Athletic Club. She hesitated.

He was alone, practicing his service rather listlessly. Each time he struck the ball he would flinch and when he moved it was with that careful, controlled motion of the seriously hung-over. Reggie looked as though he was in terrible pain, and he was. She studied him a moment, questioning herself, doubting the wisdom of approaching him one more time. But in the core of her being she knew she had no choice. She drew a breath – it was now or never – and pushed open the door.

Reggie turned at the sound and saw her come in. His head was pounding; every muscle and every joint in his body felt as though it had been pulled out of place. Still, his heart skipped a beat when he saw her. Sally was dressed pretty much as she was that first day in the restaurant, in the sweater and short skirt, her hair in a ponytail. He bounced the ball in the end of his racquet and studied her. She was a vision, he had to admit it.

"I thought you left," he said.

"I postponed my flight."

"You shouldn't of."

"Howard tells me you've been bungee jumping."

Reggie winced at that. The ball dribbled off the end of his racquet and skittered across the floor. It stopped at Sally's feet.

"I have something that needs to be said, Reggie," Sally said, and crossed her arms.

"Usually what needs to be said falls on reluctant ears."

Sally wasn't sure how to take that comment. "I knew about the affair," she said. "I heard rumors."

Reggie shrugged. "People talk too much."

"It never occurred to me that you knew," she continued. "It was courageous of you to put up with it all along."

"I'm not courageous, Sally."

"It made me sick to think what she did to you. If I had a gun I would have murdered her on the spot."

"Don't say that."

"I mean it. You know I love you."

"I know you think you do."

Sally suddenly felt very tired. And no wonder, she hadn't slept in two days, since the party. "There's no thinking involved in how I feel," she said quietly. "If I were a thinking person I'd be on a plane for Korea right now."

"You should be."

She nodded. "Maybe. But not until I say this. There is nothing binding you to her now. You've done your best to make it work. But she has thrown it away. She destroyed it. It's not your fault, Reggie, but your marriage to Eleanor is over."

Reggie thought about that a moment, then drew a very deep breath and let it pass slowly out, billowing his cheeks. The pounding in his head was intense, and he shook it once to clear it. "Sally, marriage isn't the idyllic institution you imagine it is. Maybe it was once, I don't know. But it isn't *'two becoming one'* any more. It's not that simple. Marriage today is more like *'two remaining two together.'* It's a parallel existence of separate interests, separate careers and separate bank accounts. It's two individuals living their lives and checking in with one another on occasion. Paging one another. Sending each other cryptic messages on cell phones. Leaving post-it notes. No, Sally, Eleanor hasn't destroyed our marriage. She's just carried it to its logical extreme."

"I don't agree with you."

"I wouldn't expect you to," Reggie said. "But Sally, a successful marriage today isn't bricks and mortar. It's silly putty."

The thought was repugnant to her and it showed on Sally's face. "I don't understand you. I would give up my life for you."

"Would you?"

"You doubt that?"

"If I asked you, would you sell your business and leave Korea to move here with me?"

She balked. Sally blinked. The wheels in her head turned. Finally she said, "I hadn't thought about it, but I think I would."

"But that's the point, Sally," Reggie said, smiling. "It's not you, it's *me.* I would never ask you to do it. It simply wouldn't be right. Forty years ago, maybe, if I were Ward and you were June and Wally and the Beav depended on us. *But not today.* Today both people in a marriage make small sacrifices to avoid the big one. They both bend a little to keep from breaking altogether."

Sally was unconvinced, and shrugged.

"I know only this," she said. "I love you. And *you love me, too.*"

Reggie felt his heart skip again. He looked at her a long moment and she looked back, their eyes locked. This time Sally did *not* blink or look away. Instead, she bent over and picked the little blue ball up off the floor, then tossed it to him.

"The ball is in your court, Reggie Porter," she said, and left.

201

NINETEEN

A week passed. Reggie was upstairs when the doorbell rang. "I'll get it," he called, and closed the Tourister.

"I'll get it," Reggie heard Eleanor's muffled shout from some far off location in the house. He hoisted the bag off the bed and lugged it down the steps.

"That's OK, I'll get it," he called again.

Eleanor met him in the entryway with a peeler in her hand. She had been peeling some carrots for Reggie. "Who can that be?" she asked and he shrugged. Reggie placed the suitcase alongside its twin, already packed and waiting, then opened the door.

Ralph and James stood there, beaming from ear to ear. "Surprise!" they said.

"Ralph! James! C'mon in," Reggie said, and swung the door wide for them.

James stepped inside. "We came to see you off!"

"I'll put on some coffee," Eleanor said warmly.

"Not for me, Eleanor," Ralph said, entering. "I can only stay a minute."

"Me, either," James added, and noted the luggage. "All packed and ready to go, I see."

"Uh-huh," Reggie said and patted Ralph on the back. "I sure appreciate this, Ralph," he said to the accountant.

Ralph held up both hands and closed his eyes, cutting Reggie off. "I don't want to hear a word about it," he said, and produced a key. "I just brought this by."

"I could have picked it up on the way to the airport," Reggie said, and took the key from Ralph.

"Nonsense."

James turned to Reggie's wife. "What'll you be up to while Reggie's away, Eleanor?" he asked her.

"Oh, I've got tons to keep me busy."

"It's a shame you couldn't take a few weeks off to go with your husband," Ralph said to her.

"You'll have to talk to Reggie about that," Eleanor said, "I told him I'd go if he wanted me to."

Reggie shook his head. "And blow those accounts you've been working so hard on? You'd never forgive me."

"You see? He insisted."

Ralph shrugged. "Well, maybe he'll change his mind after a day or two of eating alone."

"Maybe," Reggie said, and smiled.

"Now, Eleanor," Ralph said, "you're to call if you need anything."

"Of course," she said and kissed him on the cheek. "You're a dear."

"Turn out the lights when you leave, OK?" Ralph said to Reggie. "And try to keep from getting sand in the tub, it's a hell of a job to get it out."

"I'll do my best," Reggie said. He hugged his friend. "See you in a month."

They watched Ralph back his car out of the driveway, then James checked his watch. "When is your flight?" he asked Reggie.

"Two."

"No time for a game then."

Reggie shook his head.

"We'll play the moment you get back."

"You got it," Reggie grinned.

"Eleanor," James said, "I want you to have dinner with me."

"Surely not every night, James," Eleanor said.

"I'll call you."

"If the phone rings I pick it up."

James stood a moment and looked at her with one eyebrow raised.

Eleanor rolled her eyes. "Yes, James, I'll be good." She kissed him on the cheek, too. "Thank you for caring."

"I do care," James said, then slapped Reggie on the shoulder. "Aloha, old pal."

Reggie and Eleanor waved at James as he pulled away from the curb. Then Eleanor took her husband in her arms.

"I am curious as to why you don't want me along," she said.

"Did I say that?"

"Yes you did."

"Oh."

"I could still make arrangements, you know."

Reggie slipped out of her arms and went inside the house. She followed him, closing the door behind her.

"I'm beginning to realize that it's no good for married couples to take vacations together," Reggie said. "Nothing is more depressing than seeing two people lying on the beach, each reading books they've brought along from home."

They walked into the kitchen and Eleanor ran some carrots under a cool stream of water from the tap. "We've always had a ball on our vacations, Reggie," she said. "I don't recall any book reading."

Reggie took one of the sliced carrots and leaned up against the counter. "You're right," he said, munching a bite. "Fact is, I was afraid you'd think I wasn't supportive of your career if I asked you to go."

Eleanor looked at him and turned the corners of her lips downward. "Hoo, boy!" she said. "If it gets any deeper in here I'll need hip boots."

"No, really," Reggie insisted. "Anyway, it's too late now. My reservation's confirmed and the plane was overbooked. I was lucky to get a seat."

Eleanor glanced at the clock on the wall. She placed the sliced carrots in a baggy and wiped her hands on a cloth. "Here," she said and gave the carrots to him. "For the flight."

Reggie smiled at her. "Thanks," he said simply.

"Now, there's something I want you to do for me," she said.

"Name it."

"Well," Eleanor said and folded her arms, "I haven't heard a word from Alex since that night Jacqueline made an ass of herself."

Reggie nodded. "And?"

"And, I think it would be a huge blunder to continue our relationship."

Reggie thought about that a moment. "I can't say I'm disappointed."

"Reggie," Eleanor said, concerned, "the fact is, Alex is crazy about me."

"I admire his taste in women."

"I don't want to hurt him but under the circumstances I think we should break it off once and for all. How could I ever look you in the eye again if everything between Alex and me wasn't over forever?"

"I love you for that," Reggie said.

"I know it will be painful but he's got to be told. So I invited him over here. He'll be here in a few minutes."

Reggie stood quietly, clutching his bag of carrots and leaning on the counter with his arms folded across his chest. After a moment he said, "I understand how difficult this is for you and admire your resolve. When Alex comes I'll make myself scarce so you can tell him."

Eleanor shook her head. "That's not what I had in mind."

"Oh?"

"I think it will be easier for Alex if he hears it from you."

"Really?"

"You know," Eleanor said, and made little fists. "You can tell him if he tries to see me again you'll beat him up."

"Beat him up?"

"Uh-huh."

"But, Ely, what if he breaks down?" Reggie said. "I can't stand to see a grown man cry."

Eleanor thought about that. "It is a possibility."

"If you mean that much to him maybe I should just bow out of the picture."

Eleanor looked at him to see if he was joking. "What would possess you to say something like that?"

"I only want what's best for you," Reggie assured her. "That's all that matters."

Eleanor put her hands on her hips and walked a little circle on the kitchen floor. "Reggie, I'll put it to you straight," she said after a moment. "I'm sick and tired of Alex Newton."

"Oh!" Reggie said, his eyebrows arched. "Why don't you just tell him that?"

"Because, dammit, you know how men are!" Eleanor said and stamped her foot. "When they're sick of you they drop you like so much garbage. But if you've had enough of them their ego gets battered and there's no telling what they'll do."

At that precise moment the doorbell rang a second time. Reggie had never seen Eleanor look so frazzled.

"That's Alex!" she cried. "Tell me you'll do it!"

"OK, I'll do it." Reggie agreed.

Eleanor threw her arms around his neck and kissed him. "You're the best, Reggie," she said. "I don't deserve you."

"I know it," Reggie said, and kissed her back. "But you're stuck with me."

Reggie left her there in the kitchen and went to the front door. He opened it and Alex Newton stood before him.

"Oh, hello Reggie," Alex said and looked over Reggie's shoulder into the living room. "Nice to see you again."

"You're looking fit, Alex," Reggie said as Alex stepped inside. "Is that a new chain?"

Alex instinctively felt the chain around his neck. "Why, yes," he said. "Jacqueline gave it to me."

He looked around the room but seemed relieved not to see Eleanor. "Reggie," he said, "I need to talk to you before you go."

"Sure."

"Eleanor called me and asked me to come over."

"I see," Reggie said gravely. "Are you early?"

Alex seemed confused. "I don't know. But Reggie, I want to thank you from the bottom of my heart for how things have turned out. My marriage is stronger than ever," he said. He crossed two fingers and held them up. "Jacqueline and I are like that."

"Like that?"

Alex nodded and smiled. "I did as you suggested and packed my bags. She came to her senses just as you said she would."

"And have you forgiven her for doubting you?" Reggie asked.

"Of course I have."

"Then I'm sure you're both happy."

Alex frowned. "But there is one loose end."

"A loose end?"

"Yes," Alex said. "Eleanor."

"Eleanor?"

"I'm afraid so." Alex scratched his chin thoughtfully. "Unfortunately she's still infatuated with me," he said.

"She probably can't help herself, Alex."

"But, dammit, I have to think of myself!" Alex blurted. "She has to see that it could never be the same now."

Reggie nodded. "You're right," he said.

"I've made up my mind," Alex said resolutely. "She must know before you go."

"As much as I hate to see Eleanor hurt," Reggie said, "I see your point. I'll call her and you can speak to her."

Alex looked as if he'd seen a ghost. "Me?" he cried. "I can't tell her. I want *you* to do it!"

"Me?"

Alex nodded. "Don't you see? If I tell her, it'll break her heart. But if you tell her, you'll be a hero. You can tell her you threatened to take a nine iron to me."

"You really think so?" Reggie asked.

"I know so."

Reggie shrugged. "If you think its best."

"I do."

Reggie grinned at him slyly. "Now tell me the truth, Alex, you old fox," he said. "Why are you in such a hurry to ditch Eleanor?"

Alex studied Reggie a moment with a little sly smile of his own. He glanced around the room once again, making certain they were alone.

"Man to man?"

Reggie nodded.

"Remember Heather? From the club?"

Reggie thought a moment, then cupped his hands about a foot in front of his chest. "You mean *Heather?*"

Alex flashed his eyes and nodded. "Uh-huh."

Reggie shook his head slowly. "You are completely amoral, aren't you Alex?"

"Probably," Alex admitted.

"What about Jacqueline?"

Alex shrugged, a little miffed. "It's only sex, Reggie."

"Right."

"Now, I gotta jet," Alex said and opened the door. "You'll break it to Eleanor? I don't want her calling me."

"I'll break it," Reggie said, and smiled.

Alex hesitated at the doorway, then turned back and stuck out his hand. "I feel like I've made a true friend in you, Reggie," he said.

Reggie grinned. He took Alex's hand and shook it. "Thanks, Alex," he said, and Alex left.

Eleanor stuck her head around the corner as Reggie closed the door. "Did he go?" she asked.

"He's gone," Reggie said.

"Is it over?"

"It's over."

"How did he take it?"

"He was shocked and bewildered," Reggie said. "But I'm sure that in time he'll see it's for the best."

Eleanor nodded. "I owe you one, Reggie," she said. "But I hope you weren't cruel to him"

"I threatened him with a nine iron."

Eleanor was surprised by this, but happy. "Did you?" she said. "But that's language he'll understand."

"Right."

"And now you can go to Hawaii and not worry about me," Eleanor said. She put her arms around Reggie's waist.

"That is a load off my mind," he said, and pulled her close. She rested her head on his shoulder a moment.

"I can always count on you, Reggie Porter," she said.

"It's true," he admitted.

"You're always there for me."

"Mr. Dependable."

They kissed.

"I wish I could get away," Eleanor said. "I hate the thought of you spending a month in paradise all alone."

"Alone?" Reggie said. "Who said I'd be alone?"

Eleanor looked up at him, perplexed.

"Didn't I tell you?"

"Tell me what?"

"Sally is going with me."

Eleanor stepped back. "Sally? Sally Morgan?"

"We don't know any other Sallys, Eleanor."

Eleanor folded her arms again. "You're going to Hawaii with Sally? And who else?"

"No one else."

"Isn't that a little... strange?"

Reggie shrugged. "How so?"

"Well," Eleanor said, picking her words, "it's not *customary* for a married man to spend four weeks in a tropical island paradise with a single woman." Eleanor scratched her head. "How will it look to people?"

Reggie considered that a moment. "Come to think of it," he said, "you're the only one I've mentioned it to. And I *know* you can keep a secret."

Eleanor could feel her blood pressure rising. She walked into the kitchen. In a moment she walked back into the living room.

"Reggie," she said calmly. "I know that you and Sally have a marvelous relationship. Don't you see you stand to spoil it by doing this?"

"Nonsense," Reggie said. "You and I do it and we're best of friends."

Eleanor stiffened. "I don't mean to be dense, Darling," she said, "but you'll have to spell it out for me. Are you saying that you and Sally are lovers?"

"Certainly not."

"Oh," Eleanor said, relieved.

"Not *yet.*"

Eleanor picked up a vase and crashed it to the floor. It shattered into a hundred pieces.

"Is this pay back?" she shouted. "Is that what this is?"

Reggie shrugged. "Maybe. I don't think so."

"What makes you think I'll be here when you come back?"

"That is something you'll have to decide for yourself," Reggie said.

Eleanor picked up a lamp and crashed that to the floor also. It sputtered as it shorted out. "Do you think I'll just sit here and let that, that Judas take my husband from me? I suppose next you'll want me to kiss her cheek and wish her bon voyage."

"Something like that," Reggie said. "She's coming by in a few minutes to say goodbye to you."

Eleanor fumed. "I'll crucify her," she said.

"Eleanor, Eleanor," Reggie said, clicking his tongue. "You've forgotten how civil I was to Alex."

"I'm not you, Reggie," Eleanor stammered. "My blood is hot."

"But your brain is cold."

Eleanor sputtered. "I need a cigarette," she exclaimed, and dashed into the kitchen again.

"I thought you quit!" Reggie called after her.

"I *have* quit, dammit," she said, returning. She lit the cigarette in her mouth and put the lighter down.

"All right," she said after drawing the smoke deep into her lungs, calming herself. "Let's talk this through." She paced forward and back a moment, thinking. "Does Sally love you?"

"Yes."

"How do you know for sure?"

"She told me so."

"I'm not blind," Eleanor said. "I know that men drool over her. But not you, Reggie. She's not your type."

"What type of lover would you suggest for me?"

Eleanor looked at him and picked a bit of tobacco from her tongue. "Very funny," she said.

The doorbell chimed and the two of them froze for a second.

"I'll kill her," Eleanor said, planting her feet and squaring her shoulders.

Reggie scratched under his chin, then threw open the door. Howard was standing on the porch.

"Ready to go, Reggie?" he said.

"Sure am," Reggie said. "C'mon in."

Howard did so and had to step around the broken vase. "Oh-oh," he said. "Have an accident?"

Eleanor stepped between them. "Are you responsible for this scheme of Reggie's, Howard?" she said sternly.

Howard looked at Reggie a moment, perplexed.

"Howie doesn't know, Eleanor."

"Oh," she said, and puffed her cigarette. "Then maybe you can stop him. You're his brother."

Howard raised his palms and shrugged. "Stop him from what?"

"He's taking Sally to Hawaii with him."

Howard stood still for a moment until he fully comprehended what Eleanor had said to him. "Oh," he said finally.

"Oh? Just 'Oh'?"

Howard looked at Reggie. "I thought you and Ely had patched things up."

"We have," Reggie insisted. "Everything's fine between us."

Howard glanced at Eleanor, then at Reggie again. "Don't you love Eleanor any more, Reggie?"

"You know I do," he insisted.

"You have a bizarre way of showing it," Eleanor huffed.

"The same way you've been showing me these last six months," Reggie said flatly.

"So, I was right," Eleanor sneered. "This *is* pay back."

Reggie shrugged. "Think what you like."

"Are you in love with Sally?" Howard asked him.

Reggie thought about that and was clearly uncertain. "I don't know," he said. "But she's going back to Korea and I asked her to spend the last four weeks of her vacation with me in Hawaii. Maybe I'll find out."

Howard glanced out the window at the sound of a car. "There's a taxi," he said. "It's Sally."

"Four weeks!" Eleanor said to Reggie. Her brow was furled. "Will you leave her and come back to me in four weeks?"

Reggie looked at her and smiled. "Of course I will," he said, and glanced around the room. "This is our home."

"And you expect me to say goodbye to her as if I were blissfully unaware of her scheme?"

Reggie could see a tear forming in Eleanor's eye. He rubbed it away before it fell. "It'll be easier if you do," he said to her. "Making a scene won't keep me from going."

"Does she know I know?" Eleanor asked.

Reggie shook his head no. "She thinks it's 'our little secret.' She'd die if she thought you knew."

With that the bell chimed again. Howard opened the door.

"Oh," Sally said surprised. "Hello, Howard."

"Hi, Sally," Howard said and grabbed Reggie's two suitcases. "I'll wait for you in the pickup," he told Reggie.

Sally stepped inside. "You're just leaving?" she said to Reggie. "I'm glad I caught you. I'd hate to have missed saying goodbye to you."

Reggie smiled. "Me too," he said.

Sally looked at Eleanor and held out her hand. "My taxi's waiting," she said. "I'm on my way to the airport, too."

Eleanor took Sally's hand and squeezed it a little *too* hard. "Oh," she said casually, "maybe you're on the same flight as Reggie."

"Maybe," Sally said. She smiled at Eleanor. "You'll miss your husband, I bet."

"Horribly."

"She'll have her work to keep her mind off me," Reggie said, and put his arm around his wife.

"Duty calls," Eleanor said.

"I know what you mean," Sally agreed. "My business is in shambles." She looked at Reggie. "If we're on the same flight maybe we can sit together."

"That would be nice, Sally," Reggie said.

"Yes," Eleanor added. "You two can chat."

Sally gave Reggie a little hug, and he hugged her back. "I want to thank you both for all the kindness you've shown me," she said. "You were wonderful. You took me in like a homeless puppy and I appreciate it."

"It was nothing," Reggie said.

"You're a delight, Sally," Eleanor added.

"Perhaps you'll come visit again," Reggie continued.

Eleanor looked at him from the corner of her eye and frowned.

"I doubt it," Sally said. "But you never know."

She smiled at them both again, then turned and left. She walked past Howard's pickup and entered the taxi. Eleanor and Reggie watched it drive away.

"I didn't find that amusing at all," Eleanor said. "That crap about sitting together on the plane and all."

Reggie grinned his rakish grin and laughed. "She was faking you out!"

"Who did she think she was fooling?" Eleanor scoffed. "She's an idiot if she thought I couldn't see right through her."

"Well," Reggie said, "it would have worked on most people."

"She doesn't realize how observant I am," Eleanor stated.

"A real student of human nature," Reggie added, then checked his watch. "Well, it's time," he said.

Eleanor took him in her arms once again and kissed him. Tears began to flow freely down her cheeks. "I'll ask you again, Reggie," she whispered. *"Please don't go."*

"For twelve years we've been together, Eleanor," Reggie whispered back. "You're the wittiest woman I know. I can't think of anyone I'd rather be with than you. But once more before I die I want to be more than someone's Mr. Dependable. I want to know what it feels like to be in the arms of a woman who worships the ground I walk on. I want to stroll on the beach with my arm around her waist. I want to sit for hours and just stare into her eyes while a fire pops and sizzles nearby. I want to have sex that feels like the fourth of July. Just once more before I die I want to be in *love.*"

Eleanor began to shake in his arms. She sobbed deeply. "Reggie," she said, "let me. *I can love you like that.* I've always loved you! But I've neglected you, I can see that. I'll quit my job and come with you if you let me."

Reggie shook his head slowly. "No," he said, and pulled away from her.

"Don't do this," Eleanor said as he walked toward the pickup. "You're driving me right back into the arms of Alex."

"In that case," Reggie said and opened the pickup's door, "he'll have his hands full."

"What?" Eleanor asked, confused.

Reggie closed the door and rolled down the window. "I'll be back in four weeks," he called to her.

"I'll be gone," she called back.

"Where?"

"ANYWHERE!" she screamed. "You think I'll take you back?"

Reggie nodded and grinned that grin of his one last time. "After you've had time to mull it over."

Eleanor stamped her foot. "*Damn you!*" she said. "You are the most maddening, bullheaded man on the face of the earth!"

"See you in a month," Reggie said, and waved at her. Howard pulled away from the curb and drove away.

Eleanor stepped into the middle of the street and waved her fists, cursing. "I'll divorce you, Reggie!" she called.

"I doubt it," she heard Reggie call back as the pickup turned the corner out of sight.

TWENTY

The curtains were *not* closed. Alex thrashed about under the silk sheet, his hands on the most luscious pair of breasts he'd ever fondled. Heather rocked back and forth gently, her head thrown back, eyes fluttering. He looked up at her and twisted her nipples. She began to moan passionately.

At that moment, of course, the telephone rang shrilly.

"Damn!" Alex pushed her off and sat up on the edge of the bed. "It might be Jacqueline," he said harshly. He let the phone ring a second time, then lifted the receiver. "Hello?" he said.

Across the street, in a dingy rented office facing the St. Gregory, the tall silver haired man sat peering through the long, telephoto lens of his camera. He held the telephone to his ear. "Is this Alex Newton?" he asked.

"Yes it is," Alex said. "I'm in the middle of a meeting. What do you want?"

"I've got something I think you'd be interested in."

"What is it?" Alex asked.

"Negatives to certain photographs," the silver haired man replied.

"Photographs? I'm not interested in photographs of any sort."

"No? But these are of you."

Alex was perplexed. "Me?"

"Yes. In the company of a certain woman."

Alex felt his throat go dry. "A woman?" he croaked.

"An Eleanor… somebody."

Alex was silent a long moment. He could feel his heart pounding. Heather reached her arms around him and began nibbling his ear annoyingly. He swallowed twice and began at once to perspire. He pushed her away.

"Is this blackmail?" he said quietly.

"Certainly not," the silver haired man said. "I'm just interested in selling some photographic negatives I happen to own."

"Well, I am not interested in buying them."

"Fine. I'll just make the offer to Mrs. Newton."

Alex almost dropped the phone. "No, wait!" he said, then thought a moment. "How many photographs are we talking about?"

"Thirty-six."

Alex closed his eyes and rested his elbows on his knees. He messaged his temples, thinking. "And what is your asking price for these photographs?" he asked finally.

"Five thousand dollars."

Relief flooded over Alex. He drew a deep breath and let it out quickly. "That sounds reasonable," he said.

"A piece."

"*A piece!*" Alex became apoplectic. He did the math in his head. "That's over a hundred fifty thousand dollars!" he sputtered. "I can't *possibly* get my hands on that kind of money!"

The silver haired man interrupted him. "Calm down, Mr. Newton. I am not a difficult man to work with."

"Only my wife has access to that kind of money," Alex blurted.

"But I'm not suggesting you give me all the money at once."

Alex was confused. "Well, then, what are you talking about?"

The silver haired man looked through the lens at Alex, hunched on the edge of the bed. He could see him shaking even from this distance. "Installments," he said.

"Installments?"

"Yeah, you know. Once a month. Like car payments. I'll sell you *one* photographic negative a month for *three* years." The silver haired man smiled at himself. This was the closest thing to a retirement package he would ever see.

Alex Newton did drop the phone this time. He fell back in the bed, his head swimming.

"Are you still there, Mr. Newton?" he heard the voice on the receiver ask.

"Mr. Newton...?"

"*Mr. Newton...?*"

TWENTY-ONE

The huge engines of the jumbo jet began to whine, increasing in pitch to a deafening roar. Suddenly the jet lurched and accelerated down the runway, picking up speed, thundering as its wheels finally lifted off the pavement. At once its nose tilted skyward. Inside, Reggie Porter hunched over his seat and peered out the little window. He watched his city as it passed beneath him and, for a moment, could see the hospital construction site. The plane banked steeply then, turning into the afternoon sun.

He adjusted his seat back and put the stereo headphones over his ears, spun the little dial on the armrest until he tuned into an oldies station, then pulled the plastic baggy from his shirt pocket. He opened it.

Reggie held up the opened baggy to the beautiful passenger seated next to him. "Carrot?" he offered.

She smiled at him and declined.

About the Author

Rich Mussler was born in Sinton, Texas, just outside of Corpus, but was raised during his formative years in Oregon's lush Willamette Valley. He returned to Texas as an adult and is fond of saying, *"I got here as fast as I could."* He is proud to be a native of the Lone Star State.

Rich graduated from Oregon State University with a bachelor degree in Art (Painting) and later earned an MBA from Willamette University in Salem, Oregon. He also studied at the Dallas Theological Seminary in Dallas, Texas.

Rich lives in Flower Mound, Texas, a suburb of Dallas and Ft. Worth. You can reach him by email at musslertx@msn.com.

Printed in the United States
22388LVS00004B/328